Jospeh Winlock

Tables of Mercury

for the use of the American ephemeris and nautical almanac

Jospeh Winlock

Tables of Mercury
for the use of the American ephemeris and nautical almanac

ISBN/EAN: 9783337332457

Printed in Europe, USA, Canada, Australia, Japan

Cover: Foto ©Andreas Hilbeck / pixelio.de

More available books at **www.hansebooks.com**

TABLES

OF

MERCURY,

FOR THE USE OF

THE AMERICAN EPHEMERIS AND NAUTICAL ALMANAC.

BY

JOSEPH WINLOCK,
PROF. MATH. U. S. NAVY.

BUREAU OF NAVIGATION,
WASHINGTON.
1864.

UNIVERSITY PRESS:
WELCH, BIGELOW, AND COMPANY,
CAMBRIDGE.

PREFACE.

THE preparation of these Tables was begun in the year 1852, by order of the Superintendent of *The American Ephemeris and Nautical Almanac,* now the Chief of the Bureau of Navigation, ADMIRAL C. II. DAVIS. They have been several years in type, and have been used in computing the ephemeris of Mercury which is published in the American Ephemeris for the years 1855 – 1865 inclusive. It is hoped that they will be found especially convenient for computing an ephemeris, and as much so as the ordinary Tables for isolated places, and that the test of actual use for a number of years has rendered them unusually free from typographical errors. I am indebted to MR. CHAUNCEY WRIGHT and MR. ISAAC BRADFORD for valuable assistance in completing their publication.

JOSEPH WINLOCK,
Prof. Math. U. S. N.

CAMBRIDGE, Feb. 16, 1864.

INTRODUCTION.

CONSTRUCTION AND USE OF THE TABLES.

1. THESE Tables are based on the Theory of Mercury by U. J. LE VERRIER, Additions to the *Connaissance des Temps*, 1848. The following elements are given for the epoch 1799, Dec. 31, Paris Mean Midnight, from which the time t is reckoned in Julian years, or in units of 365.25 days: —

$$L = 110\ 13\ 17.84$$
$$\pi = 74\ 20\ 41.60 + 55.589\,t$$
$$\Omega = 45\ 57\ 37.70 + 42.511\,t$$
$$i = 7\ 0\ 4.60 + 0.0711\,t$$
$$e = 0.2056003 + 0''.0434\,t$$
$$n = 5381016''.218$$
$$a = 0.3870984$$

The coefficients of t include the constant of precession and the motion of the mean ecliptic; so that by substituting the value of t, corresponding to any date, and adding the secular inequality of precession to π and Ω, the value of the element obtained is referred to the mean equinox or the mean ecliptic of the date.

The value of the precession used is

$$50''.223\,t + 0.000122\,t^2$$

The following increments of the elements are derived from their mean motions: —

	L	π	Ω
In 100 Julian years	74 4 4.100	1 32 38.900	1 10 51.100
In a common year	1493 43 3.302	0 0 55.551	0 0 42.482
In a leap year	1497 48 35.859	0 0 55.703	0 0 42.599
In a mean day	4 5 32.557	0 0 0.152	0 0 0.117

From these numbers are deduced the values of L, Ω, and π in Table V., for the mean noon of Washington at the beginning of each year of the nineteenth century. These, as well as all the constants and arguments in the following Tables, are given for the mean noon of Jan. 0^d of each year, without excepting the leap-years, the beginnings of which, according to the general usage of astronomical tables, are assumed to be the mean noon of Jan. 1^d.

A corresponding modification is made in the Table VII. of the changes of L, π, and Ω for fractional parts of a year; so that the changes for months in Table VII. are, for common years, the changes between the mean noon of Jan. 0^d and that of the 1st day of all the months but February.

1

INTRODUCTION.

The values of the secular inequality of precession,

$$p = 0''.000122 \; t^2,$$

by which the preceding elements are reduced to the mean equinox of the date, are also given in Table V.

2. Table VI. contains for the same dates the constants dependent on the positions of the celestial equator, the equinoxes, and the plane of the orbit of Mercury; from which the computation of heliocentric rectangular coördinates can easily be effected, when the radius vector r and the true anomaly v are known, by the following formulas : —

$$x = r \, k_x \sin (K_x + v), \qquad y = r \, k_y \sin (K_y = v), \qquad z = r \, k_z \sin (K_z + v).$$

The values of k_x, K_x, &c. were computed by the method of GAUSS's *Theoria Motus* (Articles 55, 56) from the elements Ω and π of Table V., the inclination i, and the obliquity of the ecliptic given in HANSEN's Tables of the Sun. They were corrected for the secular inequality of precession by differential formulas, the coefficients of which, computed for 1850, were found not to vary sensibly during the century. In the same manner, the changes arising from the lunar nutation of the obliquity of the ecliptic, and of longitude, given in Table XLIV. of HANSEN's Tables of the Sun, were applied to log k_x, log k_y, and log k_z. From the values so computed the following constants were subtracted : —

From	K_x	20.0	from log k_x	0 units of 7th decimal place			
"	K_y	22.0	" log k_y	6	"	"	"
"	K_z	20.0	" log k_z	20	"	"	"

These constants are added in Table VIII. to the perturbations of the above quantities, so as to render them positive. The arguments H_1 and H_0 with which Table VIII. is entered, are given in Table V. They are the arguments XI. and I. of HANSEN's Tables of the Sun, interpolated to Washington time, and have respectively the periods of 6798.3 days and 365.24 days, on which depend the lunar and solar nutations.

Since the perturbations dependent on the lunar nutations are applied to the values of log k_x, log k_y, and log k_z, given in Table VI., Table VIII. contains for these quantities only the perturbations dependent on the solar nutation, which sensibly affects only log k_y and log k_z.

3. The elliptic values of the true anomaly and of the logarithm of the radius vector, given in Tables XIV. and XV., were derived from a table of the eccentric anomaly computed by the indirect method. They were computed for every unit of the argument A (12 hours), and interpolated to every tenth of the unit. The constant $20''.8$ was subtracted from the true anomaly, and the constant 0.0000111 from the log radius vector. These constants are added in the Tables X.–XIII. of the planetary perturbations, so as to render their values positive.*

Table IX. contains the logarithms of the differences of v and log r for a unit of the 5th decimal place in the argument. The characteristics of these logarithms are therefore such that, if the 5th decimal place of the argument be taken as that of the unit, the proportional part will be obtained in seconds for the anomaly, and in units of the 7th decimal place for the log radius vector.

Since logarithms given to only four places of decimals may be insufficient for the largest differences of v and log r in the most accurate computations, another Table is added, Table XVIII., with logarithms to five places, for those portions of Tables XIV. and XV. which have the largest differences.

The argument A of the elliptic Tables, given in Table V., is equal to twice the number of days elapsed from the preceding mean perihelion passage of Mercury, and its period is the anomalistic year of Mercury, namely,

$$87.969345 \text{ days, or } 175.938690 \text{ half-days.}$$

---

* Tables XIV. and XV. were computed in connection with a set of perturbation Tables in which two terms of long period were applied to the mean anomaly. In the present Tables, however, all the planetary perturbations are applied to the true anomaly; and the sums of the constants added to render the values of the perturbations positive are $30''.8$ for v, and 0.0000121 for log r. Consequently $10''.0$ should be subtracted from the sum of the perturbations of v, and 10 units of the seventh decimal place should be subtracted from those of log r, in applying them to the values of the Tables XIV. and XV.

INTRODUCTION.

Table IX. contains also the logarithms of the variations of the true anomaly, and of the log radius vector for one anomalistic year of Mercury. These were computed from the variations of v and r in 100 years, given in the following formulas, in which z denotes the mean anomaly: —

$$\delta v = 8''.54 \sin \ z + 2''.16 \sin 2z + 0''.57 \sin 3z$$
$$+ \ 0''.16 \sin 4z + 0''.04 \sin 5z + 0''.01 \sin 6z.$$

$$\delta r = 0.0000017 - 0.0000078 \cos z$$
$$- 0.0000016 \cos 2z$$
$$- 0.0000002 \cos 3z.$$

The number m of the anomalistic years of Mercury elapsed from the epoch 1800 are given for the beginning of each year in Table V.

4. The perturbations of the true anomaly are given by the following formulas, in which l, l', l'', l''', l^v denote the mean longitudes of the planets Mercury, Venus, Earth, Jupiter, and Saturn respectively, referred to the mean equinox of 1799, Dec. 31.5 Paris Mean Time. The perturbations produced by Mars are insignificant, on account of the small mass of Mars; and the action of Uranus is insensible, in consequence of its great distance from Mercury.

Perturbations of the true anomaly produced by

VENUS.

$\delta v = + \ 0''.31 \sin (l' - 76° \ 25')$
$\quad + \ 0.75 \sin (l' - l)$
$\quad - \ 0.09 \sin (l' + l + 32° \ 1')$
$\quad + \ 0.19 \sin (l' - 2l + 77° \ 28')$
$\quad - \ 0.06 \sin (l' - 3l - 38° \ 39')$

$\quad + \ 0.78 \sin (2l' + 31° \ 36')$
$\quad - \ 3.96 \sin (2l' - l - 74° \ 27')$
$\quad + \ 0.20 \sin (2l' + l - 42° \ 53')$
$\quad - \ 2.22 \sin (2l' - 2l)$
$\quad - \ 0.58 \sin (2l' - 3l + 75° \ 27')$
$\quad + \ 0.14 \sin (2l' - 4l - 30° \ 16')$
$\quad + \ 0.06 \sin (2l' - 5l + 38° \ 31')$

$\quad - \ 0.11 \sin (3l' - 37° \ 53')$
$\quad - \ 0.60 \sin (3l' - l + 32° \ 19')$
$\quad - \ 1.45 \sin (3l' - 2l - 73° \ 53')$
$\quad - \ 0.48 \sin (3l' - 3l)$
$\quad - \ 0.15 \sin (3l' - 4l + 74° \ 3')$

$= - \ 0''.10 \sin (4l' - l - 45° \ 0')$
$\quad - \ 0.54 \sin (4l' - 2l + 30° \ 57')$
$\quad + \ 0.33 \sin (4l' - 3l - 73° \ 49')$
$\quad + \ 0.05 \sin (4l' - 4l)$

$\quad + \ 0.39 \sin (5l' + 178° \ 30')$
$\quad + \ 1.55 \sin (5l' - l + 252° \ 54')$
$\quad + \ 0.09 \sin (5l' + l + 108° \ 26')$
$\quad + \ 7.72 \sin (5l' - 2l - 32° \ 54')$
$\quad + \ 3.03 \sin (5l' - 3l + 37° \ 32')$
$\quad + \ 0.75 \sin (5l' - 4l + 111° \ 40')$
$\quad + \ 0.21 \sin (5l' - 5l + 188° \ 32')$
$\quad + \ 0.06 \sin (5l' - 6l + 270° \ 0')$

$\quad + \ 0.08 \sin (6l' - 3l - 50° \ 11')$
$\quad - \ 0.09 \sin (8l' - 3l - 6° \ 44')$
$\quad + \ 0.09 \sin (10l' - 4l - 69° \ 14')$

THE EARTH.

$\delta v = + \ 0''.21 \sin (l'' - l)$

$\quad - \ 0.24 \sin (2l'' - 2l)$
$\quad - \ 0.41 \sin (2l'' - l - 74° \ 21')$

$\quad + \ 0.02 \sin (3l'' - 3l)$

$= + \ 0''.14 \sin (4l'' - 94° \cdot 33')$
$\quad + \ 0.67 \sin (4l'' - l - 20° \ 12')$
$\quad + \ 0.03 \sin (4l'' + l - 168° \ 54')$
$\quad + \ 0.35 \sin (4l'' - 2l + 48° \ 17')$
$\quad + \ 0.03 \sin (4l'' - 3l + 128° \ 30')$

3

INTRODUCTION.

JUPITER.

$$\delta v = + \overset{\prime\prime}{0}.57 \sin (l^{\text{v}} + 201° \ 44') \qquad\qquad = + \overset{\prime\prime}{0}.50 \sin (2 \ l^{\text{v}} + 30° \ 53')$$
$$+ 0.65 \sin (l^{\text{v}} - l) \qquad\qquad\qquad + 3.29 \sin (2 \ l^{\text{v}} - l + 104° \ 43')$$
$$+ 0.94 \sin (2 \ l^{\text{v}} - 2 \ l + 180° \ 0')$$

SATURN.

$$\delta v = - \overset{\prime\prime}{0}.40 \sin (2 \ l^{\text{v}} - l - 74° \ 21')$$

These expressions are put in a convenient form for computing tables of double entry by the following transformations: Let ϵ denote the mean longitude of Mercury at any epoch referred to the mean equinox of 1800 $0^{\text{d}}.5$ Paris Mean Time; let T be the number of days from that epoch, and n the daily sidereal motion in mean longitude. We then have

$$l = n \ T + \epsilon;$$

and in the same way for the other planets, —

$$l' = n' \ T' + \epsilon'$$
$$l'' = n'' \ T'' + \epsilon''$$
$$l^{\text{v}} = n^{\text{iv}} \ T^{\text{iv}} + \epsilon^{\text{iv}}$$
$$l^{\text{v}} = n^{\text{v}} \ T^{\text{v}} + \epsilon^{\text{v}}$$

Instead of double-entry tables, with two continuously variable arguments, we may, by a simple change in the formulas, construct tables for which one of the arguments shall remain constant during a period of the other. Thus, from the general form of the preceding terms of the perturbations produced by Venus,

$$k \sin (i' \ l' - i \ l + \gamma) = k \sin (i' \ n' \ T' - i \ n \ T + i' \ \epsilon' - i \ \epsilon + \gamma),$$

we may, by subtracting and adding the angle $i' \ n' \ T$, and putting the constant $i' \ \epsilon' - i \ \epsilon + \gamma = a$, obtain the form,

$$k \overset{\bullet}{\sin} [i' \ n' \ (T' - T) + (i' \ n' - i \ n) \ T + a],$$

in which the angle $n' \ (T' - T)$ is constant during a period of the argument T, and is increased for every change of period in T by the addition of the angle $n' \ 87.969$; but for a change of period in T', it is diminished by a circle, or 360°.

The epochs or the origins of the times T, T', &c., with the corresponding values of ϵ, ϵ', &c., may be taken arbitrarily and independently for the different planets. If, therefore, we take the following values of the mean longitudes and epochs and the daily sidereal motions,

$\epsilon = 354° \ 6.3$	1844	$0^{\text{d}}.5$	Paris Time	$n =$	$4° \ 5' \ 32''.42$
$\epsilon' = 145 \ 8.8$	1800	0.0	" "	$n' =$	$1 \ 36 \ 7.67$
$\epsilon'' = 98 \ 19.3$	1800	$- 1.545$	" "	$n'' =$	$0 \ 59 \ 8.15$
$\epsilon^{\text{iv}} = 81 \ 52.3$	1800	0.5	" "	$n^{\text{iv}} =$	$0 \ 4 \ 59.13$

we have for 1800 $0^{\text{d}}.0$ Washington Mean Time.

$T =$	28.11	Sidereal Period =	87.969
$T' =$	224.92	" " =	224.701
$T'' =$	367.02	" " =	365.256
$T^{\text{iv}} =$	4332.31	" " =	4332.585

From these values the tables of arguments were constructed; and the assumed values of ϵ, ϵ', &c., were substituted in the expressions of the perturbations.

4

INTRODUCTION.

By developing the preceding general form, we have

$$k \cos \left[(i' n' - i n) \, T + a \right] \sin \left[i' n' \, (T - T') \right] + k \sin \left[(i' n' - i n) \, T + a \right] \cos \left[i' n' \, (T - T') \right]$$

and if we put

$$k_\nu \cos \phi_\nu = \Sigma_i \left(k \cos \left[(i' n' - i n) \, T + a \right] \right)$$

and

$$k_\nu \sin \phi_\nu = \Sigma_i \left(k \sin \left[(i' n' - i n) \, T + a \right] \right)$$

the expressions for the perturbations become

$$\delta v = \Sigma_\nu \left(k_\nu \cos \phi_\nu \sin \left[i' n' \, (T - T') \right] + k_\nu \sin \phi_\nu \cos \left[i' n' \, (T' + T') \right] \right)$$
$$= \Sigma_\nu \left(k_\nu \sin \left[i' n' \, (T' - T) + \phi_\nu \right] \right)$$

Substituting the values of k, i, and a, we have for the perturbations produced by

VENUS.

$$k_1 \cos \varphi_1 = 0.31 \cos \left[(\quad n' \quad) \, T + 68°\; 43' \right]$$
$$+ 0.75 \cos \left[(\quad n' - \quad n) \, T + 151 \quad 2 \right]$$
$$+ 0.09 \cos \left[(\quad n' + \quad n) \, T + 351\; 16 \right]$$
$$+ 0.19 \cos \left[(\quad n' - 2 n) \, T + 234\; 24 \right]$$
$$+ 0.06 \cos \left[(\quad n' - 3 n) \, T + 304\; 11 \right]$$
$$k_2 \cos \varphi_2 = 0.78 \cos \left[(2 n' \quad) \, T + 321\; 53 \right]$$
$$+ 3.96 \cos \left[(2 n' - \quad n) \, T + 41\; 23 \right]$$
$$+ 0.20 \cos \left[(2 n' + \quad n) \, T + 241\; 31 \right]$$
$$+ 2.22 \cos \left[(2 n' - 2 n) \, T + 122 \quad 5 \right]$$
$$+ 0.58 \cos \left[(2 n' - 3 n) \, T + 203\; 26 \right]$$
$$+ 0.14 \cos \left[(2 n' - 4 n) \, T + 283\; 36 \right]$$
$$+ 0.06 \cos \left[(2 n' - 5 n) \, T + 358\; 17 \right]$$
$$k_3 \cos \varphi_3 = 0.11 \cos \left[(3 n' \quad) \, T + 217\; 34 \right]$$
$$+ 0.60 \cos \left[(3 n' - \quad n) \, T + 293\; 39 \right]$$
$$+ 1.45 \cos \left[(3 n' - 2 n) \, T + 193\; 21 \right]$$

$$+ 0.48 \cos \left[(3 n' - 3 n) \, T + 273°\; 7' \right]$$
$$+ 0.15 \cos \left[(3 n' - 4 n) \, T + 353 \quad 4 \right]$$
$$k_4 \cos \varphi_4 = 0.10 \cos \left[(4 n' - \quad n) \, T + 1\; 29 \right]$$
$$+ 0.54 \cos \left[(4 n' - 2 n) \, T + 83\; 19 \right]$$
$$+ 0.33 \cos \left[(4 n' - 3 n) \, T + 164\; 27 \right]$$
$$+ 0.05 \cos \left[(4 n' - 4 n) \, T + 244\; 10 \right]$$
$$k_5 \cos \varphi_5 = 0.39 \cos \left[(5 n' \quad) \, T + 184\; 20 \right]$$
$$+ 1.55 \cos \left[(5 n' - \quad n) \, T + 264\; 32 \right]$$
$$+ 0.09 \cos \left[(5 n' + \quad n) \, T + 108\; 16 \right]$$
$$+ 7.72 \cos \left[(5 n' - 2 n) \, T + 344\; 37 \right]$$
$$+ 3.03 \cos \left[(5 n' - 3 n) \, T + 60\; 57 \right]$$
$$+ 0.75 \cos \left[(5 n' - 4 n) \, T + 140\; 58 \right]$$
$$+ 0.21 \cos \left[(5 n' - 5 n) \, T + 223.44 \right]$$
$$+ 0.06 \cos \left[(5 n' - 6 n) \, T + 311 \quad 6 \right]$$

THE EARTH.

$$k'_1 \cos \phi'_1 = 0.21 \cos \left[(\quad n'' - \quad n) \, T + 104°\; 13' \right]$$
$$k''_2 \cos \phi''_2 = 0.41 \cos \left[(2 n'' - \quad n) \, T + 308\; 11 \right]$$
$$+ 0.24 \cos \left[(2 n'' - 2 n) \, T + 28\; 26 \right]$$
$$k''_3 \cos \phi''_3 = 0.02 \cos \left[(3 n'' - 3 n) \, T + 312\; 39 \right]$$

$$k''_4 \cos \phi''_4 = 0.14 \cos \left[(4 n''' \quad) \, T + 298°\; 44' \right]$$
$$+ 0.67 \cos \left[(4 n'' - \quad n) \, T + 18\; 59 \right]$$
$$+ 0.03 \cos \left[(4 n'' + \quad n) \, T + 218\; 29 \right]$$
$$+ 0.35 \cos \left[(4 n'' - 2 n) \, T + 93\; 22 \right]$$
$$+ 0.03 \cos \left[(4 n'' - 3 n) \, T + 179\; 28 \right]$$

JUPITER.

$$k^{iv}_1 \cos \phi^{iv}_1 = 0.57 \cos \left[(\quad n^{iv} - \quad n) \, T + 283°\; 36' \right]$$
$$+ 0.65 \cos \left[(\quad n^{iv} - \quad n) \, T + 87\; 46 \right]$$

$$k^{iv}_2 \cos \phi^{iv}_2 = 0.50 \cos \left[(2 n^{iv} \quad) \, T + 194°\; 38' \right]$$
$$+ 3.29 \cos \left[(2 n^{iv} - \quad n) \, T + 274\; 22 \right]$$
$$+ 0.94 \cos \left[(2 n^{iv} - 2 n) \, T + 355\; 32 \right]$$

By changing cos into sin in these expressions, we obtain the values of $k_1 \sin \phi_1$, $k_2 \sin \phi_2$, &c.

INTRODUCTION.

The expressions for the perturbations produced by Venus, the Earth, and Jupiter become

$$
\begin{aligned}
\delta v =\ & k_1 \sin \left[\ n' \left(T - T\right) + \phi_1\right] \\
& + k_2' \sin \left[\ 2\,n' \left(T - T\right) + \phi_2\right] \\
& + k_3 \sin \left[\ 3\,n' \left(T - T\right) + \phi_3\right] \\
& + k_4 \sin \left[\ 4\,n' \left(T - T\right) + \phi_4\right] \\
& + k_5 \sin \left[\ 5\,n' \left(T - T\right) + \phi_5\right] \\
& + 0\overset{''}{.}08 \sin \left[\ 6\,n' \left(T - T\right) + \left(\ 6\,n' - 3\,n\right)\ T + 118\overset{\circ}{\ }23\right] \\
& + 0.09 \sin \left[\ 8\,n' \left(T - T\right) + \left(\ 8\,n' - 3\,n\right)\ T + 272\ \ 7\right] \\
& + 0.09 \sin \left[10\,n' \left(T - T\right) + \left(10\,n' - 4\,n\right)\ T + 325\ 49\right] \\
& + 0''.21 \sin \left[\ n'' \left(T'' - T\right) + \left(n'' - n\right)\ T + 104^{\circ}\ 13'\right] \\
& + k_2'' \sin \left[2\,n'' \left(T'' - T\right) + \phi''_2\right] \\
& + 0''.02 \sin \left[3\,n'' \left(T'' - T\right) + \left(3\,n'' - 3\,n\right)\ T + 312^{\circ}\ 39'\right] \\
& + k''_4 \sin \left[4\,n'' \left(T'' - T\right) + \phi''_4\right] \\
& + k^{iv}_1 \sin \left[\ n^{iv} \left(T^{iv} - T\right) + \phi^{iv}_1\right] \\
& + k^{iv}_2 \sin \left[2\,n^{iv} \left(T^{iv} - T\right) + \phi^{iv}_2\right]
\end{aligned}
$$

The single term of perturbation produced by Saturn is given in a table of single entry.

Tables giving the values of k, $\sin \phi$, $k_1 \cos \phi_1$, $k_2 \sin \phi_2$, $k_4 \cos \phi_2$, or of k, ϕ, &c., for values of the argument T at suitable intervals, for the complete period of T, the computation of which is the first step in preparing double-entry tables, would, with the aid of a table of natural sines and cosines, constitute a very compact set of perturbation tables, which would be useful when a few places of a planet were to be computed, or when double-entry tables would be of inconvenient size.

Table X. contains the perturbations produced by Venus, computed for values of the angle $n'\,(T - T)$ at intervals of 3° from 0° to 360°. Tables XI. and XII. contain the perturbations produced by Jupiter and the Earth, computed for values of the angles $n^{iv}\,(T^{iv} - T)$ and $n''\,(T'' - T)$ at intervals of 6° from 0° to 360°. The intervals 3° and 6° are made the units of the vertical arguments of the tables, thus: $V = \frac{1}{2}\,n'\,(T - T)$, $J = \frac{1}{6}\,n^{iv}\,(T^{iv} - T)$, and $E = \frac{1}{6}\,n''\,(T'' - T)$; n', n^{iv}, and n'' being expressed in degrees and decimals of a degree. The period of V is therefore 120 units, and the periods of E and J are each 60 units.

The horizontal argument T of these tables has a period of 87.969 days; and for every change of period in T the arguments V, J, and E are increased by the quantities $\frac{1}{2}\,n'\,87.969$, $\frac{1}{6}\,n^{iv}\,87.969$, and $\frac{1}{6}\,n''\,87.969$ respectively. These, reduced to numbers, are for V 46.98, for J 1.22, and for E 14.45.

Table XIII. contains the term of perturbation produced by Saturn, and its argument S is given in days with a period of 89.432 days.

The arguments T, V, J, E, and S are given in Table V. for Jan. 0^d Washington Mean Noon for each year of the nineteenth century.

5. The perturbations of the logarithm of the radius vector, denoted by r, were computed in the same manner as those of the true anomaly, with the same intervals and arguments, and are placed in the same tables.

They are given in units of the seventh decimal place of the log radius vector, and are derived from the following formula : —

$$
\begin{aligned}
\delta r =\ & 4\overset{''}{.}00 \cos \left(\ l' - l\right) \\
& + 20.50 \cos \left(2\,l' - 2\,l + 180^{\circ}\right) \\
& + 11.50 \cos \left(3\,l' - 2\,l + 105^{\circ}\ 16'\right) \\
& + 4.00 \cos \left(3\,l' - 3\,l + 180^{\circ}\right) \\
& + 3.06 \cos \left(5\,l' - 1^{\circ}\ 36'\right) \\
& + 14.65 \cos \left(5\,l' - l + 72^{\circ}\ 45'\right) \\
& + 27.09 \cos \left(5\,l' - 3\,l + 35^{\circ}\ 32'\right) \\
& + 3.06 \cos \left(5\,l' - 4\,l + 115^{\circ}\ 48'\right) \\
& + 30.00 \cos \left(2\,l^{iv} - l + 105^{\circ}\ 39'\right)
\end{aligned}
$$

C

INTRODUCTION.

The coefficients are in units of the seventh decimal place of the radius vector.

Terms of perturbation are included in this formula dependent on the inequality of long period in the mean longitude,

$$7''.49 \sin (5\,l' - 2\,l - 32° 54'),$$

which LE VERRIER proposed to apply to the argument of the elliptic tables.

The terms dependent on the action of Venus are multiplied by 1.031, in order to reduce them to the new mass of Venus.

From this formula are derived the following perturbations of the logarithm of the radius vector.

$$
\begin{aligned}
\delta \log r =\; & 0.46 \cos (\; l' - 74° 21') \\
+ & 4.49 \cos (\; l' - l) \\
+ & 0.09 \cos (\; l' + l - 148° 42') \\
+ & 0.46 \cos (\; l' - 2\,l + 74° 21') \\
+ & 0.09 \cos (\; l' - 3\,l + 148° 42') \\
+ & 0.48 \cos (2\,l' + 31° 18') \\
+ & 2.35 \cos (2\,l' - l + 105° 39') \\
+ & 22.99 \cos (2\,l' - 2\,l + 180°) \\
+ & 2.35 \cos (2\,l' - 3\,l + 254° 21') \\
+ & 0.48 \cos (2\,l' - 4\,l + 328° 42') \\
+ & 0.27 \cos (3\,l' - 43° 26') \\
+ & 1.52 \cos (3\,l' - l + 30° 55') \\
+ & 13.36 \cos (3\,l' - 2\,l + 105° 20') \\
+ & 5.81 \cos (3\,l' - 3\,l + 180° \\
+ & 0.73 \cos (3\,l' - 4\,l + 254° 15') \\
+ & 0.20 \cos (3\,l' - 5\,l + 328° 42') \\
+ & 5.11 \cos (5\,l' - 1° 36') \\
+ & 16.15 \cos (5\,l' - l + 72° 58') \\
+ & 0.69 \cos (5\,l' + l - 75° 57') \\
+ & 1.44 \cos (5\,l' - 2\,l - 45° 44') \\
+ & 30.39 \cos (5\,l' - 3\,l + 35° 32') \\
+ & 6.53 \cos (5\,l' - 4\,l + 112° 54') \\
+ & 0.97 \cos (5\,l' - 5\,l + 185° 53') \\
+ & 3.44 \cos (2\,l'^v + 31° 18') \\
+ & 33.06 \cos (2\,l'^v - l + 105° 39') \\
+ & 0.70 \cos (2\,l'^v + l - 43° 3') \\
+ & 3.44 \cos (2\,l'^v - 2\,l + 180°) \\
+ & 0.70 \cos (2\,l'^v - 3\,l + 254° 21')
\end{aligned}
$$

By the same transformations as were made in the perturbations of the true anomaly we obtain the following formula:

$$
\begin{aligned}
\delta \log r =\; & k_1 \; \cos [\; n' \; (T' - T) + \phi_1 \;] \\
+ & k_2 \cdot \cos [2\,n' \; (T' - T) + \phi_2 \;] \\
+ & k_3 \; \cos [3\,n' \; (T' - T) + \phi_3 \;] \\
+ & k_5 \; \cos [5\,n' \; (T' - T) + \phi_5 \;] \\
+ & k'^v_2 \; \cos [2\,n'^v \; (T'^v - T) + \phi'^v_2]
\end{aligned}
$$

6. The reduction of the true orbit longitude to the ecliptic is given in Table XVI., and the latitude in Table XVII. If we denote the true anomaly affected by the planetary perturbations by

$$\bar v = v + \delta v$$

7

and the true argument of the latitude by

$$\omega = \bar{v} + \pi - \Omega$$

we obtain from the value of the inclination

$$7° \ 0' \ 4''.60 + 0''.0711 \, t$$

the following expression for the reduction to the ecliptic:

$$- (771''.8914 + 0.0043 \, t) \sin 2 \, \omega + 1'.44 \sin 4 \, \omega.$$

The term dependent on t is given in the column of variation for 100 years. The following are the formulas from which Table XVII. was computed: —

$$\sin \text{Lat} = \sin i \sin \omega = [9.0859733] \sin \omega$$
$$\text{variation in 100 years} = 57''.90 \tan \text{lat.}$$

The interval of one degree in the argument ω for which Tables XVI. and XVII. are constructed is such that the neglect of second differences in interpolation cannot cause an error in the reduction to the ecliptic of more than $0''.12$, but in the latitude it may cause, near the higher latitudes, an error of nearly $1''$. In both tables, however, second differences may be neglected without sensible error for those values of ω near the nodes, for which a transit of Mercury can occur.

At the heads of the columns of the argument in Table XVI. are placed the signs which belong to the reduction to the ecliptic. Thus, the reductions are negative for values of ω in the first and third quadrants, and positive for ω in the second and fourth quadrants. The latitude is positive for values of ω less than $180°$, and negative for greater values, for which the table should be entered with the argument $\omega - 180°$.

7. The true ecliptic longitude is referred to the true equinox by the addition of the nutation and the secular inequality of the precession p. Hence

$$\text{True ecliptic longitude} = \bar{v} + \pi + p + \text{Red. to Ecl.} + \text{nutation.}$$

The value of the nutation may be obtained from Table VIII., with an error of less than $0''.01$ by the formula: —

$$\text{Nutation} = d_{\flat} \, K_x + d_{\odot} \, K_x - 20''.0$$

RECAPITULATION.

The order of the tables is adapted to the work of computing ephemerides, an example of which will be given at the end of the following summary: —

Table I. contains the longitudes from Washington of the principal observatories; western longitude being considered positive.

Tables II., III., and IV. are tables of Astronomical Dates in mean solar days, from which any date given in the usual form of reference to the Christian era may be reduced to its value in days and decimals of a day of the Julian period. They are taken from PEIRCE's Lunar Tables. By adding the days given for the current year of the century to the days of the previous centennial date we obtain the number of days elapsed of the Julian Period for Jan. 0^d Mean Noon in common years and for Jan. 1^d in leap years. To this should be added the days and decimals for fractional parts of the year given in Tables III. and IV.

Table V. contains for Jan. 0^d Washington Mean Noon of each year in the present century the elements L, Ω, and π, and p the secular inequality of the precession by which these are referred to the mean equinox of date: the arguments H_1 and H_1 defined in § 2. Also, the arguments

A of Tables XI., XIV., XV., and XVIII. defined in § 3.

T the horizontal argument of Tables X., XI., and XII. defined in § 4.

V, J, E and S, the arguments of Tables X., XI., XII., and XIII. defined in § 4; and m the number of anomalistic years of Mercury completed since 1800.

INTRODUCTION.

Tables VI. and VIII. contain the quantities defined in § 2.

Table VII. is described in § 1.

Table IX. contains the logarithms of the differences of Tables XIV. and XV., and the log secular variations defined in § 3.

Tables X., XI., XII., and XIII. contain the perturbations produced by Venus, Jupiter, the Earth, and Saturn respectively, as described in § 4.

To the perturbations δv are added constants which in the aggregate amount to $30''.8$. To the perturbations $\dot{r}$ are added in the aggregate the constant 121.

Table XIV. contains the values of the true anomaly, diminished by the constant $20''.8$, at intervals of tenth of units of argument A.

Table XV. contains the values of the logarithm of the radius vector, diminished by 0.0000111, for the same intervals and arguments. (See note § 3.)

Tables XVI. and XVII. are described in § 6, and Table XVIII. in § 3.

Example.

The perturbations are conveniently computed at intervals of four days, and if the dates of the computation be so assumed that the argument I. is at the beginning nearly a multiple of four, its value will be for a long period nearly the same as those for which the tables are constructed. The interpolations for decimals of T may be performed upon the sums of the perturbations.

For January 0^d, 1865, the value of T is 17.38. For the previous day it is therefore 16.38. Assuming this as the origin of the dates, we have the following table of arguments for the year.

Day of the Year.	T	V	J	E	Day of the Year.	S	Day of the Year.	A	m
—1	16.38	69.55	28.56	57.31	—1	25.0	—1	169.467064	269
+71	0.41	116.53	29.78	11.76	+67	3.57	+3	1.528374	270
159	0.44	43.51	31.00	26.21	155	2.14	91	1.589684	271
247	0.47	90.49	32.22	40.66	243	0.71	179	1.650994	272
335	0.50	17.47	33.44	55.11	335	3.28	267	1.712304	273
367	32.50	17.47	33.44	55.11	367	35.28	355	1.773614	274

The dates preceding arguments T and S are of the assumed dates, the ones at which these arguments are changed by their respective periods. For all such changes in T the arguments V, J, and E are increased by the constants 46.98, 1.22, and 44.55 respectively, and have periods of 120.00, 60.00, and 60.00.

Argument A increases by two units each day until it exceeds its period 176.938690 which is then subtracted from it, and m is increased by a unit.

Entering the tables of perturbations for the assumed dates with the argument T successively equal to 16, 20, 24, &c., and with the constant arguments $V = 69.55$, $J = 28.56$, and $E = 57.31$; adding together the values

Day of the Year.	X.	XI.	XII.	Sum.	Diff.	Corr.	XIII.	Sum.	IX.	log sec var.	sec var.	Pert.	Diff.
—1	19.99	4.76	0.60	25.35	+0.33	+0.03	0.79	26.17	7.9487n	0.3785n	—2.4	+13.8	+3.4
+3	18.76	6.31	0.61	25.68	0.47	0.04	0.76	26.48	7.4231+	9.8545+	+0.7	17.2	3.0
7	17.65	7.86	0.64	26.15	0.65	0.06	0.69	26.90	8.0884	0.5198	3.3	20.2	2.4
11	16.85	9.17	0.78	26.80	0.75	0.07	0.61	27.48	8.2738	0.7052	5.1	22.6	1.3
15	16.54	10.07	0.94	27.55	0.62	0.06	0.50	28.11	8.3345	0.7659	5.8	23.9	+0.5
19	16.61	10.42	1.14	28.17	+0.29	+0.03	0.39	28.59	8.3355	0.7669	5.8	24.4	—0.3
23	16.82	10.32	1.32	28.46	—0.13	—0.01	0.28	28.73	8.2992	0.7306	5.4	+24.1	
—1	115	2	1	117	—6	—1		116	9.3957n	1.8255n	—67	+ 39	—11
+3	111	0	0	111	6	—1		110	9.4266	1.8580	72	28	+ 5
7	103	2	2	105	4	0		105	9.3603	1.7917	62	33	16
11	93	8	8	101	—2	0		101	9.1926	1.6240	42	49	21
15	82	17	17	99	0	0		99	8.8396n	1.2710n	—19	70	22
19	73	26	26	99	+3	0		99	8.0152+	0.4466+	+ 3	92	20
23	66	36	36	102	5	0		102	8.8646	1.2960	20	+112	

thus obtained for each date, and correcting the sums by the proportional parts of their differences for the decimal of the argument T (0.38 or 0.095 for the interval of four days), and adding the perturbations from Table XIII.; we obtain the sums given in the ninth columns of the above example. These are further corrected by the secular variations, and diminished by the constants $10''.0$ for δv and 10 units for $\dot r$. The logarithms of the secular variations are obtained by adding log m to the values of log sec. var. in Table IX.

The values of the perturbations should be interpolated to intervals of a day, and added to the values of v and log r given in Tables XVI. and XV. These tables are entered with the nearest values in tenths of units of argument A, for every day, and interpolated to the true values of the argument by means of Table IX., according to the precept of § 3. Thus for 1865 we have

Day of the Year.	A	log P. P.			P. P.	Pert.	v		P. P.	Pert.	log r
		v	log r								
0	171.5	2.5710n	2.5134	345 57 28.0	—372.4	+14.7	345 51 30.3	9.4900665	+326	+34	9.4901025
1	173.5	2.5740	2.2585	352 15 50.5	375.0	15.6	352 9 51.1	9.4885231	181	31	9.4885443
2	175.5	2.5753n	1.5155	358 36 8.1	—376.1	16.4	358 30 8.4	9.4878713	33	29	9.4878775
3	1.5	2.5102+	1.9844	4 45 7.2	+323.7	17.2	4 50 48.1	9.4881048	96	28	9.4881172
4	3.5	2.5079	2.3483	11 4 35.4	322.0	18.0	11 10 15.4	9.4892328	223	28	9.4892579
5	5.5	2.5038	2.5873	17 21 19.6	+319.0	+18.8	17 26 57.4	9.4912368	+345	+29	9.4912742

The true values of K_x, log k_x, &c. are conveniently computed from Tables VI. and VIII., at intervals of ten days, and interpolated to intervals of one day. This being done, we have, for 1865,

Day of the Year.	K_x	K_y	K_z	log k_x	log k_y	log k_z
0	165 8 15.1	77 52 13.2	65 45 46.6	9.9982821	9.9453473	9.6812330
10	165 8 16.9	77 52 15.0	65 45 48.1	9.9982821	9.9453474	9.6812328
20	165 8 18.6	77 52 16.7	65 45 49.6	9.9982821	9.9453474	9.6812328

Day of the Year.	$v + K_x$	$v + K_y$	$v + K_z$	log $k_x \sin (v + K_x)$	log $k_y \sin (v + K_y)$	log $k_z \sin (v + K_z)$
0	150 59 45.4	63 43 43.5	51 37 16.9	9.6839088	9.8979986	9.5755075
1	157 18 6.4	70 2 4.5	57 55 37.9	9.5847315	9.9184284	9.6093082
2	163 38 23.9	76 22 22.0	64 15 55.3	9.4480260	9.9329462	9.6358685
3	169 59 3.7	82 43 1.8	70 36 35.2	9.2386241	9.9418294	9.6558733
4	176 18 31.2	89 2 29.3	76 56 2.6	8.8070423	9.9452865	9.6698412
5	182 35 13.4	95 19 11.5	83 12 44.8	8.652817Gn	9.9434726	9.6781784

Day of the Year.	log x	log y	log z	x	y	z
0	9.1740113	9.3881011	9.0656100	+0.1492833	+0.2444000	+0.1163081
1	9.0732758	9.4069727	9.0978525	0.1183793	0.2552541	0.1252715
2	8.9359035	9.4208237	9.1237460	0.0862787	0.2635261	0.1329677
3	8.7267413	9.4299466	9.1439905	0.0533017	0.2691204	0.1393126
4	8.2963002	9.4345444	9.1590991	+0.0197834	0.2719846	0.1442445
5	8.1440918n	9.4347468	9.1694526	—0.0139345	+0.2721114	+0.1477245

The computation of an ephemeris may be completed by the following formulas, in which X, Y, and Z denote the sun's coördinates, a, δ, and Δ the right ascension, declination, and geocentric distance of the planet.

$$x + X = \Delta \cos \delta \cos a.$$
$$y + Y = \Delta \cos \delta \sin a.$$
$$z + Z = \Delta \sin \delta.$$

Aberration $= -8.22 \times \Delta \times$ minute motion in A. R. or Dec.

Semidiameter $= \dfrac{3''.34}{\Delta}$.

Horizontal Parallax $= \dfrac{8''.58}{\Delta}$.

TABLES OF MERCURY.

.

Place.	Longitude from Washington in Time.	Decimal of a Day.	Place.	Longitude from Washington in Time.	Decimal of a Day.
	h. m. s.	d.		h. m. s.	d.
Åbo,	—6 37 20.0	—0.275926	Kremsmünster,	—6 4 44.6	—0.253294
Albany,	0 13 12.6	0.009174	Leipsic,	5 57 39.7	0.248376
Altona,	—5 47 57.4	—0.241637	Leyden,	5 26 8.6	0.226488
Ann Arbor,	+0 27 12.0	+0.018889	Liverpool,	4 56 11.1	0.205684
Athens,	—6 43 6.4	—0.279935	London,	5 7 34.1	0.213589
Berlin,	6 1 46.1	0.251228	Madras,	10 29 8.2	0.436900
Bilk,	5 35 16.1	0.232825	Mannheim,	5 42 2.7	0.237531
Bonn,	5 36 35.7	0.233747	Markree,	4 34 22.8	0.190542
Breslau,	6 16 21.2	0.261356	Marseilles,	5 29 40.2	0.228937
Brussels,	5 25 38.8	0.226144	Milan,	5 44 57.8	0.239558
Cambridge (Mass.),	0 23 41.5	0.016453	Modena,	5 51 55.2	0.244389
Cambridge (Eng.),	5 8 34.7	0.214291	Moscow,	7 38 28.5	0.318385
Cape of Good Hope,	6 22 7.2	0.265361	Munich,	5 54 37.0	0.246269
Christiania,	—5 51 6.0	—0.243819	Naples,	6 5 12.1	0.253612
Cincinnati,	+0 29 46.9	+0.020682	Olmutz,	6 17 11.3	0.261809
Copenhagen,	—5 58 30.5	—0.248964	Oxford,	5 3 8.6	0.210516
Cracow,	6 28 2.4	0.269472	Padua,	5 55 40.2	0.246993
Dorpat,	6 55 5.8	0.288262	Palermo,	—6 1 36.7	—0.251119
Dublin,	4 42 49.2	0.196403	Paramatta,	+8 47 42.6	+0.366465
Durham,	5 1 53.2	0.209644	Paris,	—5 17 32.7	—0.220517
Edinburgh,	4 55 28.2	0.205187	St. Petersburg,	7 9 24.7	0.298203
Florence,	5 53 12.9	0.245288	Philadelphia,	0 7 33.6	0.005250
Geneva,	—5 32 48.9	—0.231122	Prague,	6 5 53.2	0.254088
Georgetown,	+0 0 6.2	+0.000072	Pulkowa,	7 9 20.9	0.298263
Göttingen,	—5 47 57.3	—0.241635	Rome,	5 58 .5.9	0.248679
Gotha,	5 51 6.9	0.243830	San Fernando,	4 43 22.1	0.196784
Greenwich,	5 8 11.2	0.214019	Santiago,	0 25 37.4	0.017966
Hamburg,	—5 48 4.8	—0.241722	Senftenberg,	6 14 1.1	0.259735
Hudson,	+0 17 32.1	+0.012177	Vienna,	6 18 43.7	0.259534
Kasan,	—8 24 43.1	—0.350499	Washington,	0 0 0.0	0.000000
Königsberg,	—6 30 11.6	—0.270968	Wilna,	—6 49 23.0	—0.284294

TABLE II. 3

Year.	Date in Mean Solar Days.	Year.	Date in Mean Solar Days.	YEAR IN THE CENTURY.		Days from previous Centennial Date.	YEAR IN THE CENTURY.		Days from previous Centennial Date.
				If Negative.	If Positive.		If Negative.	If Positive.	
—4713B.	0	—1000	1356173	100	1	0	50	51	18262
—4712	365	— 900	1392698	99	2	365	49B.	52B.	18628
—4711	730	— 800	1429223	98	3	730	48	53	18993
—4710	1095	— 700	1465748	97B.	4B.	1096	47	54	19358
—4709B.	1461	— 600	1502273	96	5	1461	46	55	19723
—4708	1826	— 500	1538798°	95	6	1826	45B.	56B.	20089
—4707	2191	— 400	1575323	94	7	2191	44	57	20454
—4706	2556	— 300	1611848	93B.	8B.	2557	43	58	20819
—4705B.	2922	— 200	1648373	92	9	2922	42	59	21184
—4704	3287	— 100	1684898	91	10	3287	41B.	60B.	21550
—4703	3652	1	1721423	90	11	3652	40	61	21915
—4702	4017	101	1757948	89B.	12B.	4018	39	62	22280
—4701B.	4383	201	1794473	88	13	4383	38	63	22645
—4700	4748	301	1830998	87	14	4748	37B.	64B.	23011
—4600	41273	401	1867523	86	15	5113	36	65	23376
—4500	77798	501	1904048	85B.	16B.	5479	35	66	23741
—4400	114323	601	1940573	84	17	5844	34	67	24106
—4300	150848	701	1977098	83	18	6209	33B.	68B.	24472
—4200	187373	801	2013623	82	19	6574	32	69	24837
—4100	223898	901	2050148	81B.	20B.	6940	31	70	25202
—4000	260423	1001	2086673	80	21	7305	30	71	25567
—3900	296948	1101	2123198	79	22	7670	29B.	72B.	25933
—3800	333473	1201	2159723	78	23	8035	28	73	26298
—3700	369998	1301	2196248	77B.	24B.	8401	27	74	26663
—3600	406523	1401	2232773	76	25	8766	26	75	27028
—3500	443048	1501	2269298	75	26	9131	25B.	76B.	27394
—3400	479573	1583	2299238	74	27	9496	24	77	27759
—3300	516098	1584B.	2299604	73B.	28B.	9862	23	78	28124
—3200	552623	1585	2299969	72	29	10227	22	79	28489
—3100	589148	1586	2300334	71	30	10592	21B.	80B.	28855
—3000	625673	1587	2300699	70	31	10957	20	81	29220
—2900	662198	1588B.	2301065	69B.	32B.	11323	19	82	29585
—2800	698723	1589	2301430	68	33	11688	18	83	29950
—2700	735248	1590	2301795	67	34	12053	17B.	84B.	30316
—2600	771773	1591	2302160	66	35	12418	16	85	30681
—2500	808298	1592B.	2302526	65B.	36B.	12784	15	86	31046
—2400	844823	1593	2302891	64	37	13149	14	87	31411
—2300	881348	1594	2303256	63	38	13514	13B.	88B.	31777
—2200	917873	1595	2303621	62	39	13879	12	89	32142
—2100	954398	1596B.	2303987	61B.	40B.	14245	11	90	32507
—2000	1090923	1597	2304352	60	41	14610	10	91	32872
—1900	1127448	1598 ·	2304717	59	42	14975	9B.	92B.	33238
—1800	1163973	1599	2305082	58	43	15340	8	93	33603
—1700	1200498	1600B.	2305448	57B.	44B.	15706	7	94	33968
—1600	1237023	1601	2305813	56	45	16071	6	95	34333
—1500	1273548	1701	2342337	55	46	16436	5B.	96B.	34699
—1400	1210073	1801	2378861	54	47	16801	4	97	35064
—1300	1246598	1901	2415385	53B.	48B.	17167	3	98	35429
—1200	1283123			52	49	17532	2	99	35794
—1100	1319648			51	50	17897	1B.	100B.	36160
—1000	1356173			50	51	18262		100	36159

4   TABLE III.

Day of Month	JANUARY Common Year	JANUARY Bissextile Year	FEBRUARY Common Year	FEBRUARY Bissextile Year	MARCH	APRIL	MAY	JUNE	JULY	AUGUST	SEPTEMBER	OCTOBER	NOVEMBER	DECEMBER	1582. OCTOBER	1582. NOVEMBER	1582. DECEMBER
1	1	0	32	31	60	91	121	152	182	213	244	274	305	335	274	295	325
2	2	1	33	32	61	92	122	153	183	214	245	275	306	336	275	296	326
3	3	2	34	33	62	93	123	154	184	215	246	276	307	337	276	297	327
4	4	3	35	34	63	94	124	155	185	216	247	277	308	338	277	298	328
5	5	4	36	35	64	95	125	156	186	217	248	278	309	339		299	329
6	6	5	37	36	65	96	126	157	187	218	249	279	310	340		300	330
7	7	6	38	37	66	97	127	158	188	219	250	280	311	341		301	331
8	8	7	39	38	67	98	128	159	189	220	251	281	312	342		302	332
9	9	8	40	39	68	99	129	160	190	221	252	282	313	343		303	333
10	10	9	41	40	69	100	130	161	191	222	253	283	314	344		304	334
11	11	10	42	41	70	101	131	162	192	223	254	284	315	345		305	335
12	12	11	43	42	71	102	132	163	193	224	255	285	316	346		306	336
13	13	12	44	43	72	103	133	164	194	225	256	286	317	347		307	337
14	14	13	45	44	73	104	134	165	195	226	257	287	318	348		308	338
15	15	14	46	45	74	105	135	166	196	227	258	288	319	349	278	309	339
16	16	15	47	46	75	106	136	167	197	228	259	289	320	350	279	310	340
17	17	16	48	47	76	107	137	168	198	229	260	290	321	351	280	311	341
18	18	17	49	48	77	108	138	169	199	230	261	322	322	352	281	312	342
19	19	18	50	49	78	109	139	170	200	231	262	292	323	353	282	313	343
20	20	19	51	50	79	110	140	171	201	232	263	293	324	354	283	314	344
21	21	20	52	51	80	111	141	172	202	233	264	294	325	355	284	315	345
22	22	21	53	52	81	112	142	173	203	234	265	295	326	356	285	316	346
23	23	22	54	53	82	113	143	174	204	235	266	296	327	357	286	317	347
24	24	23	55	54	83	114	144	175	205	236	267	297	328	358	287	318	348
25	25	24	56	55	84	115	145	176	206	237	268	298	329	359	288	319	349
26	26	25	57	56	85	116	146	177	207	238	269	299	330	360	289	320	350
27	27	26	58	57	86	117	147	178	208	239	270	300	331	361	290	321	351
28	28	27	59	58	87	118	148	179	209	240	271	301	332	362	291	322	352
29	29	28		59	88	119	149	180	210	241	272	302	333	363	292	323	353
30	30	29			89	120	150	181	211	242	273	303	334	364	293	324	354
31	31	30			90		151		212	243		304		365	294		355

TABLE IV.

5

Hours and Minutes	Decimal of a Day.	Minutes.	Decimal of a Day.	Minutes and Seconds	Decimal of a Day.	Seconds.	Decimal of a Day.
h.		m.		m.		s.	
1	.041666667	13	.009027778	50	.034722222	23	.000266204
2	.083333333	14	.009722222	51	.035416667	24	.000277778
3	.125000000	15	.010416667	52	.036111111	25	.000289352
4	.166666667	16	.011111111	53	.036805556	26	.000300926
5	.208333333	17	.011805556	54	.037500000	27	.000312500
6	.250000000	18	.012500000	55	.038494444	28	.000324074
7	.291666667	19	.013194444	56	.038888889	29	.000335648
8	.333333333	20	.013888889	57	.039583333	30	.000347222
9	.375000000	21	.014583333	58	.040277778	31	.000358796
10	.416666667	22	.015277778	59	.040972222	32	.000370310
11	.458333333	23	.015972222	60	.041666667	33	.000381944
12	.500000000	24	.016666667			34	.000393519
13	.541666667	25	.017361111			35	.000405093
14	.583333333	26	.018055556			36	.000416667
15	.625000000	27	.018750000			37	.000428241
16	.666666667	28	.019444444	s.		38	.000439815
17	.708333333	29	.020138889	1	.000011574	39	.000451389
18	.750000000	30	.020833333	2	.000023148	40	.000462963
19	.791666667	31	.021527778	3	.000034722	41	.000474537
20	.833333333	32	.022222222	4	.000046296	42	.000486111
				5	.000057870		
21	.875000000	33	.022916667	6	.000069444	43	.000497685
22	.916666666	34	.023611111	7	.000081019	44	.000509259
23	.958333333	35	.024305556	8	.000092593	45	.000520833
24	1.000000000	36	.025000000	9	.000104167	46	.000532407
		37	.025694444	10	.000115741	47	.000543981
m.							
1	.000694444	38	.026388889	11	.000127315	48	.000555556
2	.001388889	39	.027083333	12	.000138889	49	.000567130
3	.002083333	40	.027777778	13	.000150463	50	.000578704
4	.002777778	41	.028472222	14	.000162037	51	.000590278
5	.003472222	42	.029166667	15	.000173611	52	.000601852
6	.004166667	43	.029861111	16	.000185185	53	.000613426
7	.004861111	44	.030555556	17	.000196759	54	.000625000
8	.005555556	45	.031230000	18	.000208333	55	.000636574
9	.006250000	46	.031944444	19	.000219907	56	.000648148
10	.006944444	47	.032638889	20	.000231481	57	.000659722
11	.007638889	48	.033333333	21	.000243056	58	.000671296
12	.008333333	49	.034027778	22	.000254630	59	.000682870
13	.009027778	50	.034722222	23	.000266204	60	.000694444

6 TABLE V.

Year.	L	Ω	π	p	H_1	H_2
1800	109° 4′ 40.35″	45° 57′ 37.67″	74° 20′ 41.55″	0.00	6170	1.7
1801	162 47 43.65	45 58 20.15	74 21 37.10	0.00	6535	1.5
1802	216 30 46.95	45 59 2.63	74 22 32.65	0.00	102	1.3
1803	270 13 50.26	45 59 45.11	74 23 28.20	0.00	468	1.0
1804 B	323 56 53.56	46 0 27.60	74 24 23.75	0.00	832	0.8
1805	21 45 29.42	46 1 10.19	74 25 19.46	0.00	1198	1.5
1806	75 28 32.72	46 1 52.68	74 26 15.01	0.00	1563	1.3
1807	129 11 36.02	46 2 35.16	74 27 10.56	0.00	1929	1.0
1808 B	182 54 39.32	46 3 17.64	74 28 6.11	0.00	2293	0.8
1809	240 43 15.18	46 4 0.24	74 29 1.81	0.00	2659	1.6
1810	294 26 18.48	46 4 42.72	74 29 57.36	0.01	3024	1.3
1811	348 9 21.79	46 5 25.20	74 30 52.91	0.01	3390	1.1
1812 B	41 52 25.09	46 6 7.68	74 31 48.47	0.01	3754	0.8
1813	99 41 0.95	46 6 50.28	74 32 44.17	0.02	4120	1.6
1814	153 24 4.25	46 7 32.77	74 33 39.72	0.02	4485	1.3
1815	207 7 7.55	46 8 15.25	74 34 35.27	0.03	4851	1.1
1816 B	260 50 10.85	46 8 57.73	74 35 30.82	0.03	5215	0.9
1817	318 36 46.71	46 9 40.33	74 36 26.52	0.04	5581	1.6
1818	12 21 50.01	46 10 22.81	74 37 22.08	0.04	5946	1.4
1819	66 4 53.32	46 11 5.29	74 38 17.63	0.05	6312	1.1
1820 B	119 47 56.62	46 11 47.77	74 39 13.18	0.05	6676	0.9
1821	177 36 32.48	46 12 30.37	74 40 8.88	0.05	214	1.6
1822	231 19 35.78	46 13 12.86	74 41 4.43	0.06	609	1.4
1823	285 2 39.08	46 13 55.34	74 41 59.98	0.06	974	1.2
1824 B	338 45 42.38	46 14 37.82	74 42 55.53	0.07	1339	0.9
1825	36 34 18.24	46 15 20.42	74 43 51.24	0.08	1705	1.7
1826	90 17 21.54	46 16 2.90	74 44 46.79	0.08	2070	1.4
1827	144 0 24.85	46 16 45.38	74 45 42.34	0.08	2435	1.2
1828 B	197 43 28.15	46 17 27.86	74 46 37.89	0.09	2800	0.9
1829	255 32 4.00	46 18 10.46	74 47 33.59	0.10	3166	1.7
1830	309 15 7.31	46 18 52.95	74 48 29.14	0.11	3531	1.5
1831	2 58 10.61	46 19 35.43	74 49 24.69	0.11	3897	1.2
1832 B	56 41 13.91	46 20 17.91	74 50 20.25	0.12	4261	1.0
1833	114 29 49.77	46 21 0.51	74 51 15.95	0.13	4627	1.7
1834	168 12 53.07	46 21 42.99	74 52 11.50	0.14	4992	1.5
1835	221 55 56.38	46 22 25.47	74 53 7.05	0.15	5358	1.2
1836 B	275 38 59.68	46 23 7.95	74 54 2.60	0.15	5722	1.0
1837	333 27 35.54	46 23 50.55	74 54 58.31	0.16	6088	1.8
1838	27 10 38.84	46 24 33.04	74 55 53.86	0.17	6453	1.5
1839	80 53 42.14	46 25 15.52	74 56 49.41	0.18	20	1.3
1840 B	134 36 45.44	46 25 58.00	74 57 44.96	0.19	385	1.0
1841	192 25 21.30	46 26 40.60	74 58 40.66	0.20	751	1.8
1842	246 8 24.60	46 27 23.08	74 59 36.21	0.21	1116	1.5
1843	299 51 27.91	46 28 5.56	75 0 31.76	0.22	1481	1.3
1844 B	353 34 31.21	46 28 48.04	75 1 27.31	0.23	1846	1.1
1845	51 23 7.07	46 29 30.64	75 2 23.02	0.24	2212	1.8
1846	105 6 10.37	46 30 13.13	75 3 18.57	0.25	2577	1.6
1847	158 49 13.67	46 30 55.61	75 4 14.12	0.26	2942	1.3
1848 B	212 32 16.97	46 31 38.09	75 5 9.67	0.28	3307	1.1
1849	270 20 52.83	46 32 20.69	75 6 5.37	0.29	3673	1.8
1850	324 3 56.13	46 33 3.17	75 7 0.92	0.30	4038	1.6

TABLE V.

7

Year.	A	T	V	J	E	S	m
1800	16.974666	28.11	105.10	59.66	55.66	73.8	0
1801	43.219906	41.23	53.02	4.48	53.47	81.1	4
1802	69.465146	54.35	0.94	9.36	51.28	88.4	8
1803	95.710386	67.47	68.86	14.24	49.09	6.2	12
1804 B	121.955626	80.59	16.78	19.12	46.89	13.5	16
1805	150.200667	6.75	11.68	25.20	59.13	21.8	20
1806	0.507417	19.87	79.59	30.08	56.94	29.0	25
1807	26.752657	33.00	27.51	34.96	54.74	36.3	29
1808 B	52.997697	46.12	95.42	39.84	52.54	43.6	33
1809	81.243137	60.24	43.35	44.72	50.35	51.9	37
1810	107.488377	73.36	111.26	49.60	48.15	59.1	41
1811	133.733617	86.49	59.18	54.48	45.95	66.4	45
1812 B	159.978857	11.64	54.08	0.52	58.18	73.7	49
1813	12.285407	25.76	2.00	5.40	56.00	82.0	54
1814	38.530648	38.88	69.92	10.27	53.81	89.2	58
1815	64.775868	52.01	17.83	15.16	51.61	7.0	62
1816 B	91.021128	65.13	85.75	20.02	49.40	14.3	66
1817	119.266368	79.25	33.67	24.90	47.21	22.6	70
1818	145.511608	4.41	28.56	30.99	59.46	29.9	74
1819	171.756848	17.53	96.48	35.86	57.27	37.2	78
1820 B	22.063398	30.65	44.41	40.75	55.06	44.4	83
1821	50.306638	44.77	112.32	45.63	52.86	52.7	87
1822	76.553879	57.90	60.24	50.52	50.66	60.0	91
1823	102.799119	71.02	8.16	55.40	48.46	67.3	95
1824 B	129.044359	84.14	76.08	0.21	46.27	74.5	99
1825	157.269599	10.29	70.97	6.31	58.53	82.8	103
1826	7.596148	23.42	18.68	11.18	56.34	0.6	109
1827	33.841389	36.54	86.80	16.07	54.12	7.9	112
1828 B	60.086629	49.66	34.72	20.94	51.93	15.2	116
1829	88.331869	63.78	102.64	25.81	49.73	23.5	120
1830	114.577110	76.91	50.56	30.69	47.55	30.7	124
1831	140.822350	2.06	45.46	36.78	59.80	38.0	128
1832 B	167.067590	15.19	113.37	41.67	57.60	45.3	132
1833	19.374140	29.31	61.29	46.55	55.39	53.6	137
1834	45.619380	42.43	9.22	51.43	53.19	60.8	141
1835	71.864620	55.55	77.14	56.30	51.00	68.1	145
1836 B	98.109860	68.67	25.05	1.12	48.82	75.4	149
1837	126.355100	82 80	92.97	6.00	46.61	83.7	153
1838	152.600341	7.95	87.87	12.11	58.85	1.5	157
1839	2.906891	21.07	35.79	16.97	56.67	8.8	162
1840 B	29.152131	34.20	103.70	21.85	54.46	16.0	166
1841	57.397371	48.32	51.62	26.73	52.25	24.3	170
1842	83.642611	61.44	119.54	31.61	50.06	31.6	174
1843	109.887851	74.56	67.46	36.50	47.87	38.9	178
1844 B	136.133091	87.69	15.36	41.36	45.67	46.1	182
1845	164.378331	13.84	10.26	47.45	57.92	54.4	186
1846	14.681882	26.96	78.18	52.34	55.72	61.7	191
1847	40.930122	40.08	26.10	57.22	53.52	68.9	195
1848 B	67.175362	53.21	94.01	2.03	51.34	76.2	199
1849	95.420602	67.33	41.93	6.91	49.13	84.5	203
1850	121.665842	80.45	109.85	11.79	46.94	2.3	207

8

TABLE V.

Year.	I,	Ω	π	p	H₁	H₂
1850	324 3 56.13	46 33 3.17	75 7 0.92	0.30	4036	1.6
1851	17 46 59.44	46 33 45.65	75 7 56.47	0.31	4403	1.4
1852 B	71 30 2.74	46 34 28.14	75 8 52.03	0.33	4768	1.1
1853	129 18 38.60	46 35 10.73	75 9 47.73	0.34	5134	1.9
1854	183 1 41.90	46 35 53.22	75 10 43.28	0.36	5499	1.6
1855	236 44 45.20	46 36 35.70	75 11 38.83	0.37	5864	1.4
1856 B	290 27 48.50	46 37 18.18	75 12 34.38	0.38	6229	1.1
1857	348 16 21.36	46 38 0.78	75 13 30.08	0.40	6595	1.9
1858	41 59 27.66	46 38 43.26	75 14 25.64	0.42	162	1.7
1859	95 42 30.97	46 39 25.74	75 15 21.19	0.43	527	1.4
1860 B	149 25 34.27	46 40 8.22	75 16 16.74	0.44	891	1.2
1861	207 14 10.13	46 40 50.82	75 17 12.44	0.46	1258	1.9
1862	260 57 13.43	46 41 33.31	75 18 7.99	0.47	1623	1.7
1863	314 40 16.73	46 42 15.79	75 19 3.54	0.48	1988	1.4
1864 B	8 23 20.03	46 42 58.27	75 19 59.09	0.49	2353	1.2
1865	66 11 55.89	46 43 40.87	75 20 54.80	0.51	2719	2.0
1866	119 54 59.19	46 44 23.35	75 21 50.35	0.53	3084	1.7
1867	173 38 2.50	46 45 5.83	75 22 45.90	0.55	3449	1.5
1868 B	227 21 5.80	46 45 48.31	75 23 41.45	0.56	3814	1.2
1869	285 9 41.66	46 46 30.91	75 24 37.15	0.58	4180	2.0
1870	338 52 44.96	46 47 13.40	75 25 32.70	0.60	4545	1.7
1871	32 35 48.26	46 47 55.88	75 26 28.25	0.62	4910	1.5
1872 B	86 18 51.56	46 48 38.36	75 27 23.81	0.63	5275	1.3
1873	144 7 27.42	46 49 20.96	75 28 19.51	0.65	5641	2.0
1874	197 50 30.72	46 50 3.44	75 29 15.06	0.67	6006	1.8
1875	251 33 34.03	46 50 45.92	75 30 10.61	0.68	6371	1.5
1876 B	305 16 37.33	46 51 28.40	75 31 6.16	0.70	6736	1.3
1877	3 5 13.19	46 52 11.00	75 32 1.86	0.72	304	2.1
1878	56 48 16.49	46 52 53.49	75 32 57.42	0.74	669	1.8
1879	110 31 19.79	46 53 35.97	75 33 52.97	0.76	1034	1.6
1880 B	164 14 23.09	46 54 18.45	75 34 48.52	0.78	1398	1.3
1881	222 2 58.95	46 55 1.05	75 35 44.22	0.80	1765	2.1
1882	275 46 2.25	46 55 43.53	75 36 39.77	0.82	2130	1.8
1883	329 29 5.56	46 56 26.01	75 37 35.32	0.84	2495	1.6
1884 B	23 12 8.86	46 57 8.49	75 38 30.87	0.86	2859	1.4
1885	81 0 44.72	46 57 51.09	75 39 26.58	0.88	3226	2.1
1886	134 43 48.02	46 58 33.58	75 40 22.13	0.90	3591	1.9
1887	188 26 51.32	46 59 16.06	75 41 17.68	0.92	3956	1.6
1888 B	242 9 54.62	46 59 58.54	75 42 13.23	0.94	4321	1.4
1889	299 58 30.48	47 0 41.14	75 43 8.93	0.97	4687	2.1
1890	353 41 33.78	47 1 23.62	75 44 4.48	0.99	5052	1.9
1891	47 24 37.09	47 2 6.10	75 45 0.03	1.01	5417	1.7
1892 B	101 7 40.39	47 2 48.58	75 45 55.59	1.03	5782	1.4
1893	158 56 16.25	47 3 31.18	75 46 51.29	1.05	6148	2.2
1894	212 39 19.55	47 4 13.67	75 47 46.84	1.07	6513	1.9
1895	266 22 22.85	47 4 56.15	75 48 42.39	1.10	80	1.7
1896 B	320 5 26.15	47 5 38.63	75 49 37.94	1.12	444	1.4
1897	17 54 2.01	47 6 21.23	75 50 33.64	1.14	811	2.2
1898	71 37 5.31	47 7 3.71	75 51 29.20	1.17	1176	2.0
1899	125 20 8.62	47 7 46.19	75 52 24.75	1.19	1541	1.7
1900	179 3 11.92	47 8 28.67	75 53 20.30	1.22	1906	1.5

TABLE V.

Year.	A	T	V	J	E	S	m
1850	121.665842	80.45	109.85	11.79	46.94	2.3	207
1851	147.911082	5.60	104.75	17.87	59.19	9.6	211
1852 B	174.156322	18.73	52.66	22.76	56.98	16.9	215
1853	26.462873	32.85	0.58	27.65	54.78	25.2	220
1854	52.708113	45.97	68.50	32.52	52.60	32.4	224
1855	78.953353	59.10	16.41	37.40	50.39	39.7	228
1856 B	105.198593	72.22	84.33	42.28	48.20	47.0	232
1857	133.443833	86.34	32.25	47.17	45.99	55.3	236
1858	159.689073	11.49	27.15	53.24	58.25	62.5	240
1859	9.995623	24.62	95.07	58.12	56.05	69.8	245
1860 B	36.240863	37.74	42.98	2.95	53.86	77.1	249
1861	61.486104	51.86	110.90	7.83	51.67	85.3	253
1862	90.731344	64.99	58.81	12.71	49.47	3.2	257
1863	116.976584	78.11	6.73	17.57	47.26	10.5	261
1864 B	143.221824	3.26	1.63	23.67	59.52	17.7	265
1865	171.467064	17.38	69.55	28.56	57.31	26.0	269
1866	21.773614	30.51	17.46	33.43	55.10	33.3	274
1867	48.018854	43.63	85.39	38.31	52.92	40.6	278
1868 B	74.264094	56.75	33.30	43.19	50.73	47.8	282
1869	102.509335	70.87	101.22	48.07	48.53	56.1	286
1870	128.754575	84.00	49.13	52.95	46.33	63.4	290
1871	154.999815	9.15	44.04	59.04	58.58	70.6	294
1872 B	5.306365	22.27	111.96	3.87	56.40	77.9	299
1873	33.551605	36.39	59.87	8.74	54.19	86.2	303
1874	59.796845	49.52	7.78	13.62	51.99	4.0	307
1875	86.042085	62.64	75.70	18.49	49.80	11.3	311
1876 B	112.287325	75.76	23.62	23.37	47.60	18.6	315
1877	140.532566	1.92	18.52	29.47	59.84	26.9	319
1878	166.777806	15.04	86.44	34.36	57.64	34.1	323
1879	17.084356	28.16	34.36	39.23	55.45	41.4	328
1880 B	43.329596	41.28	102.27	44.10	53.26	48.7	332
1881	71.574836	55.41	50.18	48.98	51.07	56.9	336
1882	97.820076	68.53	118.10	53.86	48.86	64.2	340
1883	121.065316	81.66	66.02	58.74	46.65	71.5	344
1884 B	150.310556	6.81	60.92	4.78	58.90	78.8	348
1885	2.617106	20.93	8.84	9.66	56.72	87.0	353
1886	28.862347	34.05	76.76	14.53	54.53	4.9	357
1887	55.107587	47.17	24.68	19.41	52.32	12.2	361
1888 B	81.352827	60.29	92.60	24.29	50.12	19.4	365
1889	109.598067	74.42	40.51	29.16	47.93	27.7	369
1890	135.843307	87.54	108.42	34.05	45.73	35.0	373
1891	162.088547	12.69	103.33	40.13	58.00	42.2	377
1892 B	12.395097	25.82	51.24	45.01	55.77	49.5	383
1893	40.640337	39.94	119.16	49.89	53.58	57.8	386
1894	66.885578	53.06	67.08	54.77	51.38	65.1	390
1895	93.130818	66.18	15.00	59.65	49.20	72.3	394
1896 B	119.376058	79.31	82.92	4.47	46.99	79.6	398
1897	147.621298	5.46	77.82	10.57	59.25	87.9	402
1898	173.866538	18.58	25.73	15.44	57.01	5.7	406
1899	24.173088	31.70	93.65	20.31	54.85	13.0	411
1900	50.418328	44.82	41.57	25.20	52.65	20.3	415

Year.	K_x	K_y	K_z	log k_x	log k_y	log k_z
1800	161° 7′ 30″.0	76° 49′ 50″.6	64° 53′ 56″.6	9.9983264	9.9450101	9.6821729
1801	164 8 25.5	76 50 47.6	64 54 44.0	.9983258	.9450140	.6821624
1802	164 9 21.1	76 51 44.7	64 55 31.4	.9983251	.9450191	.6821484
1803	164 10 16.7	76 52 41.7	64 56 18.8	.9983243	.9450255	.6821301
1804 B	164 11 12.2	76 53 38.8	64 57 6.2	.9983235	.9450327	.6821092
1805	164 12 7.9	76 54 36.0	64 57 53.7	.9983226	.9450407	.6820854
1806	164 13 3.5	76 55 33.0	64 58 41.1	.9983221	.9450489	.6820606
1807	164 13 59.1	76 56 30.1	64 59 28.5	.9983214	.9450574	.6820354
1808 B	164 14 54.6	76 57 27.1	65 0 15.9	.9983208	.9450652	.6820118
1809	164 15 50.3	76 58 24.3	65 1 3.4	.9983202	.9450725	.6819901
1810	164 16 45.9	76 59 21.4	65 1 50.8	.9983195	.9450792	.6819721
1811	164 17 41.5	77 0 18.4	65 2 38.2	.9983190	.9450833	.6819583
1812 B	164 18 37.0	77 1 15.5	65 3 25.6	.9983184	.9450871	.6819484
1813	164 19 32.7	77 2 12.7	65 4 13.2	.9983177	.9450898	.6819423
1814	164 20 28.3	77 3 9.7	65 5 0.6	.9983171	.9450921	.6819386
1815	164 21 23.8	77 4 6.8	65 5 48.0	.9983165	.9450931	.6819370
1816 B	164 22 19.4	77 5 3.8	65 6 35.4	.9983158	.9450942	.6819356
1817	164 23 15.1	77 6 1.1	65 7 22.9	.9983151	.9450960	.6819326
1818	164 24 10.7	77 6 58.1	65 8 10.3	.9983144	.9450983	.6819278
1819	164 25 6.2	77 7 55.2	65 8 57.7	.9983136	.9451017	.6819197
1820 B	164 26 1.8	77 8 52.2	65 9 45.1	.9983128	.9451063	.6819078
1821	164 26 57.5	77 9 49.4	65 10 32.7	.9983121	.9451120	.6818921
1822	164 27 53.1	77 10 46.5	65 11 20.1	.9983113	.9451187	.6818728
1823	164 28 48.7	77 11 43.5	65 12 7.5	.9983105	.9451263	.6818506
1824 B	164 29 44.3	77 12 40.5	65 12 54.9	.9983097	.9451345	.6818261
1825	164 30 40.0	77 13 37.8	65 13 42.8	.9983089	.9451430	.6818009
1826	164 31 35.5	77 14 34.8	65 14 29.9	.9983083	.9451510	.6817761
1827	164 32 31.0	77 15 31.9	65 15 17.3	.9983078	.9451588	.6817527
1828 B	164 33 26.7	77 16 28.9	65 16 4.7	.9983072	.9451656	.6817326
1829	164 34 22.4	77 17 26.1	65 16 52.3	.9983066	.9451710	.6817162
1830	164 35 18.0	77 18 23.2	65 17 39.7	.9983059	.9451759	.6817035
1831	164 36 13.6	77 19 20.2	65 18 27.1	.9983053	.9451789	.6816953
1832 B	164 37 9.1	77 20 17.3	65 19 14.5	.9983047	.9451811	.6816901
1833	164 38 4.8	77 21 14.5	65 20 2.1	.9983041	.9451827	.6816876
1834	164 39 0.4	77 22 11.5	65 20 49.5	.9983036	.9451840	.6816858
1835	164 39 56.0	77 23 8.5	65 21 36.9	.9983029	.9451855	.6816839
1836 B	164 40 51.6	77 24 5.6	65 22 24.4	.9983022	.9451875	.6816803
1837	164 41 47.3	77 25 2.8	65 23 11.9	.9983015	.9451903	.6816743
1838	164 42 42.8	77 25 59.8	65 23 59.3	.9983007	.9451939	.6816660
1839	164 43 38.4	77 26 56.8	65 24 46.8	.9982999	.9451990	.6816514
1840 B	164 44 34.0	77 27 53.9	65 25 34.2	.9982991	.9452052	.6816338
1841	164 45 29.7	77 28 51.1	65 26 21.7	.9982983	.9452124	.6816132
1842	164 46 25.2	77 29 48.1	65 27 9.1	.9982977	.9452201	.6815901
1843	164 47 20.8	77 30 45.2	65 27 56.6	.9982969	.9452284	.6815650
1844 B	164 48 16.4	77 31 42.2	65 28 44.0	.9982962	.9452367	.6815396
1845	164 49 12.1	77 32 39.4	65 29 31.6	.9982955	.9452448	.6815154
1846	164 50 7.7	77 33 36.5	65 30 19.0	.9982949	.9452524	.6814935
1847	164 51 3.3	77 34 33.5	65 31 6.4	.9982944	.9452585	.6814743
1848 B	164 51 56.9	77 35 30.6	65 31 53.8	.9982938	.9452637	.6814593
1849	164 52 54.5	77 36 27.7	65 32 41.4	.9982932	.9452678	.6814484
1850	164 53 50.1	77 37 24.8	65 33 28.8	9.9982925	9.9452706	9.6814414

TABLE VI.   11

Year.	K_x	K_y	K_z	$\log k_x$	$\log k_y$	$\log k_z$
1850	164° 53′ 50″.1	77° 37′ 24″.8	65° 33′ 28″.8	9.9982925	9.9452706	9.6814414
1851	164 54 45.7	77 38 21.8	65 34 16.2	.9982919	.9452727	.6814372
1852 B	164 55 41.3	77 39 18.8	65 35 3.7	.9982914	.9452741	.6814352
1853	164 56 37.0	77 40 16.0	65 35 51.3	.9982907	.9452756	.6814334
1854	164 57 32.6	77 41 13.1	65 36 38.7	.9982900	.9452772	.6814310
1855	164 58 28.1	77 42 10.1	65 37 26.1	.9982892	.9452794	.6814263
1856 B	164 59 23.7	77 43 7.1	65 38 13.5	.9982884	.9452825	.6814191
1857	165 0 19.4	77 44 4.3	65 39 1.1	.9982877	.9452867	.6814079
1858	165 1 15.0	77 45 1.3	65 39 48.5	.9982870	.9452921	.6813931
1859	165 2 10.6	77 45 58.4	65 40 36.0	.9982862	.9452987	.6813744
1860 B	165 3 6.1	77 46 55.4	65 41 23.4	.9982854	.9453060	.6813526
1861	165 4 1.9	77 47 52.6	65 42 11.0	.9982846	.9453142	.6813285
1862	165 4 57.4	77 48 49.6	65 42 58.4	.9982840	.9453229	.6813032
1863	165 5 53.0	77 49 46.6	65 43 45.9	.9982833	.9453310	.6812778
1864 B	165 6 48.6	77 50 43.7	65 44 33.3	.9982827	.9453387	.6812543
1865	165 7 44.3	77 51 40.9	65 45 20.9	.9982821	.9453460	.6812330
1866	165 8 39.9	77 52 37.9	65 46 8.3	.9982815	.9453519	.6812156
1867	165 9 35.5	77 53 35.0	65 46 55.8	.9982809	.9453567	.6812022
1868 B	165 10 31.1	77 54 32.0	65 47 43.2	.9982803	.9453602	.6811927
1869	165 11 26.8	77 55 29.2	65 48 30.8	.9982797	.9453627	.6811868
1870	165 12 22.4	77 56 26.2	65 49 18.2	.9982791	.9453645	.6811832
1871	165 13 18.0	77 57 23.3	65 50 5.7	.9982785	.9453658	.6811817
1872 B	165 14 13.5	77 58 20.3	65 50 53.1	.9982778	.9453672	.6811798
1873	165 15 9.3	77 59 17.5	65 51 40.7	.9982771	.9453692	.6811765
1874	165 16 4.9	78 0 14.5	65 52 28.1	.9982763	.9453717	.6811709
1875	165 17 0.5	78 1 11.6	65 53 15.6	.9982756	.9453753	.6811620
1876 B	165 17 56.0	78 2 8.6	65 54 3.0	.9982748	.9453799	.6811494
1877	165 18 51.8	78 3 5.8	65 54 50.6	.9982740	.9453858	.6811329
1878	165 19 47.4	78 4 2.8	65 55 39.1	.9982734	.9453927	.6811129
1879	165 20 43.0	78 4 59.9	65 56 25.5	.9982726	.9454003	.6810902
1880 B	165 21 38.6	78 5 56.9	65 57 13.0	.9982718	.9454087	.6810653
1881	165 22 34.3	78 6 54.1	65 58 0.6	.9982711	.9454171	.6810399
1882	165 23 29.9	78 7 51.1	65 58 48.1	.9982705	.9454253	.6810150
1883	165 24 25.5	78 8 48.1	65 59 35.5	.9982699	.9454329	.6809921
1884 B	165 25 21.1	78 9 45.2	66 0 23.0	.9982692	.9454396	.6809723
1885	165 26 16.8	78 10 42.4	66 1 10.6	.9982687	.9454451	.6809562
1886	165 27 12.4	78 11 39.4	66 1 58.0	.9982680	.9454494	.6809442
1887	165 28 8.0	78 12 36.4	66 2 45.5	.9982674	.9454525	.6809362
1888 B	165 29 3.6	78 13 33.4	66 3 32.9	.9982668	.9454546	.6809313
1889	165 29 59.4	78 14 30.6	66 4 20.5	.9982662	.9454562	.6809289
1890	165 30 54.9	78 15 27.7	66 5 8.0	.9982656	.9454575	.6809270
1891	165 31 50.5	78 16 24.7	66 5 55.5	.9982649	.9454591	.6809248
1892 B	165 32 46.1	78 17 21.7	66 6 42.9	.9982641	.9454612	.6809207
1893	165 33 41.9	78 18 18.9	66 7 30.5	.9982633	.9454642	.6809139
1894	165 34 37.4	78 19 15.9	66 8 18.0	.9982626	.9454683	.6809034
1895	165 35 33.0	78 20 13.0	66 9 5.5	.9982619	.9454733	.6808892
1896 B	165 36 28.6	78 21 10.0	66 9 52.9	.9982611	.9454796	.6808713
1897	165 37 24.4	78 22 7.2	66 10 40.5	.9982603	.9454870	.6808499
1898	165 38 20.0	78 23 4.2	66 11 28.0	.9982595	.9454949	.6808262
1899	165 39 15.6	78 24 1.2	66 12 15.5	.9982588	.9455033	.6808012
1900	165 40 11.2	78 24 58.3	66 13 2.9	9.9982581	9.9455115	9.6807761

TABLE VII.

Months.	C.	D.	L	π	Ω	Hours.	L	Hours.	L.
Jan.	0	0	0° 0′ 0.00″	0.00″	0.00″	1	0° 10′ 13.86″	13	2 13 0.13
Feb.	0	0	126 51 49.27	4.72	3.61	2	0 20 27.71	14	2 23 13.99
March	1	0	215 32 33.42	9.13	6.98	3	0 30 41.57	15	2 33 27.85
April	1	0	12 24 22.69	13.85	10.59	4	0 40 55.43	16	2 43 41.70
May	1	0	135 10 39.40	18.42	14.08	5	0 51 9.28	17	2 53 55.56
June	1	0	262 2 28.66	23.13	17.69	6	1 1 23.14	18	3 4 9.42
July	1	0	24 48 45.37	27.70	21.18	7	1 11 37.00	19	3 14 23.27
Aug.	1	0	151 40 34.64	32.42	24.79	8	1 21 50.85	20	3 24 37.13
Sept.	1	0	278 32 23.91	37.14	28.40	9	1 32 4.71	21	3 34 50.99
Oct.	1	0	41 18 40.62	41.70	31.89	10	1 42 18.56	22	3 45 4.84
Nov.	1	0	168 10 29.88	46.42	35.50	11	1 52 32.42	23	3 55 18.70
Dec.	1	0	290 56 46.59	50.99	38.99	12	2 2 46.28	24	4 5 32.56

Days.	L	π	Ω	Minutes, Seconds.	L	L	Minutes, Seconds.	L	L
1	4° 5′ 32.56″	0.15	0.12	1	0′ 10.23″	0.17″	31	5′ 17.16″	5.29″
2	8 11 5.11	0.30	0.23	2	0 20.46	0.34	32	5 27.39	5.46
3	12 16 37.67	0.46	0.35	3	0 30.69	0.51	33	5 37.62	5.63
4	16 22 10.23	0.61	0.47	4	0 40.92	0.68	34	5 47.85	5.80
5	20 27 42.78	0.76	0.58	5	0 51.15	0.85	35	5 58.08	5.97
6	24 33 15.34	0.91	0.70	6	1 1.39	1.02	36	6 8.31	6.14
7	28 38 47.90	1.07	0.81	7	1 11.62	1.19	37	6 18.54	6.31
8	32 44 20.46	1.22	0.93	8	1 21.85	1.36	38	6 28.78	6.48
9	36 49 53.01	1.37	1.05	9	1 32.08	1.53	39	6 39.01	6.65
10	40 55 25.57	1.52	1.16	10	1 42.31	1.70	40	6 49.24	6.82
11	45 0 58.13	1.67	1.28	11	1 52.54	1.88	41	6 59.47	6.99
12	49 6 30.68	1.83	1.40	12	2 2.77	2.05	42	7 9.70	7.16
13	53 12 3.24	1.98	1.51	13	2 13.00	2.22	43	7 19.93	7.33
14	57 17 35.80	2.13	1.63	14	2 23.23	2.39	44	7 30.16	7.50
15	61 23 8.35	2.28	1.75	15	2 33.46	2.56	45	7 40.39	7.67
16	65 28 40.91	2.44	1.86	16	2 43.69	2.73	46	7 50.62	7.84
17	69 34 13.47	2.59	1.98	17	2 53.93	2.90	47	8 0.85	8.01
18	73 39 46.03	2.74	2.10	18	3 4.16	3.07	48	8 11.08	8.18
19	77 45 18.58	2.89	2.21	19	3 14.39	3.24	49	8 21.32	8.35
20	81 50 51.14	3.04	2.33	20	3 24.62	3.41	50	8 31.55	8.53
21	85 56 23.70	3.20	2.44	21	3 34.85	3.58	51	8 41.78	8.70
22	90 1 56.25	3.34	2.56	22	3 45.08	3.75	52	8 52.01	8.87
23	94 7 28.81	3 50	2.68	23	3 55.31	3.92	53	9 2.24	9.04
24	98 13 1.37	3.65	2.79	24	4 5.54	4.09	54	9 12.47	9.21
25	102 18 33.92	3.80	2.91	25	4 15.77	4.26	55	9 22.70	9.38
26	106 24 6.48	3.96	3.03	26	4 26.00	4.43	56	9 32.93	9.55
27	110 29 39.04	4.11	3.14	27	4 36.24	4.60	57	9 43.16	9.72
28	114 35 11.60	4.26	3.26	28	4 46.47	4.77	58	9 53.39	9.89
29	118 40 44.15	4.41	3.38	29	4 56.70	4.94	59	10 3.62	10.06
30	122 46 16.71	4.57	3.49	30	5 6.93	5.12	60	10 13.86	10.23
31	126 51 49.27	4.72	3.61						

TABLE VIII.   13

H_1	$d_C K_x$	$d_C K_y$	$d_C K_z$	H_1	$d_C K_x$	$d_C K_y$	$d_C K_z$	H_1	$d_C K_x$	$d_C K_y$	$d_C K_z$
0	18.00	21.03	21.52	2400	32.02	33.88	27.28	4800	1.22	2.34	3.38
100	19.56	22.64	22.78	2500	31.00	32.75	26.19	4900	0.89	2.11	3.44
200	21.11	24.24	24.00	2600	29.87	31.53	25.03	5000	0.71	2.01	3.62
300	22.65	25.82	25.17	2700	28.63	30.17	23.82	5100	0.66	2.08	3.93
400	24.12	27.31	26.29	2800	27.29	28.72	22.53	5200	0.79	2.30	4.34
500	25.57	28.77	27.34	2900	25.87	27.20	21.20	5300	1.05	2.65	4.89
600	26.94	30.13	28.30	3000	24.38	25.61	19.86	5400	1.45	3.15	5.53
700	28.25	31.45	29.20	3100	22.83	23.98	18.49	5500	1.99	3.81	6.27
800	29.47	32.65	29.98	3200	21.24	22.31	17.12	5600	2.67	4.58	7.12
900	30.60	33.76	30.68	3300	19.62	20.62	15.75	5700	3.47	5.51	8.04
1000	31.63	34.74	31.26	3400	17.98	18.92	14.39	5800	4.39	6.54	9.07
1100	32.55	35.62	31.75	3500	16.35	17.23	13.09	5900	5.42	7.69	10.16
1200	33.35	36.37	32.12	3600	14.73	15.57	11.81	6000	6.56	8.93	11.30
1300	34.02	36.97	32.36	3700	13.14	13.95	10.59	6100	7.78	10.25	12.51
1400	34.56	37.44	32.50	3800	11.59	12.37	9.44	6200	9.09	11.65	13.76
1500	34.96	37.76	32.52	3900	10.10	10.87	8.36	6300	10.47	13.13	15.03
1600	35.21	37.91	32.39	4000	8.68	9.45	7.36	6400	11.91	14.66	16.30
1700	35.32	37.94	32.15	4100	7.35	8.13	6.46	6500	13.40	16.24	17.64
1800	35.29	37.81	31.80	4200	6.11	6.93	5.69	6600	14.92	17.83	18.96
1900	35.10	37.52	31.32	4300	4.98	5.81	5.00	6700	16.47	19.45	20.26
2000	31.77	37.08	30.73	4400	3.96	4.84	4.43	6800	18.03	21.07	21.54
2100	31.29	36.50	30.01	4500	3.07	3.99	3.97	6900	19.59	22.68	22.81
2200	33.67	35.77	29.21	4600	2.32	3.30	3.67	7000	21.14	24.27	24.03
2300	32.91	34.89	28.29	4700	1.70	2.75	3.47	7100	22.66	25.82	25.19
2400	32.02	33.86	27.28	4800	1.22	2.34	3.38	7200	24.14	27.33	26.30

H_1	$d_\odot K_x$	$d_\odot K_y$	$d_\odot K_z$	$d_\odot \log k_y$	$d_\odot \log k_z$	H_1	$d_\odot K_x$	$d_\odot K_y$	$d_\odot K_z$	$d_\odot \log k_y$	$d_\odot \log k_z$
0	2.36	2.31	2.08	13	0	190	2.64	2.62	2.34	12	1
10	2.76	2.74	2.44	12	2	200	2.96	2.96	2.64	11	4
20	3.06	3.07	2.75	11	6	210	3.16	3.19	2.86	10	9
30	3.22	3.25	2.98	9	13	220	3.24	3.29	3.00	8	16
40	3.24	3.30	3.03	7	20	230	3.19	3.25	3.01	6	23
50	3.12	3.17	2.98	5	27	240	3.00	3.08	2.93	3	30
60	2.83	2.91	2.82	3	33	250	2.69	2.77	2.73	2	35
70	2.46	2.54	2.56	1	38	260	2.31	2.39	2.45	1	39
80	2.04	2.11	2.24	0	41	270	1.88	1.94	2.10	0	41
90	1.61	1.65	1.87	0	41	280	1.47	1.52	1.74	0	40
100	1.23	1.25	1.53	1	38	290	1.11	1.12	1.41	2	37
110	0.95	0.95	1.25	2	34	300	0.85	0.84	1.14	3	31
120	0.79	0.76	1.04	4	28	310	0.74	0.71	0.98	5	25
130	0.76	0.71	0.95	6	21	320	0.79	0.74	0.95	7	17
140	0.87	0.80	0.99	8	15	330	0.98	0.91	1.04	9	11
150	1.11	1.04	1.12	10	8	340	1.28	1.21	1.23	11	5
160	1.45	1.39	1.36	11	3	350	1.67	1.61	1.52	12	1
170	1.85	1.79	1.66	12	0	360	2.13	2.08	1.89	12	0
180	2.26	2.21	2.00	13	0	370	2.56	2.53	2.28	12	0

A	.0 Log Diff.		.1 Log Diff.		.2 Log Diff.		.3 Log Diff.		.4 Log Diff.		Log Sec. var.
	v	Log r	v	Log r	v	Log r	v	Log r	v	Log r	v
0	9.0578	.....	9.0578	7.3522	9.0578	7.0589	9.0578	7.8357	9.0578	7.9591	.....
1	9.0576	8.3561	9.0575	8.3971	9.0575	8.4354	9.0574	8.4698	9.0574	8.5018	7.1299
2	9.0569	8.6556	9.0568	8.6767	9.0567	8.6968	9.0566	8.7160	9.0565	8.7340	7.4231
3	9.0558	8.8300	9.0556	8.8439	9.0555	8.8574	9.0553	8.8701	9.0552	8.8828	7.5965
4	9.0542	8.9518	9.0540	8.9622	9.0538	8.9725	9.0536	8.9823	9.0534	8.9917	7.7182
5	9.0522	9.0453	9.0519	9.0533	9.0517	9.0613	9.0514	9.0691	9.0512	9.0768	7.8131
6	9.0497	9.1198	9.0494	9.1266	9.0491	9.1331	9.0489	9.1394	9.0486	9.1460	7.8896
7	9.0469	9.1816	9.0466	9.1873	9.0463	9.1927	9.0459	9.1981	9.0456	9.2035	7.9522
8	9.0437	9.2337	9.0433	9.2384	9.0430	9.2429	9.0426	9.2475	9.0423	9.2521	8.0039
9	9.0401	9.2781	9.0397	9.2822	9.0393	9.2863	9.0389	9.2903	9.0385	9.2942	8.0491
10	9.0361	9.3166	9.0357	9.3201	9.0352	9.3236	9.0348	9.3270	9.0344	9.3303	8.0884
11	9.0318	9.3499	9.0313	9.3529	9.0309	9.3560	9.0304	9.3590	9.0299	9.3619	8.1236
12	9.0271	9.3789	9.0266	9.3816	9.0261	9.3843	9.0256	9.3870	9.0251	9.3897	8.1540
13	9.0222	9.4043	9.0217	9.4067	9.0212	9.4090	9.0206	9.4113	9.0201	9.4136	8.1810
14	9.0170	9.4266	9.0164	9.4286	9.0159	9.4307	9.0153	9.4327	9.0148	9.4347	8.2045
15	9.0115	9.4460	9.0109	9.4478	9.0104	9.4497	9.0098	9.4514	9.0092	9.4530	8.2256
16	9.0058	9.4630	9.0052	9.4646	9.0046	9.4662	9.0040	9.4676	9.0034	9.4692	8.2438
17	8.9999	9.4778	8.9993	9.4791	8.9987	9.4805	8.9981	9.4818	8.9975	9.4831	8.2596
18	8.9938	9.4905	8.9932	9.4917	8.9926	9.4928	8.9919	9.4940	8.9913	9.4951	8.2738
19	8.9876	9.5015	8.9869	9.5025	8.9863	9.5035	8.9856	9.5045	8.9850	9.5054	8.2864
20	8.9811	9.5108	8.9804	9.5116	8.9798	9.5125	8.9791	9.5133	8.9785	9.5141	8.2971
21	8.9746	9.5186	8.9739	9.5193	8.9733	9.5200	8.9726	9.5207	8.9720	9.5214	8.3065
22	8.9680	9.5251	8.9673	9.5257	8.9666	9.5262	8.9660	9.5268	8.9653	9.5273	8.3142
23	8.9612	9.5303	8.9605	9.5308	8.9598	9.5312	8.9592	9.5316	8.9585	9.5320	8.3207
24	8.9544	9.5343	8.9537	9.5346	8.9530	9.5350	8.9523	9.5353	8.9516	9.5356	8.3262
25	8.9475	9.5372	8.9468	9.5374	8.9461	9.5377	8.9454	9.5379	8.9447	9.5381	8.3311
26	8.9406	9.5392	8.9399	9.5393	8.9392	9.5395	8.9385	9.5396	8.9378	9.5397	8.3345
27	8.9337	9.5402	8.9330	9.5403	8.9323	9.5403	8.9316	9.5403	8.9309	9.5404	8.3374
28	8.9268	9.5404	8.9261	9.5404	8.9255	9.5403	8.9247	9.5403	8.9240	9.5402	8.3393
29	8.9198	9.5397	8.9191	9.5396	8.9184	9.5395	8.9177	9.5394	8.9170	9.5392	8.3403
30	8.9129	9.5384	8.9122	9.5382	8.9115	9.5380	8.9108	9.5379	8.9101	9.5377	8.3403
31	8.9060	9.5363	8.9053	9.5361	8.9046	9.5358	8.9039	9.5355	8.9032	9.5353	8.3403
32	8.8991	9.5335	8.8984	9.5332	8.8977	9.5328	8.8971	9.5325	8.8964	9.5322	8.3388
33	8.8923	9.5302	8.8916	9.5298	8.8910	9.5294	8.8903	9.5290	8.8896	9.5286	8.3374
34	8.8856	9.5262	8.8849	9.5257	8.8843	9.5253	8.8836	9.5248	8.8829	9.5244	8.3355
35	8.8789	9.5217	8.8782	9.5212	8.8776	9.5207	8.8769	9.5202	8.8763	9.5197	8.3325
36	8.8723	9.5167	8.8716	9.5161	8.8710	9.5156	8.8703	9.5150	8.8697	9.5145	8.3291
37	8.8658	9.5111	8.8651	9.5105	8.8645	9.5099	8.8638	9.5093	8.8632	9.5087	8.3252
38	8.8593	9.5051	8.8587	9.5044	8.8580	9.5038	8.8574	9.5031	8.8568	9.5025	8.3207
39	8.8530	9.4986	8.8524	9.4979	8.8517	9.4972	8.8511	9.4965	8.8505	9.4958	8.3162
40	8.8467	9.4916	8.8461	9.4909	8.8455	9.4901	8.8449	9.4894	8.8443	9.4886	8.3111
41	8.8406	9.4842	8.8400	9.4834	8.8394	9.4826	8.8388	9.4819	8.8382	9.4811	8.3055
42	8.8345	9.4764	8.8339	9.4756	8.8333	9.4748	8.8327	9.4739	8.8321	9.4732	8.2992
43	8.8286	9.4682	8.8280	9.4673	8.8274	9.4665	8.8269	9.4656	8.8263	9.4648	8.2923
44	8.8228	9.4596	8.8222	9.4587	8.8217	9.4578	8.8211	9.4569	8.8205	9.4560	8.2853
45	8.8171	9.4506	8.8165	9.4497	8.8160	9.4487	8.8154	9.4478	8.8149	9.4468	8.2777
46	8.8115	9.4412	8.8109	9.4402	8.8104	9.4392	8.8098	9.4383	8.8093	9.4373	8.2699
47	8.8060	9.4314	8.8055	9.4304	8.8049	9.4294	8.8044	9.4283	8.8039	9.4273	8.2619
48	8.8007	9.4212	8.8002	9.4201	8.7997	9.4191	8.7991	9.4180	8.7986	9.4170	8.2533
49	8.7955	9.4107	8.7950	9.4096	8.7945	9.4085	8.7940	9.4074	8.7935	9.4063	8.2444
50	8.7904	9.3997	8.7899	9.3986	8.7894	9.3974	8.7889	9.3963	8.7884	9.3951	8.2342
51	8.7854	9.3883	8.7849	9.3871	8.7844	9.3860	8.7840	9.3848	8.7835	9.3836	8.2237
52	8.7806	9.3766	8.7801	9.3753	8.7797	9.3742	8.7792	9.3729	8.7787	9.3717	8.2136
53	8.7759	9.3644	8.7754	9.3631	8.7750	9.3619	8.7745	9.3606	8.7741	9.3594	8.2032
54	8.7713	9.3518	8.7709	9.3505	8.7704	9.3492	8.7700	9.3479	8.7695	9.3466	8.1910
55	8.7669	9.3388	8.7665	9.3374	8.7660	9.3361	8.7656	9.3347	8.7652	9.3334	8.1803
56	8.7626	9.3253	8.7622	9.3239	8.7618	9.3225	8.7613	9.3211	8.7609	9.3198	8.1677
57	8.7584	9.3114	8.7580	9.3100	8.7576	9.3085	8.7572	9.3071	8.7568	9.3057	8.1540
58	8.7544	9.2969	8.7540	9.2954	8.7536	9.2939	8.7532	9.2924	8.7528	9.2909	8.1406
59	8.7505	9.2819	8.7501	9.2804	8.7498	9.2788	8.7494	9.2773	8.7490	9.2758	8.1268
60	8.7468	9.2664	8.7464	9.2648	8.7461	9.2632	8.7457	9.2616	8.7453	9.2600	8.1125

TABLE IX.   15

A	.5		.6		.7		.8		.9		Log sec. var.
	Log Diff.		Log Diff.		Log Diff.		Log Diff.		Log Diff.		
	v	Log r	v	Log r	v	Log r	v	Log r	v	Log r	Log r
0	9.0577	6.0550	9.0577	8.1336	9.0577	8.2001	9.0577	8.2589	9.0576	8.3107	9.4294n
1	9.0573	8.5315	9.0572	8.5593	9.0572	8.5860	9.0571	8.6107	9.0570	8.6335	9.4286
2	9.0564	8.7555	9.0562	8.7687	9.0561	8.7847	9.0560	8.8001	9.0559	8.8153	9.4256
3	9.0550	8.8954	9.0548	8.9074	9.0547	8.9188	9.0545	8.9302	9.0543	8.9413	9.4235
4	9.0532	9.0012	9.0530	9.0105	9.0528	9.0193	9.0526	9.0280	9.0524	9.0367	9.4187
5	9.0509	9.0844	9.0507	9.0917	9.0504	9.0990	9.0502	9.1062	9.0499	9.1130	9.4123
6	9.0483	9.1522	9.0480	9.1582	9.0477	9.1642	9.0475	9.1701	9.0472	9.1760	9.4041
7	9.0453	9.2086	9.0450	9.2138	9.0447	9.2190	9.0443	9.2239	9.0440	9.2288	9.3950
8	9.0420	9.2567	9.0416	9.2612	9.0412	9.2656	9.0409	9.2698	9.0405	9.2740	9.3847
9	9.0381	9.2980	9.0377	9.3018	9.0373	9.3055	9.0369	9.3091	9.0365	9.3129	9.3734
10	9.0339	9.3338	9.0335	9.3371	9.0331	9.3404	9.0327	9.3434	9.0322	9.3467	9.3603
11	9.0294	9.3649	9.0290	9.3678	9.0285	9.3706	9.0280	9.3735	9.0276	9.3762	9.3455
12	9.0246	9.3922	9.0242	9.3946	9.0237	9.3970	9.0232	9.3994	9.0227	9.4019	9.3291
13	9.0196	9.4158	9.0191	9.4181	9.0186	9.4202	9.0180	9.4224	9.0175	9.4245	9.3111
14	9.0142	9.4367	9.0137	9.4386	9.0131	9.4405	9.0126	9.4423	9.0120	9.4442	9.2913
15	9.0086	9.4548	9.0081	9.4565	9.0075	9.4581	9.0069	9.4597	9.0064	9.4614	9.2699
16	9.0028	9.4707	9.0023	9.4720	9.0017	9.4735	9.0011	9.4750	9.0005	9.4764	9.2462
17	8.9968	9.4843	8.9962	9.4856	8.9956	9.4869	8.9950	9.4881	8.9944	9.4893	9.2205
18	8.9907	9.4962	8.9901	9.4973	8.9895	9.4984	8.9888	9.4994	8.9882	9.5005	9.1926
19	8.9843	9.5064	8.9837	9.5073	8.9830	9.5082	8.9824	9.5091	8.9817	9.5099	9.1620
20	8.9778	9.5149	8.9772	9.5157	8.9765	9.5164	8.9759	9.5172	8.9752	9.5179	9.1291
21	8.9713	9.5220	8.9706	9.5227	8.9700	9.5233	8.9693	9.5239	8.9687	9.5245	9.0027
22	8.9646	9.5279	8.9639	9.5284	8.9632	9.5289	8.9626	9.5294	8.9619	9.5298	9.0519
23	8.9578	9.5324	8.9571	9.5328	8.9564	9.5332	8.9558	9.5336	8.9551	9.5340	9.0070
24	8.9510	9.5359	8.9503	9.5362	8.9496	9.5364	8.9489	9.5367	8.9482	9.5370	8.9569
25	8.9440	9.5383	8.9434	9.5385	8.9427	9.5387	8.9420	9.5389	8.9413	9.5390	8.9015
26	8.9372	9.5398	8.9365	9.5399	8.9358	9.5400	8.9351	9.5401	8.9344	9.5401	8.8396
27	8.9302	9.5404	8.9296	9.5404	8.9289	9.5404	8.9282	9.5404	8.9275	9.5404	8.7691
28	8.9233	9.5402	8.9226	9.5401	8.9219	9.5400	8.9212	9.5399	8.9205	9.5398	8.6849
29	8.9163	9.5391	8.9157	9.5390	8.9150	9.5388	8.9143	9.5387	8.9136	9.5386	8.5804
30	8.9094	9.5375	8.9088	9.5372	8.9081	9.5370	8.9074	9.5368	8.9067	9.5365	8.4462
31	8.9025	9.5350	8.9019	9.5347	8.9012	9.5344	8.9005	9.5341	8.8998	9.5338	8.2568
32	8.8957	9.5318	8.8950	9.5315	8.8943	9.5312	8.8937	9.5309	8.8930	9.5305	7.9132n
33	8.8889	9.5282	8.8883	9.5278	8.8876	9.5274	8.8869	9.5270	8.8863	9.5266	7.0807+
34	8.8823	9.5239	8.8816	9.5235	8.8809	9.5230	8.8802	9.5226	8.8796	9.5221	8.0152
35	8.8756	9.5192	8.8749	9.5187	8.8743	9.5182	8.8736	9.5177	8.8730	9.5172	8.2793
36	8.8690	9.5139	8.8684	9.5133	8.8677	9.5128	8.8671	9.5122	8.8664	9.5117	8.4386
37	8.8625	9.5081	8.8619	9.5075	8.8612	9.5069	8.8606	9.5063	8.8599	9.5057	8.5520
38	8.8561	9.5018	8.8555	9.5012	8.8549	9.5005	8.8543	9.4999	8.8536	9.4992	8.6304
39	8.8498	9.4951	8.8492	9.4944	8.8486	9.4937	8.8480	9.4930	8.8473	9.4923	8.7101
40	8.8436	9.4879	8.8430	9.4872	8.8424	9.4865	8.8418	9.4857	8.8412	9.4849	8.7709
41	8.8375	9.4803	8.8369	9.4795	8.8363	9.4787	8.8357	9.4760	8.8351	9.4772	8.8210
42	8.8315	9.4723	8.8310	9.4715	8.8304	9.4707	8.8298	9.4698	8.8292	9.4690	8.8646
43	8.8257	9.4630	8.8251	9.4630	8.8245	9.4622	8.8240	9.4613	8.8234	9.4605	8.9015
44	8.8199	9.4551	8.8194	9.4542	8.8188	9.4533	8.8182	9.4524	8.8177	9.4515	8.9331
45	8.8143	9.4459	8.8137	9.4450	8.8132	9.4440	8.8126	9.4431	8.8121	9.4421	8.9615
46	8.8087	9.4363	8.8082	9.4353	8.8076	9.4343	8.8071	9.4334	8.8065	9.4324	8.9870
47	8.8033	9.4263	8.8028	9.4253	8.8023	9.4243	8.8018	9.4232	8.8012	9.4222	9.0101
48	8.7981	9.4159	8.7976	9.4149	8.7971	9.4138	8.7965	9.4128	8.7960	9.4117	9.0320
49	8.7929	9.4052	8.7924	9.4041	8.7919	9.4030	8.7914	9.4019	8.7909	9.4008	9.0519
50	8.7879	9.3940	8.7874	9.3929	8.7869	9.3917	8.7864	9.3906	8.7859	9.3894	9.0692
51	8.7830	9.3824	8.7825	9.3813	8.7820	9.3801	8.7816	9.3789	8.7811	9.3778	9.0850
52	8.7782	9.3705	8.7778	9.3693	8.7773	9.3681	8.7768	9.3668	8.7764	9.3656	9.0991
53	8.7736	9.3581	8.7731	9.3568	8.7727	9.3556	8.7722	9.3543	8.7718	9.3531	9.1125
54	8.7691	9.3453	8.7687	9.3440	8.7682	9.3427	8.7678	9.3414	8.7673	9.3401	9.1244
55	8.7647	9.3320	8.7643	9.3307	8.7639	9.3293	8.7635	9.3280	8.7630	9.3266	9.1360
56	8.7605	9.3184	8.7601	9.3170	8.7597	9.3156	8.7592	9.3142	8.7588	9.3128	9.1459
57	8.7564	9.3042	8.7560	9.3028	8.7556	9.3013	8.7552	9.2998	8.7548	9.2984	9.1555
58	8.7524	9.2894	8.7521	9.2879	8.7517	9.2864	8.7513	9.2840	8.7509	9.2834	9.1649
59	8.7486	9.2742	8.7483	9.2727	8.7479	9.2711	8.7475	9.2695	8.7472	9.2680	9.1734
60	8.7449	9.2584	8.7446	9.2568	8.7442	9.2552	8.7438	9.2536	8.7435	9.2520	9.1810+

A	.0 Log Diff.		.1 Log Diff.		.2 Log Diff.		.3 Log Diff.		.4 Log Diff.		Log Sec. var.
	v	Log r	v	Log r	v	Log r	v	Log r	v	Log r	v
60	8.7468	9.2664	8.7464	9.2648	8.7461	9.2632	8.7457	9.2616	8.7453	9.2600	8.1125
61	8.7431	9.2503	8.7428	9.2486	8.7424	9.2470	8.7421	9.2453	8.7417	9.2437	8.0977
62	8.7396	9.2336	8.7393	9.2319	8.7389	9.2302	8.7386	9.2285	8.7383	9.2267	8.0824
63	8.7363	9.2162	8.7360	9.2144	8.7357	9.2126	8.7353	9.2106	8.7350	9.2090	8.0656
64	8.7331	9.1981	8.7328	9.1962	8.7325	9.1944	8.7322	9.1925	8.7318	9.1906	8.0482
65	8.7300	9.1793	8.7297	9.1774	8.7294	9.1754	8.7291	9.1735	8.7288	9.1715	8.0301
66	8.7270	9.1596	8.7267	9.1576	8.7264	9.1555	8.7262	9.1535	8.7259	9.1514	8.0111
67	8.7242	9.1390	8.7239	9.1369	8.7237	9.1348	8.7234	9.1327	8.7231	9.1305	7.9913
68	8.7215	9.1175	8.7212	9.1153	8.7210	9.1131	8.7207	9.1108	8.7205	9.1086	7.9705
69	8.7190	9.0948	8.7187	9.0925	8.7185	9.0901	8.7182	9.0878	8.7180	9.0854	7.9487
70	8.7165	9.0709	8.7163	9.0684	8.7160	9.0660	8.7158	9.0635	8.7156	9.0610	7.9258
71	8.7142	9.0457	8.7140	9.0431	8.7138	9.0405	8.7136	9.0378	8.7134	9.0352	7.9015
72	8.7121	9.0190	8.7119	9.0162	8.7117	9.0135	8.7115	9.0107	8.7113	9.0078	7.8738
73	8.7101	8.9906	8.7099	8.9877	8.7097	8.9847	8.7095	8.9817	8.7093	8.9787	7.8471
74	8.7082	8.9603	8.7080	8.9571	8.7078	8.9540	8.7077	8.9508	8.7075	8.9475	7.8163
75	8.7064	8.9277	8.7062	8.9243	8.7061	8.9209	8.7059	8.9174	8.7058	8.9139	7.7831
76	8.7048	8.8926	8.7046	8.8889	8.7045	8.8852	8.7043	8.8815	8.7042	8.8777	7.7491
77	8.7033	8.8545	8.7032	8.8504	8.7030	8.8464	8.7029	8.8426	8.7027	8.8382	7.7121
78	8.7019	8.8126	8.7018	8.8082	8.7017	8.8042	8.7015	8.7994	8.7014	8.7945	7.6695
79	8.7007	8.7664	8.7006	8.7616	8.7005	8.7567	8.7004	8.7517	8.7003	8.7467	7.6247
80	8.6996	8.7152	8.6995	8.7093	8.6994	8.7037	8.6993	8.6981	8.6992	8.6924	7.5720
81	8.6986	8.6564	8.6985	8.6507	8.6984	8.6440	8.6984	8.6375	8.6983	8.6310	7.5120
82	8.6978	8.5894	8.6977	8.5821	8.6977	8.5746	8.6976	8.5665	8.6975	8.5587	7.4462
83	8.6971	8.5092	8.6970	8.5004	8.6970	8.4914	8.6969	8.4820	8.6969	8.4735	7.3685
84	8.6965	8.4116	8.6964	8.4006	8.6964	8.3892	8.6963	8.3775	8.6963	8.3655	7.2682
85	8.6960	8.2856	8.6960	8.2707	8.6959	8.2553	8.6959	8.2393	8.6959	8.2214	7.1451
86	8.6957	8.1072	8.6957	8.0846	8.6957	8.0607	8.6956	8.0355	8.6956	8.0086	7.0615
87	8.6955	7.7094	8.6955	7.7521	8.6955	7.7404	8.6955	7.6858	8.6955	7.5682	6.6605
88	8.6955	6.3011n	8.6955	6.9294n	8.6955	7.1761n	8.6955	7.3325n	8.6955	7.4472n	.....
89	8.6955	7.8261	8.6955	7.8663	8.6955	7.9031	8.6956	7.9370	8.6956	7.9685	6.6827n
90	8.6957	8.1206	8.6957	8.1415	8.6958	8.1614	8.6958	8.1804	8.6958	8.1987	6.9728
91	8.6960	8.2945	8.6961	8.3086	8.6961	8.3222	8.6962	8.3355	8.6962	8.3483	7.1526
92	8.6965	8.4183	8.6966	8.4290	8.6966	8.4402	8.6967	8.4503	8.6967	8.4594	7.2738
93	8.6971	8.5146	8.6972	8.5231	8.6972	8.5291	8.6973	8.5404	8.6974	8.5478	7.3720
94	8.6978	8.5927	8.6979	8.6010	8.6980	8.6075	8.6981	8.6149	8.6982	8.6217	7.4499
95	8.6987	8.6604	8.6988	8.6665	8.6989	8.6726	8.6990	8.6790	8.6991	8.6849	7.5152
96	8.6997	8.7181	8.6998	8.7239	8.6999	8.7292	8.7000	8.7340	8.7001	8.7400	7.5748
97	8.7008	8.7694	8.7009	8.7742	8.7010	8.7793	8.7012	8.7839	8.7013	8.7885	7.6272
98	8.7020	8.8153	8.7021	8.8199	8.7023	8.8242	8.7024	8.8284	8.7026	8.8325	7.6717
99	8.7034	8.8569	8.7035	8.8608	8.7037	8.8648	8.7038	8.8687	8.7040	8.8725	7.7141
100	8.7049	8.8948	8.7051	8.8984	8.7052	8.9020	8.7054	8.9056	8.7055	8.9091	7.7509
101	8.7065	8.9298	8.7067	8.9332	8.7069	8.9365	8.7070	8.9398	8.7072	8.9431	7.7848
102	8.7083	8.9622	8.7085	8.9653	8.7087	8.9684	8.7089	8.9715	8.7091	8.9745	7.8179
103	8.7102	8.9924	8.7104	8.9953	8.7106	8.9982	8.7108	9.0011	8.7110	9.0039	7.8486
104	8.7122	9.0206	8.7124	9.0233	8.7126	9.0261	8.7129	9.0288	8.7131	9.0315	7.8759
105	8.7144	9.0473	8.7146	9.0499	8.7149	9.0524	8.7151	9.0550	8.7153	9.0575	7.9028
106	8.7167	9.0724	8.7169	9.0748	8.7172	9.0772	8.7174	9.0797	8.7177	9.0821	7.9270
107	8.7191	9.0962	8.7194	9.0985	8.7196	9.1008	8.7199	9.1031	8.7201	9.1053	7.9499
108	8.7217	9.1188	8.7220	9.1210	8.7222	9.1232	8.7225	9.1254	8.7228	9.1275	7.9716
109	8.7244	9.1403	8.7247	9.1424	8.7250	9.1445	8.7252	9.1466	8.7255	9.1486	7.9924
110	8.7272	9.1608	8.7275	9.1628	8.7278	9.1648	8.7281	9.1668	8.7284	9.1688	8.0121
111	8.7301	9.1805	8.7304	9.1824	8.7307	9.1843	8.7310	9.1862	8.7313	9.1881	8.0310
112	8.7332	9.1993	8.7336	9.2011	8.7338	9.2030	8.7342	9.2048	8.7345	9.2066	8.0492
113	8.7365	9.2173	8.7368	9.2191	8.7372	9.2208	8.7375	9.2226	8.7378	9.2243	8.0665
114	8.7398	9.2346	8.7401	9.2363	8.7405	9.2379	8.7408	9.2396	8.7412	9.2412	8.0833
115	8.7435	9.2513	8.7437	9.2529	8.7440	9.2545	8.7444	9.2561	8.7448	9.2577	8.0985
116	8.7470	9.2674	8.7474	9.2689	8.7477	9.2705	8.7481	9.2720	8.7485	9.2736	8.1133
117	8.7507	9.2829	8.7511	9.2844	8.7513	9.2859	8.7519	9.2874	8.7523	9.2889	8.1276
118	8.7547	9.2978	8.7551	9.2992	8.7555	9.3007	8.7559	9.3021	8.7563	9.3036	8.1414
119	8.7587	9.3122	8.7591	9.3136	8.7595	9.3150	8.7600	9.3164	8.7604	9.3178	8.1548
120	8.7629	9.3261n	8.7633	9.3274n	8.7638	9.3288n	8.7642	9.3301n	8.7646	9.3315n	8.1685n

TABLE IX.   17

A	.5 v	.5 Log r	.6 v	.6 Log r	.7 v	.7 Log r	.8 v	.8 Log r	.9 v	.9 Log r	Log Sec. var. Log r
	Log Diff.		Log Diff.		Log Diff.		Log Diff.		Log Diff.		
60	8.7449	9.2584	8.7446	9.2568	8.7442	9.2552	8.7438	9.2536	8.7435	9.2520	9.1810
61	8.7414	9.2420	8.7410	9.2404	8.7407	9.2387	8.7403	9.2370	8.7400	9.2353	9.1879
62	8.7379	9.2250	8.7376	9.2232	8.7373	9.2215	8.7370	9.2197	8.7366	9.2180	9.1939
63	8.7347	9.2072	8.7344	9.2054	8.7341	9.2036	8.7337	9.2018	8.7334	9.1999	9.1999
64	8.7315	9.1888	8.7312	9.1869	8.7309	9.1850	8.7306	9.1831	8.7303	9.1812	9.2058
65	8.7285	9.1696	8.7282	9.1676	8.7279	9.1656	8.7276	9.1636	8.7273	9.1616	9.2110
66	8.7256	9.1494	8.7253	9.1473	8.7250	9.1453	8.7248	9.1432	8.7245	9.1411	9.2155
67	8.7228	9.1284	8.7226	9.1263	8.7223	9.1241	8.7220	9.1219	8.7218	9.1197	9.2199
68	8.7202	9.1063	8.7200	9.1040	8.7197	9.1017	8.7195	9.0994	8.7192	9.0971	9.2237
69	8.7177	9.0830	8.7175	9.0806	8.7172	9.0782	8.7170	9.0758	8.7167	9.0734	9.2274
70	8.7153	9.0585	8.7151	9.0559	8.7149	9.0534	8.7147	9.0508	8.7144	9.0482	9.2317
71	8.7131	9.0325	8.7129	9.0299	8.7127	9.0272	8.7125	9.0245	8.7123	9.0217	9.2354
72	8.7111	9.0050	8.7109	9.0022	8.7107	8.9993	8.7105	8.9964	8.7103	8.9935	9.2384
73	8.7092	8.9757	8.7090	8.9727	8.7088	8.9696	8.7086	8.9665	8.7084	8.9634	9.2408
74	8.7073	8.9443	8.7071	8.9410	8.7069	8.9377	8.7068	8.9344	8.7066	8.9311	9.2432
75	8.7056	8.9105	8.7054	8.9069	8.7054	8.9034	8.7051	8.8998	8.7050	8.8962	9.2456
76	8.7040	8.8739	8.7039	8.8701	8.7037	8.8663	8.7036	8.8624	8.7034	8.8585	9.2474
77	8.7026	8.8341	8.7025	8.8300	8.7023	8.8255	8.7022	8.8215	8.7020	8.8173	9.2498
78	8.7013	8.7903	8.7012	8.7857	8.7011	8.7811	8.7009	8.7764	8.7008	8.7712	9.2509
79	8.7001	8.7416	8.7000	8.7364	8.6999	8.7312	8.6998	8.7255	8.6997	8.7206	9.2527
80	8.6991	8.6871	8.6990	8.6813	8.6989	8.6753	8.6988	8.6689	8.6987	8.6628	9.2539
81	8.6982	8.6243	8.6981	8.6176	8.6980	8.6107	8.6980	8.6037	8.6979	8.5966	9.2544
82	8.6974	8.5515	8.6974	8.5429	8.6973	8.5347	8.6972	8.5278	8.6972	8.5179	9.2556
83	8.6968	8.4632	8.6967	8.4541	8.6967	8.4441	8.6966	8.4338	8.6966	8.4225	9.2568
84	8.6962	8.3541	8.6962	8.3415	8.6961	8.3274	8.6961	8.3139	8.6960	8.3000	9.2579
85	8.6958	8.2055	8.6958	8.1876	8.6958	8.1673	8.6958	8.1492	8.6957	8.1288	9.2585
86	8.6956	7.9800	8.6956	7.9404	8.6956	7.9165	8.6955	7.8806	8.6955	7.8420	9.2591
87	8.6955	7.4914	8.6955	7.3802	8.6955	7.2553	8.6955	7.0792	8.6955	6.6532	9.2591
88	8.6955	7.5185n	8.6955	7.5966n	8.6955	7.6767n	8.6955	7.7324n	8.6955	7.7818n	9.2591
89	8.6956	7.9979	8.6956	8.0253	8.6956	8.0512	8.6957	8.0756	8.6957	8.0987	9.2591
90	8.6958	8.2149	8.6958	8.2330	8.6959	8.2492	8.6959	8.2637	8.6960	8.2799	9.2591
91	8.6963	8.3608	8.6963	8.3739	8.6964	8.3847	8.6964	8.3962	8.6965	8.4083	9.2585
92	8.6968	8.4691	8.6969	8.4786	8.6969	8.4879	8.6970	8.4977	8.6970	8.5065	9.2579
93	8.6975	8.5557	8.6975	8.5641	8.6976	8.5712	8.6977	8.5781	8.6977	8.5866	9.2568
94	8.6982	8.6284	8.6983	8.6350	8.6984	8.6415	8.6985	8.6484	8.6986	8.6542	9.2556
95	8.6992	8.6902	8.6993	8.6959	8.6994	8.7020	8.6995	8.7070	8.6996	8.7127	9.2544
96	8.7002	8.7447	8.7004	8.7494	8.7005	8.7548	8.7006	8.7597	8.7007	8.7646	9.2533
97	8.7014	8.7931	8.7015	8.7976	8.7016	8.8021	8.7018	8.8065	8.7019	8.8109	9.2521
98	8.7027	8.8367	8.7028	8.8408	8.7030	8.8448	8.7031	8.8488	8.7033	8.8528	9.2509
99	8.7041	8.8763	8.7043	8.8801	8.7044	8.8838	8.7046	8.8875	8.7047	8.8912	9.2492
100	8.7057	8.9127	8.7059	8.9162	8.7060	8.9196	8.7062	8.9230	8.7063	8.9264	9.2474
101	8.7074	8.9463	8.7076	8.9496	8.7078	8.9528	8.7079	8.9559	8.7081	8.9591	9.2456
102	8.7092	8.9776	8.7094	8.9806	8.7096	8.9836	8.7098	8.9865	8.7100	8.9895	9.2432
103	8.7112	9.0067	8.7114	9.0096	8.7116	9.0123	8.7118	9.0151	8.7120	9.0179	9.2406
104	8.7133	9.0341	8.7135	9.0368	8.7137	9.0395	8.7140	9.0421	8.7142	9.0447	9.2384
105	8.7155	9.0600	8.7158	9.0626	8.7160	9.0650	8.7162	9.0675	8.7165	9.0700	9.2354
106	8.7179	9.0845	8.7181	9.0868	8.7184	9.0892	8.7186	9.0915	8.7189	9.0939	9.2317
107	8.7204	9.1076	8.7207	9.1098	8.7209	9.1121	8.7212	9.1144	8.7214	9.1166	9.2280
108	8.7230	9.1297	8.7233	9.1318	8.7236	9.1340	8.7239	9.1361	8.7241	9.1382	9.2243
109	8.7258	9.1507	8.7261	9.1527	8.7264	9.1548	8.7266	9.1568	8.7269	9.1588	9.2199
110	8.7286	9.1708	8.7289	9.1727	8.7292	9.1747	8.7295	9.1766	8.7298	9.1786	9.2155
111	8.7316	9.1900	8.7320	9.1919	8.7323	9.1938	8.7326	9.1956	8.7329	9.1975	9.2110
112	8.7349	9.2084	8.7352	9.2102	8.7355	9.2120	8.7359	9.2138	8.7362	9.2155	9.2058
113	8.7381	9.2261	8.7385	9.2278	8.7388	9.2295	8.7391	9.2312	8.7395	9.2329	9.1999
114	8.7415	9.2429	8.7419	9.2446	8.7422	9.2463	8.7426	9.2480	8.7429	9.2496	9.1939
115	8.7451	9.2593	8.7455	9.2610	8.7459	9.2626	8.7463	9.2642	8.7466	9.2658	9.1879
116	8.7488	9.2751	8.7492	9.2767	8.7496	9.2782	8.7500	9.2798	8.7503	9.2813	9.1810
117	8.7527	9.2903	8.7531	9.2918	8.7535	9.2933	8.7539	9.2948	8.7543	9.2963	9.1734
118	8.7567	9.3050	8.7571	9.3064	8.7575	9.3079	8.7579	9.3093	8.7583	9.3108	9.1649
119	8.7608	9.3191	8.7612	9.3205	8.7616	9.3219	8.7621	9.3233	8.7625	9.3247	9.1555
120	8.7650	9.3328n	8.7655	9.3342n	8.7659	9.3355n	8.7663	9.3369n	8.7668	9.3382n	9.1451

A	.0		.1		.2		.3		.4		Log Sec. var.
	Log Diff.		Log Diff.		Log Diff.		Log Diff.		Log Diff.		
	v	Log r	v	Log r	v	Log r	v	Log r	v	Log r	v
120	8.7629	9.3261n	8.7633	9.3274n	8.7638	9.3288n	8.7642	9.3301n	8.7646	9.3315n	8.1685n
121	8.7672	0.3396	8.7676	9.3409	8.7681	9.3422	8.7685	9.3435	8.7690	9.3448	8.1810
122	8.7716	9.3526	8.7720	9.3539	8.7725	9.3551	8.7730	9.3564	8.7734	9.3576	8.1926
123	8.7762	9.3652	8.7767	9.3664	8.7771	9.3676	8.7776	9.3688	8.7781	9.3700	8.2039
124	8.7809	9.3773	8.7814	9.3785	8.7819	9.3797	8.7823	9.3808	8.7828	9.3820	8.2142
125	8.7857	9.3891	8.7862	9.3902	8.7867	9.3914	8.7872	9.3925	8.7877	9.3936	8.2243
126	8.7907	9.4004	8.7912	9.4015	8.7917	9.4026	8.7922	9.4037	8.7927	9.4048	8.2348
127	8.7958	9.4113	8.7963	9.4123	8.7968	9.4134	8.7974	9.4144	8.7979	9.4155	8.2450
128	8.8010	9.4218	8.8015	9.4228	8.8021	9.4238	8.8026	9.4249	8.8031	9.4259	8.2539
129	8.8063	9.4320	8.8068	9.4330	8.8074	9.4340	8.8079	9.4349	8.8085	9.4359	8.2625
130	8.8118	9.4418	8.8124	9.4427	8.8129	9.4437	8.8135	9.4446	8.8140	9.4456	8.2704
131	8.8174	9.4512	8.8180	9.4521	8.8185	9.4530	8.8191	9.4539	8.8197	9.4548	8.2782
132	8.8231	9.4601	8.8237	9.4610	8.8243	9.4618	8.8248	9.4627	8.8254	9.4636	8.2859
133	8.8289	9.4688	8.8295	9.4696	8.8301	9.4704	8.8307	9.4712	8.8313	9.4720	8.2929
134	8.8349	9.4769	8.8355	9.4777	8.8361	9.4785	8.8367	9.4792	8.8373	9.4800	8.2997
135	8.8409*	9.4847	8.8415	9.4854	8.8421	9.4862	8.8428	9.4869	8.8434	9.4876	8.3060
136	8.8471	0.4920	8.8477	9.4927	8.8483	9.4934	8.8490	9.4941	8.8496	9.4948	8.3116
137	8.8533	9.4990	8.8539	9.4996	8.8546	9.5003	8.8552	9.5009	8.8559	9.5016	8.3167
138	8.8597	9.5054	8.8603	9.5060	8.8610	9.5066	8.8616	9.5072	8.8623	9.5078	8.3212
139	8.8662	9.5115	8.8668	9.5120	8.8675	9.5126	8.8681	9.5131	8.8688	9.5137	8.3257
140	8.8727	9.5170	8.8734	9.5175	8.8740	9.5180	8.8747	9.5185	8.8753	9.5190	8.3291
141	8.8793	9.5220	8.8800	9.5224	8.8806	9.5229	8.8813	9.5233	8.8820	9.5238	8.3326
142	8.8860	9.5265	8.8867	9.5269	8.8873	9.5273	8.8880	9.5277	8.8887	9.5281	8.3355
143	8.8927	9.5304	8.8934	9.5307	8.8941	9.5311	8.8948	9.5314	8.8955	9.5317	8.3374
144	8.8996	9.5337	8.9002	9.5340	8.9010	9.5343	8.9016	9.5345	8.9023	9.5348	8.3388
145	8.9064	9.5365	8.9071	9.5367	8.9078	9.5370	8.9085	9.5372	8.9092	9.5374	8.3403
146	8.9133	9.5385	8.9140	9.5387	8.9147	9.5388	8.9154	9.5390	8.9161	9.5391	8.3407
147	8.9202	9.5398	8.9209	9.5399	8.9216	9.5400	8.9223	9.5401	8.9230	9.5401	8.3403
148	8.9272	9.5404	8.9279	9.5404	8.9286	9.5404	8.9293	9.5404	8.9300	9.5404	8.3393
149	8.9341	9.5402	8.9348	9.5401	8.9355	9.5401	8.9362	9.5400	8.9369	9.5399	8.3374
150	8.9410	9.5391	8.9417	9.5389	8.9424	9.5388	8.9431	9.5386	8.9438	9.5384	8.3345
151	8.9479	9.5371	8.9486	9.5368	8.9493	9.5366	8.9500	9.5363	8.9506	9.5360	8.3311
152	8.9548	9.5340	8.9555	9.5336	8.9562	9.5333	8.9568	9.5329	8.9575	9.5325	8.3257
153	8.9616	9.5300	8.9623	9.5295	8.9630	9.5290	8.9636	9.5285	8.9643	9.5280	8.3202
154	8.9684	9.5247	8.9691	9.5241	8.9697	9.5235	8.9704	9.5229	8.9710	9.5222	8.3137
155	8.9750	9.5181	8.9756	9.5174	8.9763	9.5166	8.9769	9.5159	8.9776	9.5151	8.3060
156	8.9815	9.5102	8.9821	9.5093	8.9828	9.5084	8.9834	9.5075	8.9841	9.5066	8.2966
157	8.9880	9.5008	8.9886	9.4998	8.9892	9.4987	8.9899	9.4977	8.9905	9.4966	8.2859
158	8.9942	9.4898	8.9948	9.4886	8.9954	9.4874	8.9960	9.4861	8.9966	9.4849	8.2732
159	9.0003	9.4769	9.0009	9.4755	9.0015	9.4741	9.0021	9.4726	9.0027	9.4712	8.2585
160	9.0062	9.4620	9.0068	9.4604	9.0073	9.4587	9.0079	9.4571	9.0085	9.4554	8.2426
161	9.0119	9.4449	9.0124	9.4430	9.0130	9.4412	9.0135	9.4393	9.0141	9.4374	8.2237
162	9.0173	9.4253	9.0178	9.4232	9.0183	9.4210	9.0189	9.4189	9.0194	9.4166	8.2032
163	9.0225	9.4029	9.0230	9.4005	9.0235	9.3980	9.0240	9.3955	9.0245	9.3930	8.1797
164	9.0274	9.3772	9.0279	9.3745	9.0283	9.3717	9.0288	0.3689	9.0292	9.3660	8.1526
165	9.0320	9.3479	9.0324	9.3448	9.0329	9.3416	9.0333	9.3389	9.0337	9.3351	8.1221
166	9.0363	9.3143	9.0367	9.3107	9.0371	9.3071	9.0375	9.3032	9.0379	9.2994	8.0859
167	9.0403	9.2755	9.0407	9.2714	9.0410	9.2672	9.0414	9.2628	9.0417	9.2584	8.0463
168	9.0439	9.2308	9.0442	9.2259	9.0445	9.2209	9.0449	9.2158	9.0452	9.2106	8.0008
169	9.0471	0.1783	9.0474	9.1725	9.0477	9.1665	9.0479	9.1605	9.0481	9.1546	7.9487
170	9.0499	9.1158	9.0501	9.1098	9.0504	9.1018	9.0506	9.0947	9.0509	9.0873	7.8855
171	9.0523	9.0400	9.0525	9.0316	9.0527	9.0229	9.0529	9.0139	9.0531	9.0050	7.8082
172	9.0543	8.9453	9.0544	8.9345	9.0546	8.9233	9.0548	8.9118	9.0549	8.9001	7.7121
173	9.0558	8.8209	9.0559	8.8062	9.0561	8.7910	9.0561	8.7749	9.0562	8.7582	7.5865
174	9.0569	8.6425	9.0570	8.6196	9.0570	8.5955	9.0571	8.5700	9.0572	8.5422	7.4111
175	9.0576	8.3284n	9.0576	8.2799n	9.0576	8.2240n	9.0576	8.1614n	9.0576	8.0882n	7.1060n
176	9.0578	7.1140	9.0578	7.5623	9.0578	7.7745	9.0578	7.9165	9.0578	8.0212	5.8568
177	9.0575	8.3766	9.0575	8.4183	9.0574	8.4281	9.0574	8.4942	9.0573	8.5211	7.1526
178	9.0568	8.6702	9.0567	8.6920	9.0566	8.7093	9.0565	8.7259	9.0564	8.7419	7.4348
179	9.0557	8.8401	9.0555	8.8525	9.0554	8.8645	9.0552	8.8762	9.0551	8.8910	7.6044
180	9.0541	8.9619	9.0539	8.9694	9.0537	8.9786	9.0535	8.9877	0.0532	8.9042	7.7241

TABLE IX.   19

A	.5		.6		.7		.8		.9		Log Sec. var.
	Log Diff.		Log Diff.		Log Diff.		Log Diff.		Log Diff.		
	v	Log r	v	Log r	v	Log r	v	Log r	v	Log r	Log r
120	8.7600	9.3328n	8.7655	9.3342n	8.7659	9.3355n	8.7663	9.3369n	8.7668	9.3382n	9.1451
121	8.7694	9.3461	8.7698	9.3474	8.7703	9.3487	8.7707	9.3500	8.7712	9.3513	9.1345
122	8.7739	9.3589	8.7744	9.3602	8.7748	9.3614	8.7753	9.3627	8.7757	9.3639	9.1236
123	8.7785	9.3712	8.7790	9.3725	8.7795	9.3737	8.7800	9.3749	8.7804	9.3761	9.1117
124	8.7833	9.3832	8.7838	9.3844	8.7843	9.3856	8.7847	9.3867	8.7852	9.3879	9.0985
125	8.7882	9.3947	8.7887	9.3959	8.7892	9.3970	8.7897	9.3981	8.7902	9.3993	9.0841
126	8.7932	9.4058	8.7938	9.4069	8.7943	9.4080	8.7948	9.4091	8.7953	9.4102	9.0683
127	8.7984	9.4165	8.7989	9.4176	8.7994	9.4186	8.8000	9.4197	8.8005	9.4207	9.0510
128	8.8036	9.4269	8.8042	9.4279	8.8047	9.4289	8.8052	9.4300	8.8058	9.4310	9.0320
129	8.8090	9.4369	8.8096	9.4379	8.8101	9.4389	8.8107	9.4398	8.8112	9.4408	9.0101
130	8.8146	9.4465	8.8152	9.4474	8.8157	9.4484	8.8163	9.4493	8.8168	9.4503	8.9859
131	8.8202	9.4556	8.8208	9.4565	8.8214	9.4574	8.8220	9.4583	8.8225	9.4592	8.9608
132	8.8260	9.4644	8.8266	9.4653	8.8272	9.4662	8.8277	9.4671	8.8283	9.4679	8.9319
133	8.8319	9.4728	8.8325	9.4737	8.8331	9.4745	8.8337	9.4753	8.8343	9.4761	8.8989
134	8.8379	9.4808	8.8385	9.4816	8.8391	9.4824	8.8397	9.4831	8.8403	9.4839	8.8603
135	8.8440	9.4883	8.8446	9.4891	8.8452	9.4898	8.8459	9.4905	8.8465	9.4913	8.8163
136	8.8502	9.4955	8.8508	9.4962	8.8514	9.4969	8.8521	9.4976	8.8527	9.4983	8.7655
137	8.8565	9.5022	8.8571	9.5028	8.8578	9.5035	8.8584	9.5041	8.8591	9.5048	8.7060
138	8.8629	9.5084	8.8636	9.5091	8.8642	9.5097	8.8649	9.5103	8.8655	9.5109	8.6346
139	8.8694	9.5142	8.8701	9.5148	8.8707	9.5153	8.8714	9.5159	8.8720	9.5164	8.5461
140	8.8760	9.5195	8.8767	9.5200	8.8773	9.5205	8.8780	9.5210	8.8786	9.5215	8.4309
141	8.8826	9.5242	8.8833	9.5247	8.8840	9.5251	8.8847	9.5256	8.8853	9.5260	8.2682
142	8.8893	9.5284	8.8900	9.5288	8.8907	9.5292	8.8914	9.5296	8.8920	9.5300	7.9945
143	8.8961	9.5320	8.8968	9.5324	8.8975	9.5327	8.8982	9.5330	8.8989	9.5334	6.6827
144	8.9030	9.5351	8.9037	9.5354	8.9044	9.5357	8.9050	9.5359	8.9057	9.5362	7.9499n
145	8.9098	9.5376	8.9105	9.5378	8.9112	9.5380	8.9119	9.5382	8.9126	9.5383	8.2682
146	8.9167	9.5392	8.9174	9.5394	8.9181	9.5395	8.9188	9.5396	8.9195	9.5397	8.4536
147	8.9237	9.5402	8.9244	9.5402	8.9251	9.5403	8.9258	9.5403	8.9265	9.5404	8.5858
148	8.9306	9.5404	8.9313	9.5404	8.9320	9.5403	8.9327	9.5403	8.9334	9.5403	8.6892
149	8.9375	9.5398	8.9382	9.5397	8.9389	9.5395	8.9396	9.5394	8.9403	9.5393	8.7726
150	8.9444	9.5382	8.9451	9.5380	8.9458	9.5378	8.9465	9.5376	8.9472	9.5373	8.8441
151	8.9513	9.5357	8.9520	9.5354	8.9527	9.5350	8.9534	9.5347	8.9541	9.5344	8.9054
152	8.9582	9.5321	8.9589	9.5317	8.9596	9.5313	8.9602	9.5308	8.9609	9.5304	8.9603
153	8.9650	9.5275	8.9657	9.5270	8.9664	9.5264	8.9670	9.5259	8.9677	9.5253	9.0101
154	8.9717	9.5216	8.9724	9.5209	8.9730	9.5202	8.9737	9.5195	8.9743	9.5188	9.0538
155	8.9782	9.5143	8.9789	9.5135	8.9795	9.5127	8.9802	9.5119	8.9808	9.5110	9.0943
156	8.9847	9.5057	8.9854	9.5047	8.9860	9.5038	8.9867	9.5028	8.9873	9.5018	9.1307
157	8.9911	9.4955	8.9917	9.4944	8.9923	9.4933	8.9930	9.4921	8.9936	9.4910	9.1635
158	8.9972	9.4836	8.9979	9.4823	8.9985	9.4810	8.9991	9.4796	8.9997	9.4783	9.1939
159	9.0032	9.4697	9.0038	9.4682	9.0044	9.4667	9.0050	9.4651	9.0056	9.4636	9.2212
160	9.0090	9.4537	9.0096	9.4520	9.0102	9.4503	9.0108	9.4485	9.0113	9.4467	9.2468
161	9.0146	9.4351	9.0151	9.4334	9.0157	9.4314	9.0162	9.4294	9.0168	9.4274	9.2704
162	9.0199	9.4144	9.0204	9.4121	9.0209	9.4098	9.0215	9.4075	9.0220	9.4052	9.2923
163	9.0249	9.3904	9.0254	9.3878	9.0259	9.3853	9.0264	9.3826	9.0269	9.3800	9.3116
164	9.0297	9.3632	9.0302	9.3602	9.0306	9.3571	9.0311	9.3540	9.0315	9.3510	9.3296
165	9.0341	9.3317	9.0346	9.3283	9.0350	9.3249	9.0354	9.3213	9.0359	9.3179	9.3460
166	9.0383	9.2957	9.0387	9.2918	9.0391	9.2878	9.0395	9.2836	9.0399	9.2796	9.3608
167	9.0421	9.2540	9.0425	9.2495	9.0428	9.2449	9.0432	9.2403	9.0435	9.2356	9.3743
168	9.0455	9.2054	9.0458	9.2001	9.0461	9.1948	9.0465	9.1894	9.0468	9.1839	9.3860
169	9.0485	9.1483	9.0488	9.1419	9.0491	9.1355	9.0493	9.1291	9.0496	9.1224	9.3957
170	9.0511	9.0797	9.0513	9.0721	9.0516	9.0645	9.0518	9.0564	9.0521	9.0483	9.4050
171	9.0533	8.9957	9.0535	8.9859	9.0537	8.9761	9.0539	8.9662	9.0541	8.9560	9.4128
172	9.0550	8.8876	9.0552	8.8754	9.0553	8.8625	9.0555	8.8488	9.0556	8.8351	9.4191
173	9.0563	8.7406	9.0565	8.7231	9.0566	8.7046	9.0567	8.6844	9.0568	8.6637	9.4235
174	9.0572	8.5132	9.0573	8.4829	9.0574	8.4495	9.0575	8.4125	9.0575	8.3720	9.4266
175	9.0576	7.9978n	9.0577	7.8865n	9.0577	7.7324n	9.0577	7.4914n	9.0577	6.9543n	9.4266
176	9.0577	8.1055	9.0577	8.1761	9.0577	8.2368	9.0577	8.2912	9.0576	8.3395	9.4294
177	9.0573	8.5465	9.0572	8.5705	9.0571	8.5999	9.0570	8.6253	9.0569	8.6454	9.4266
178	9.0563	8.7649	9.0561	8.7796	9.0560	8.8007	9.0559	8.8075	9.0559	8.8249	9.4266
179	9.0549	8.9042	9.0547	8.9149	9.0546	8.9253	9.0544	8.9355	9.0543	8.9513	9.4231
180	9.0531	9.0051	9.0529	9.0162	9.0527	9.0261	9.0525	9.0342	9.0523	9.0422	9.4183n

TABLE X.

T	0			4			8			12			16			20		
V	δv	Diff.	ṙ	δv	Diff.	ṙ	δv	Diff.	ṙ	δv	Diff.	ṙ	δv	Diff.	ṙ	δv	Diff.	ṙ
0	25.19	+1.95	68	25.95	+2.40	77	26.50	+2.91	86	26.61	+3.48	95	23.90	+4.06	102	24.41	+4.18	106
1	27.16	1.92	56	28.36	2.35	63	29.44	2.88	72	30.14	3.47	83	29.94	4.00	95	28.71	4.28	104
2	29.03	1.74	43	30.66	2.15	49	32.26	2.65	58	33.56	3.24	72	33.90	3.79	87	32.98	4.14	101
3	30.64	1.43	31	32.66	2.78	35	34.75	2.23	44	36.63	2.70	59	37.52	3.33	78	37.00	3.73	97
4	31.89	1.02	20	34.22	1.28	23	36.73	1.65	30	39.14	2.15	47	40.57	2.67	69	40.45	3.08	93
5	32.67	+0.52	12	35.23	0.70	13	38.06	0.96	20	40.93	1.36	37	42.86	1.82	60	43.16	2.24	87
6	32.93	-0.01	7	35.62	+0.06	6	38.65	+0.20	12	41.86	+0.47	28	44.21	+0.85	52	44.93	1.24	80
7	32.64	0.34	6	35.55	-0.59	2	38.46	-0.58	7	41.87	-0.45	21	44.56	-0.12	45	45.64	+0.21	74
8	31.84	1.03	8	34.44	1.20	2	37.49	1.32	5	40.96	1.32	17	43.88	1.17	39	45.35	-0.53	67
9	30.57	1.46	13	32.96	1.72	5	35.82	1.96	6	39.24	2.10	16	42.23	2.08	35	43.99	1.82	60
10	28.92	1.78	21	31.01	2.13	13	33.56	2.49	11	36.76	2.80	18	39.73	2.85	32	41.70	2.68	54
11	27.04	1.95	32	28.71	2.40	23	30.85	2.85	19	33.71	3.24	22	36.53	3.45	33	38.63	3.39	49
12	25.01	2.04	45	26.22	2.51	36	27.86	3.04	30	30.28	3.51	29	32.84	3.62	34	34.98	3.82	45
13	22.96	1.90	51	23.69	2.47	50	24.78	3.02	42	26.69	3.56	38	28.89	3.96	36	30.99	4.05	43
14	21.04	1.82	74	21.27	2.29	65	21.81	2.34	56	23.15	3.41	48	24.93	3.55	43	26.89	4.02	41
15	19.33	1.54	88	19.10	1.98	80	19.10	2.49	70	19.87	3.10	59	21.18	3.53	49	22.94	3.76	42
16	17.97	1.16	100	17.31	1.54	93	16.83	1.99	83	17.04	2.52	70	17.87	2.99	56	19.36	3.16	43
17	17.01	0.73	111	16.02	1.01	105	15.11	1.89	95	14.82	1.85	80	15.19	2.29	63	16.64	2.60	44
18	16.51	-0.26	118	15.28	-0.45	114	14.05	-0.70	104	13.34	1.07	89	13.29	1.46	70	14.15	1.70	51
19	16.50	+0.23	123	15.12	+0.14	120	13.70	+0.01	111	12.68	-0.20	96	12.26	-0.56	76	12.79	-0.56	55
20	16.97	0.88	124	15.56	0.71	122	14.06	0.70	114	12.83	+0.56	101	12.16	+0.34	82	12.37	+0.05	61
21	17.87	1.09	122	16.54	1.21	121	15.09	1.52	115	13.70	1.31	103	12.91	1.19	86	12.89	0.95	67
22	19.15	1.40	116	17.97	1.61	116	16.69	1.83	112	15.45	1.95	102	14.64	1.94	88	14.27	1.75	72
23	20.67	1.50	108	19.76	1.80	108	18.75	2.20	106	17.68	2.42	99	16.82	2.52	89	16.39	2.41	77
24	22.34	1.67	98	21.75	2.01	98	21.09	2.38	97	19.28	2.60	94	19.58	2.90	86	19.08	2.84	80
25	24.02	1.61	86	23.78	2.90	86	23.51	2.37	89	23.00	2.74	86	22.59	3.02	85	22.37	3.07	83
26	25.55	1.40	74	25.67	1.75	74	25.84	2.17	75	25.77	2.58	76	25.61	2.90	81	25.21	3.02	85
27	26.82	1.08	61	27.29	1.40	61	27.80	1.78	63	28.39	2.20	68	28.39	2.55	76	28.15	2.74	84
28	27.70	0.65	52	28.47	0.92	50	29.42	1.24	52	30.17	1.61	59	30.71	1.94	70	30.69	2.36	83
29	28.12	+0.16	43	29.13	+0.35	40	30.37	+0.60	42	31.46	0.91	50	32.37	1.25	64	32.61	1.53	80
30	28.02	-0.36	37	29.18	-0.20	33	30.65	-0.11	34	32.99	+0.11	42	33.21	+0.39	57	33.75	+0.09	76

T	48			52			56			60			64			68		
V	δv	Diff.	ṙ	δv	Diff.	ṙ	δv	Diff.	ṙ	δv	Diff.	ṙ	δv	Diff.	ṙ	δv	Diff.	ṙ
0	18.86	+1.77	64	19.19	+1.50	59	19.49	+1.49	57	19.68	+1.47	58	19.76	+1.47	62	19.80	+1.52	70
1	20.75	1.86	71	20.89	1.77	65	21.09	1.65	60	21.24	1.60	58	21.32	1.60	60	21.40	1.64	65
2	22.78	2.04	81	22.72	1.84	72	22.78	1.70	65	22.88	1.63	60	22.96	1.63	59	23.07	1.65	62
3	24.82	1.09	91	24.56	1.78	79	24.48	1.64	70	24.51	1.57	62	24.58	1.56	58	24.70	1.57	59
4	26.76	1.82	100	26.29	1.53	86	26.12	1.49	75	26.03	1.42	65	26.08	1.39	59	26.22	1.40	56
5	28.47	1.55	108	27.82	1.38	93	27.46	1.25	80	27.36	1.17	69	27.36	1.14	60	27.50	1.13	55
6	29.87	1.20	114	29.06	1.06	99	28.58	0.95	86	28.40	0.88	73	28.36	0.84	62	28.48	0.61	55
7	30.87	0.79	119	29.94	0.69	104	29.51	0.60	90	29.12	0.54	76	29.04	0.50	65	29.07	+0.47	56
8	31.45	+0.37	121	30.44	+0.31	107	29.80	+0.25	94	29.49	+0.20	80	29.37	+0.16	68	29.42	-0.13	58
9	31.61	-0.06	121	30.55	-0.07	109	29.87	-0.08	95	29.52	-0.13	83	29.36	-0.18	71	29.38	0.21	61
10	31.33	0.46	119	30.30	0.42	110	29.61	0.41	99	29.24	0.42	86	29.05	0.45	75	29.00	0.51	64
11	30.69	0.80	115	29.71	0.73	108	29.05	0.68	100	28.69	0.67	88	28.46	0.69	78	28.37	0.73	68
12	29.73	1.08	109	28.85	1.07	105	28.37	0.89	99	27.90	0.87	90	27.68	0.86	81	27.55	0.90	72
13	28.53	1.28	102	27.78	1.14	101	27.27	1.03	97	26.96	0.95	90	26.74	0.98	83	26.58	1.01	76
14	27.17	1.40	94	26.58	1.24	95	26.19	1.11	95	25.94	1.04	90	25.73	1.02	85	25.54	1.03	79
15	25.74	1.43	86	25.31	1.25	90	25.06	1.12	92	24.88	1.04	89	24.70	1.01	86	24.51	1.01	82
16	24.31	1.38	77	24.07	1.19	83	23.95	1.06	88	23.85	0.98	88	23.71	0.94	86	23.52	0.92	84
17	22.98	1.24	70	22.92	1.08	78	22.93	0.95	84	22.91	0.87	86	22.83	0.81	86	22.67	0.77	85
18	21.83	1.03	64	21.91	0.89	73	22.05	0.78	81	22.11	0.70	83	22.10	0.64	85	21.97	0.60	85
19	20.92	0.76	60	21.13	0.67	69	21.37	0.56	78	21.50	0.49	81	21.55	0.44	84	21.37	0.38	85
20	20.31	0.44	58	20.00	0.38	67	20.92	0.31	75	21.13	0.25	79	21.22	-0.20	82	21.20	-0.15	84
21	20.03	-0.11	57	20.37	-0.08	66	20.74	-0.05	74	21.00	-0.01	78	21.15	+0.05	80	21.17	+0.10	82
22	20.08	+0.32	60	20.43	+0.21	67	20.72	+0.21	74	21.11	+0.23	71	21.31	0.27	79	21.39	0.38	80
23	20.46	0.53	65	20.78	0.46	69	21.15	0.44	77	21.45	0.44	76	21.69	0.47	78	21.92	0.52	78
24	21.13	0.78	70	21.39	0.70	73	21.70	0.63	77	21.99	0.62	77	22.25	0.63	77	22.43	0.67	76
25	22.02	0.96	77	22.18	0.85	78	22.41	0.76	80	22.68	0.73	78	22.94	0.73	77	23.15	0.75	74
26	23.04	1.06	85	23.09	0.93	85	23.22	0.82	84	23.44	0.76	80	23.68	0.73	77	23.93	0.76	73
27	24.13	1.06	93	24.04	0.92	90	24.04	0.88	88	24.20	0.72	83	24.41	0.69	79	24.67	0.69	73
28	25.16	0.98	101	24.94	0.84	96	24.83	0.71	93	24.89	0.62	87	25.06	0.57	81	25.36	0.57	73
29	26.06	0.79	108	25.72	0.68	102	25.48	0.55	98	25.45	0.46	91	25.56	0.40	84	25.76	0.39	75
30	26.75	+0.56	113	26.30	+0.46	107	25.94	+0.34	103	25.82	+0.26	95	25.86	-0.18	87	26.01	+0.12	78

NOTE. — When T exceeds 86, subtract 86 from it, and add 46.98 to V.

TABLE X.   **21**

T	24			28			32			36			40			44		
V	δv	Diff.	r	δv	Diff.	r	δv	Diff.	r	δv	Diff.	r	δv	Diff.	r	δv	Diff.	r
0	22.60	+4.08	100	21.01	3.74	102	19.90	5.27	95	15.25	2.78	87	18.89	2.36	78	18.81	2.08	70
1	26.83	4.26	110	24.91	3.96	110	23.33	8.50	107	22.19	3.02	100	21.40	2.59	90	20.98	2.24	81
2	31.12	4.18	113	28.92	3.94	119	26.00	8.63	118	25.28	8.07	112	24.06	2.65	103	23.29	2.32	92
3	35.19	3.84	114	32.80	3.66	125	30.39	8.34	128	28.34	2.94	124	26.71	2.57	115	25.61	2.25	103
4	38.80	3.27	114	36.29	3.21	129	33.59	2.97	136	31.17	3.64	134	29.20	2.94	126	27.79	2.05	113
5	41.73	2.50	112	39.22	2.56	132	36.33	2.42	142	33.63	2.20	142	31.39	1.97	134	29.71	1.74	122
6	43.80	1.58	109	41.40	1.74	131	38.43	1.78	144	35.58	1.63	146	33.14	1.49	140	31.27	1.83	126
7	44.89	+0.58	103	42.70	+0.83	127	39.80	0.96	142	36.90	+0.98	147	34.37	0.95	143	32.38	0.87	132
8	44.96	−0.45	96	43.07	−0.09	121	40.36	+0.16	139	37.55	−0.30	144	35.04	+0.37	142	33.01	+0.37	133
9	44.00	1.42	88	42.52	0.99	112	40.12	−0.63	130	37.51	0.37	138	35.12	−0.20	138	33.13	−0.12	132
10	42.12	2.28	79	41.09	1.81	102	39.11	1.34	118	36.81	0.99	128	34.85	0.73	131	32.77	0.58	127
11	39.44	2.00	70	38.90	2.50	90	37.42	1.97	106	35.53	1.53	117	33.67	1.10	121	31.98	0.97	120
12	36.13	3.51	61	36.10	3.01	77	35.17	2.46	92	33.75	1.96	103	32.27	1.57	109	30.84	1.29	111
13	32.42	3.80	52	32.88	3.34	64	32.51	2.78	77	31.61	2.26	88	30.54	1.83	96	29.41	1.52	101
14	28.53	3.86	45	29.43	3.46	52	29.61	2.93	63	29.24	2.41	73	28.61	1.98	83	27.80	1.65	90
15	24.70	3.68	39	25.97	3.36	42	26.66	2.90	49	26.79	2.42	59	26.58	2.01	70	26.11	1.68	79
16	21.17	3.29	35	22.70	3.07	34	23.81	2.70	38	24.40	2.29	47	24.59	1.91	58	24.44	1.61	69
17	18.11	2.71	34	19.83	2.59	28	21.26	2.33	30	22.21	2.02	37	22.75	1.08	48	22.89	1.44	60
18	15.74	1.97	35	17.51	1.97	26	19.14	1.84	25	20.36	1.63	31	21.17	1.40	41	21.55	1.19	53
19	14.17	1.13	37	15.88	1.25	26	17.58	1.24	23	18.95	1.15	27	19.94	1.02	37	20.50	0.87	49
20	13.47	−0.34	42	15.01	−0.40	36	16.66	−0.63	25	18.00	0.81	28	19.12	−0.55	36	19.81	0.50	49
21	13.68	+0.04	49	14.95	+0.32	36	16.41	+0.09	31	17.73	−0.05	32	18.77	+0.12	39	19.50	−0.10	48
22	14.74	1.46	56	15.65	1.07	44	16.84	0.74	39	17.95	+0.49	39	18.88	0.34	44	19.58	+0.27	52
23	16.60	2.10	64	17.08	1.73	55	17.89	1.31	49	18.70	0.98	49	19.44	0.75	52	20.04	0.63	58
24	18.94	2.59	72	19.72	2.19	66	19.45	1.75	62	19.90	1.47	61	20.38	1.09	63	20.83	0.92	66
25	21.72	2.87	80	20.46	2.43	77	21.39	2.05	75	21.44	1.44	74	21.61	1.83	74	21.88	1.15	75
26	24.67	2.90	86	23.05	2.59	88	23.55	2.18	88	22.18	1.77	87	23.03	1.45	86	23.06	1.23	85
27	27.52	2.60	92	26.64	2.47	97	25.74	2.11	100	24.98	1.75	100	24.51	1.45	95	24.44	1.23	95
28	30.06	2.28	95	28.99	2.13	104	27.78	1.88	109	26.68	1.58	112	25.93	1.33	108	25.55	1.18	105
29	32.08	1.67	96	30.91	1.55	109	29.50	1.49	117	28.15	1.20	119	27.17	1.09	117	26.60	0.92	113
30	33.40	+0.01	95	32.29	+1.03	111	30.77	+0.99	120	29.26	+0.88	124	28.12	+0.77	122	27.40	+0.55	118

T	72			76			80			84			88			92		
V	δv	Diff.	r	δv	Diff.	r	δv	Diff.	r	δv	Diff.	r	δv	Diff.	r	δv	Diff.	r
0	19.73	+1.61	80	19.47	+1.78	92	18.86	1.99	104	17.73	+2.24	116	16.13	+2.52	127	14.08	+2.88	132
1	21.42	1.72	74	21.33	1.80	84	20.94	2.12	95	20.08	2.40	106	18.79	2.73	117	17.09	3.11	123
2	23.17	1.74	67	23.25	1.80	76	23.09	2.12	85	22.53	2.42	95	21.59	2.78	105	20.29	3.20	112
3	24.90	1.65	62	25.12	1.78	68	25.18	2.00	75	24.92	2.33	83	24.35	2.65	92	23.48	3.00	100
4	26.47	1.44	57	26.82	1.56	65	27.09	1.76	66	27.12	2.09	72	26.90	2.38	80	26.46	2.80	88
5	27.79	1.16	54	28.24	1.25	55	28.68	1.40	58	28.99	1.66	62	29.11	1.98	69	29.08	2.37	77
6	28.79	0.82	51	29.32	0.88	50	29.90	1.00	51	30.44	1.20	54	30.86	1.47	59	31.20	1.81	68
7	29.43	0.45	51	30.00	+0.47	48	30.68	0.55	47	31.40	+0.70	48	32.06	0.86	52	32.69	1.17	56
8	29.70	+0.09	51	30.27	−0.07	47	31.00	+0.10	44	31.84	−0.19	34	32.57	+0.33	47	33.53	+0.51	54
9	29.61	−0.26	53	30.14	0.31	48	30.88	−0.33	44	31.29	0.29	43	32.72	−0.21	46	33.71	−0.14	52
10	29.18	0.57	56	29.66	0.63	50	30.35	0.69	46	31.27	0.71	45	32.25	0.72	47	33.26	0.72	53
11	28.48	0.80	60	28.88	0.90	54	29.50	0.98	51	30.37	1.05	49	31.29	1.13	51	32.27	1.21	57
12	27.58	0.97	65	27.87	1.08	60	28.40	1.10	56	29.17	1.30	55	30.00	1.42	57	30.85	1.56	63
13	26.54	1.07	70	26.73	1.17	65	27.13	1.31	63	27.77	1.45	62	28.45	1.60	65	29.15	1.79	71
14	25.45	1.09	74	25.53	1.19	71	25.79	1.32	70	26.28	1.48	70	26.80	1.65	74	27.27	1.89	80
15	24.36	1.06	78	24.34	1.14	77	24.46	1.26	77	24.80	1.42	79	25.15	1.59	83	25.38	1.83	89
16	23.34	0.95	82	23.24	1.02	81	23.26	1.12	83	23.44	1.26	86	23.61	1.43	92	23.61	1.64	99
17	22.40	0.79	85	22.30	0.83	86	22.23	0.91	88	22.28	1.03	93	22.29	1.16	99	23.10	1.81	106
18	21.76	0.58	86	21.57	0.60	88	21.44	0.66	92	21.38	0.74	98	21.26	0.82	105	20.95	0.96	112
19	21.29	−0.35	90	21.09	0.34	90	20.93	0.35	94	20.80	0.30	100	20.65	0.43	108	20.23	−0.47	116
20	21.05	+0.10	86	20.88	−0.00	89	20.73	−0.04	94	20.59	−0.01	100	20.41	−0.02	108	20.01	0.09	116
21	21.08	0.16	84	20.96	+0.23	87	20.85	+0.28	91	20.75	+0.33	98	20.63	+0.42	105	20.29	0.53	113
22	21.37	0.40	81	21.33	0.48	83	21.29	0.57	82	21.08	0.67	92	21.25	0.80	99	21.06	0.90	107
23	21.87	0.59	78	21.91	0.68	75	21.99	0.80	81	22.08	0.94	85	22.22	1.12	91	22.26	1.38	98
24	22.55	0.74	75	22.69	0.81	74	22.89	0.97	75	23.13	1.13	77	23.49	1.35	81	23.81	1.65	87
25	23.56	0.81	71	23.56	1.05	67	23.92	1.05	67	24.33	1.22	67	24.91	1.45	69	25.56	1.79	74
26	24.16	0.60	68	24.50	0.80	64	24.98	1.01	59	25.56	1.19	56	26.39	1.42	56	27.38	1.77	56
27	24.69	0.72	66	25.37	0.75	59	25.95	0.89	52	26.71	1.05	46	27.76	1.27	43	29.10	1.61	45
28	25.61	0.58	65	26.08	0.80	56	26.76	0.68	46	27.67	0.81	38	28.93	1.00	31	30.60	1.20	32
29	26.07	0.33	65	26.07	0.35	54	27.32	0.89	42	28.33	0.48	31	29.96	0.61	22	31.67	0.63	18
30	26.28	+0.08	66	26.78	+0.05	53	27.54	+00.5	40	28.63	+0.08	26	30.16	+0.15	11	32.26	+0.30	8

NOTE. — When T exceeds 88, subtract 88 from it, and add 46.98 to V.

T	0			4			8			12			16			20		
V	δv	Diff.	ṙ	δv	Diff.	ṙ	δv	Diff.	ṙ	δv	Diff.	ṙ	δv	Diff.	ṙ	δv	Diff.	ṙ
30	28.02	−0.86	37	29.18	−0.26	33	30.63	−0.11	34	32.99	+0.11	42	33.21	+0.99	57	33.75	+0.69	76
31	27.40	0.87	35	28.61	0.85	29	30.15	0.85	29	31.68	−0.72	36	33.16	−0.51	51	34.00	−0.28	71
32	26.28	1.34	35	27.43	1.46	28	28.94	1.55	26	30.55	1.55	33	32.10	1.44	47	33.30	1.21	60
33	24.72	1.79	39	25.70	1.95	31	27.06	2.18	27	28.58	1.29	31	30.33	2.26	43	31.69	2.04	60
34	22.81	2.03	46	23.53	2.33	37	21.62	2.66	32	25.98	2.88	33	27.68	2.98	41	29.23	2.86	55
35	20.66	2.21	56	21.04	2.59	46	21.74	3.01	39	22.82	3.34	37	24.38	3.53	40	26.08	3.44	50
36	18.39	2.26	68	18.36	2.69	58	18.61	3.17	49	19.30	3.60	43	20.68	3.88	42	22.36	3.86	46
37	16.14	2.18	80	15.66	2.63	71	15.40	3.15	61	15.02	3.64	51	16.63	3.99	45	18.34	4.00	42
38	14.03	1.98	94	13.00	2.42	85	12.30	2.95	74	12.01	3.46	61	12.65	3.88	49	14.24	4.02	41
39	12.19	1.65	107	10.81	2.05	100	9.50	2.56	87	8.69	3.08	72	8.87	3.51	55	10.80	3.74	41
40	10.74	1.21	119	8.97	1.56	113	7.17	2.02	100	5.85	2.50	82	5.58	2.96	62	6.76	3.23	42
41	09.78	0.68	130	7.68	0.96	124	5.46	1.93	112	3.68	1.76	93	2.95	2.21	69	3.83	2.52	45
42	09.38	−0.09	137	7.04	−0.28	134	4.50	−0.55	122	2.32	−0.85	102	1.16	1.90	76	1.71	1.64	49
43	09.60	+0.52	141	7.11	+0.44	140	4.35	+0.29	130	1.88	+0.04	110	0.35	−0.30	63	0.53	−0.63	54
44	10.43	1.13	142	7.91	1.16	143	5.07	1.13	135	2.39	0.99	116	0.56	+0.73	90	0.38	+0.37	61
45	11.87	1.65	140	9.42	1.82	142	6.60	1.91	136	3.85	1.90	120	1.80	1.72	96	1.27	1.39	67
46	14.83	2.17	134	11.55	2.39	139	8.89	2.60	133	6.18	2.70	121	4.00	2.62	100	3.16	2.32	75
47	16.21	2.52	127	14.20	2.89	132	11.80	3.14	131	9.24	3.33	121	7.03	3.35	104	5.91	3.10	82
48	18.88	2.73	116	17.21	3.10	123	15.16	3.49	124	12.84	3.77	118	10.70	3.88	106	9.36	3.08	88
49	21.67	2.78	105	20.40	3.18	112	18.77	3.62	116	16.78	3.93	115	14.78	4.15	106	13.28	4.03	93
50	24.43	2.66	92	23.57	3.07	100	22.40	3.53	106	20.80	3.98	108	19.00	4.16	100	17.41	4.10	100
51	26.98	2.38	80	26.54	2.78	88	25.84	3.24	96	24.64	3.64	102	23.11	3.92	105	21.48	3.91	104
52	29.18	1.97	69	29.14	2.34	77	28.89	2.77	86	28.09	3.17	95	26.85	3.45	103	25.27	3.53	107
53	30.91	1.46	59	31.23	1.78	67	31.38	2.15	78	30.98	2.52	89	30.01	2.78	100	28.48	2.86	109
54	32.10	0.90	52	32.70	1.14	59	33.19	1.44	71	33.13	1.74	84	32.42	1.99	98	31.00	2.11	110
55	32.70	+0.32	48	33.52	+0.49	54	34.26	+0.60	66	34.46	+0.91	80	33.99	1.12	96	32.70	1.25	110
56	32.73	−0.23	46	33.68	−0.15	52	34.57	−0.05	64	34.95	+0.00	78	34.66	+0.23	95	33.50	+0.36	110
57	32.24	0.72	47	33.22	0.73	53	34.17	0.71	64	34.54	−0.68	78	34.06	−0.60	94	33.43	−0.48	109
58	31.28	1.13	51	32.22	1.21	57	33.13	1.29	67	33.60	1.54	80	33.47	1.32	94	32.55	1.22	107
59	29.98	1.43	57	30.80	1.57	63	31.59	1.78	72	31.97	1.85	83	31.82	1.90	96	30.99	1.80	106
60	28.43	−1.62	65	29.09	−1.79	71	29.68	−2.01	79	29.91	−2.10	88	29.68	−2.30	98	28.80	−2.27	105

T	48			52			56			60			64			68		
V	δv	Diff.	ṙ	δv	Diff.	ṙ	δv	Diff.	ṙ	δv	Diff.	ṙ	δv	Diff.	ṙ	δv	Diff.	ṙ
30	26.75	+0.56	113	26.30	+0.40	107	25.94	+0.34	108	23.82	+0.26	95	25.86	+0.18	87	26.01	+0.12	78
31	27.18	+0.28	117	26.55	+0.21	111	26.17	+0.11	107	25.97	−0.02	99	25.92	−0.06	91	26.00	−0.03	80
32	27.31	−0.03	118	26.72	−0.06	114	26.17	−0.13	110	25.87	0.22	102	25.74	0.30	95	25.74	0.36	85
33	27.13	0.84	118	26.53	0.33	114	25.92	0.37	112	25.54	0.44	106	25.32	0.52	99	25.24	0.62	90
34	26.64	0.63	114	26.06	0.58	113	25.43	0.59	113	25.06	0.64	108	24.70	0.71	103	24.50	0.82	95
35	25.87	0.86	109	25.37	0.80	110	24.75	0.77	112	24.27	0.80	109	23.90	0.87	106	23.61	0.95	100
36	24.88	1.09	102	24.47	0.97	105	23.90	0.91	110	23.40	0.92	109	22.97	0.96	109	22.60	1.04	105
37	23.70	1.23	93	23.44	1.08	99	22.92	0.99	106	22.44	0.97	108	21.98	1.00	110	21.54	1.07	110
38	22.42	1.30	83	22.32	1.13	92	21.92	1.01	101	21.46	0.96	107	20.98	0.97	111	20.46	1.03	113
39	21.11	1.28	73	21.18	1.10	84	20.92	0.98	96	20.52	0.92	104	20.03	0.89	111	19.48	0.92	116
40	19.85	1.20	63	20.11	1.01	76	19.99	0.86	90	19.65	0.79	100	19.19	0.75	109	18.62	0.76	117
41	18.71	1.03	53	19.15	0.86	68	19.19	0.70	83	18.93	0.61	95	18.53	0.55	107	17.96	0.55	117
42	17.79	0.79	45	18.39	0.62	60	18.58	0.49	76	18.48	0.38	100	18.08	0.32	113	17.83	0.35	115
43	17.13	0.49	36	17.88	0.36	54	18.21	−0.23	70	18.16	−0.18	84	17.89	−0.05	99	17.42	+0.02	112
44	16.80	−0.15	34	17.66	−0.00	48	18.12	+0.06	65	18.17	+0.15	79	17.98	+0.24	94	17.59	0.32	108
45	16.89	+0.21	31	17.76	+0.26	45	18.32	0.35	60	18.46	0.43	73	18.37	0.53	88	18.06	0.62	103
46	17.21	0.55	31	18.18	0.56	42	18.81	0.62	56	19.03	0.69	66	19.03	0.79	83	18.83	0.89	97
47	17.92	0.85	33	18.82	0.82	42	19.55	0.85	53	19.84	0.91	64	19.94	1.00	77	19.85	1.10	91
48	18.91	1.10	37	19.82	1.08	43	20.51	1.08	52	20.84	1.08	60	21.03	1.14	72	21.03	1.23	84
49	20.11	1.25	42	20.93	1.15	45	21.60	1.12	51	21.99	1.16	58	22.21	1.21	67	22.31	1.30	78
50	21.40	1.30	48	22.12	1.18	49	22.75	1.19	52	23.15	1.15	52	23.44	1.19	63	23.62	1.27	71
51	22.70	1.25	55	23.29	1.12	53	23.86	1.05	54	24.26	1.04	55	24.50	1.07	59	24.86	1.13	66
52	23.91	1.11	62	24.36	0.97	58	24.85	0.89	56	25.23	0.87	55	25.59	0.89	57	25.92	0.94	61
53	24.93	0.89	69	25.24	0.76	62	25.65	0.67	58	26.01	0.65	55	26.37	0.65	55	26.75	0.68	57
54	25.90	0.61	75	25.88	0.49	66	26.20	0.41	61	26.53	0.48	56	26.89	0.37	54	27.29	0.38	55
55	26.23	+0.29	79	26.23	+0.20	70	26.47	+0.13	63	26.77	+0.09	57	27.11	+0.07	54	27.52	+0.06	53
56	26.29	−0.03	82	26.29	−0.10	72	26.46	−0.15	65	26.72	−0.19	59	27.04	−0.21	55	27.44	−0.21	52
57	26.11	0.34	83	26.04	0.38	73	26.17	0.42	66	26.40	0.40	60	26.70	0.47	56	27.10	0.40	53
58	25.32	0.62	82	25.53	0.63	74	25.63	0.64	67	25.85	0.65	61	26.11	0.68	57	26.48	0.67	56
59	24.87	0.85	79	24.78	0.82	72	24.80	0.82	67	25.10	0.83	62	25.34	0.85	58	25.66	0.88	56
60	23.92	−1.03	76	23.89	−0.97	70	24.00	−0.95	66	24.20	−0.95	62	24.42	−0.96	50	24.72	−0.99	58

Note. — When T exceeds 89, subtract 88 from it, and add 46.98 to V

TABLE X.   (UNIVERSITY OF CALIFORNIA) 23

T	24			28			32			36			40			44		
V	dv	Diff.	r	dv	Diff.	r	dv	Diff.	r	dv	Diff.	r	dv	Diff.	r	dv	Diff.	r
30	33.40	+0.91	95	32.59	+1.03	111	30.77	+0.99	120	29.26	+0.88	124	28.12	+0.77	122	27.40	+0.68	118
31	33.90	+0.06	92	32.97	+0.28	109	31.48	+0.39	121	29.92	+0.40	126	28.71	+0.38	125	27.90	+0.32	122
32	33.52	−0.82	87	32.85	−0.50	105	31.55	−0.27	117	30.07	−0.12	124	28.88	−0.05	124	28.05	−0.04	122
33	32.27	1.67	80	31.97	1.26	97	30.95	0.90	111	29.69	0.64	118	28.62	0.48	121	27.83	0.40	120
34	30.18	2.44	71	30.34	1.96	88	29.75	1.49	101	28.80	1.14	109	27.93	0.89	113	27.26	0.74	115
35	27.39	3.06	62	28.05	2.56	75	27.97	2.02	88	27.42	1.68	97	26.85	1.25	103	26.35	1.06	107
36	24.03	3.54	53	25.22	3.02	64	25.71	2.44	74	25.65	1.92	83	25.44	1.54	91	25.17	1.29	97
37	20.52	3.80	45	22.02	3.28	51	23.10	2.71	59	23.59	2.16	68	23.78	1.74	77	23.78	1.40	85
38	16.43	3.84	37	18.64	3.40	39	20.30	2.83	44	21.33	2.28	53	21.96	1.84	63	22.26	1.54	73
39	12.64	3.64	31	15.23	3.20	28	17.45	2.77	31	18.03	2.25	38	20.10	1.83	49	20.70	1.58	61
40	9.14	3.25	27	12.05	2.97	19	14.75	2.55	19	16.82	2.09	25	18.29	1.72	36	19.19	1.43	49
41	6.16	2.62	25	9.28	2.48	13	12.35	2.22	9	14.84	1.80	14	16.66	1.48	25	17.83	1.24	38
42	3.89	1.84	25	7.08	1.84	10	10.40	1.66	4	13.21	1.40	7	15.31	1.16	16	16.71	0.96	30
43	2.47	−0.95	28	5.60	1.07	10	9.02	1.04	1	12.04	0.90	2	14.33	0.76	11	15.91	0.61	24
44	1.99	+0.01	33	4.93	−0.24	13	8.32	−0.35	2	11.40	−0.34	2	13.80	−0.29	8	15.48	−0.22	20
45	2.49	0.98	41	5.12	+0.62	20	8.32	+0.37	8	11.35	+0.25	4	13.75	+0.19	9	15.46	+0.19	19
46	3.95	1.88	49	6.16	1.43	29	9.05	1.06	16	11.89	0.81	12	14.18	0.46	12	15.86	0.60	21
47	6.25	2.05	59	7.97	2.18	40	10.43	1.66	27	12.97	1.82	22	15.06	1.08	21	16.65	0.95	26
48	9.25	3.28	69	10.42	2.48	53	12.37	2.15	40	14.52	1.72	33	16.33	1.42	31	17.75	1.23	32
49	12.73	3.62	80	13.33	3.04	67	14.72	2.47	55	16.41	2.00	47	17.82	1.65	42	19.11	1.42	41
50	16.48	3.74	91	16.50	3.20	79	17.30	2.62	70	18.51	2.12	61	19.62	1.75	54	20.59	1.40	50
51	20.22	3.62	100	19.73	3.13	93	19.95	2.58	84	20.65	2.09	75	21.38	1.71	67	22.09	1.45	60
52	23.73	3.28	107	22.77	2.86	104	22.46	2.36	97	22.69	1.91	86	23.04	1.56	78	23.49	1.30	69
53	26.79	2.74	114	25.46	2.41	114	24.68	2.00	108	24.48	1.60	99	24.50	1.29	88	24.70	1.07	78
54	29.22	2.05	118	27.60	1.82	120	26.46	1.61	115	25.90	1.20	107	25.63	0.95	96	25.63	0.76	85
55	30.89	1.26	120	29.10	1.15	123	27.71	0.95	121	26.88	+0.73	113	26.40	0.55	103	26.22	0.41	90
56	31.75	+0.45	120	29.90	+0.43	125	28.36	+0.35	123	27.37	−0.24	115	26.74	+0.13	106	26.45	+0.04	93
57	31.79	−0.36	111	29.97	−0.27	123	28.41	−0.24	122	27.36	0.26	115	26.66	−0.28	106	26.31	−0.32	93
58	31.05	1.07	116	29.36	0.91	120	27.88	0.70	118	26.86	0.71	111	26.19	0.65	103	25.82	0.64	92
59	29.66	1.66		28.15	1.45	114	26.84	1.24	112	25.95	1.08	105	25.36	0.87	97	25.03	0.90	88
60	27.74	−2.00	108	26.47	−1.85	108	25.40	−1.58	104	24.70	−1.88	97	24.25	−1.21	90	24.02	−1.11	82

T	72			76			80			84			88			92		
V	dv	Diff.	r	dv	Diff.	r	dv	Diff.	r	dv	Diff.	r	dv	Diff.	r	dv	Diff.	r
30	26.28	+0.08	66	26.78	+0.05	53	27.54	+0.05	40	28.63	+0.08	26	30.16	+0.15	14	32.26	+0.30	8
31	26.23	−0.20	69	26.68	−0.26	55	27.42	−0.81	40	28.51	−0.83	16	30.07	−0.84	20	32.27	−0.30	2
32	25.89	0.48	73	26.26	0.57	59	26.93	0.67	42	27.97	0.74	17	29.48	0.84	19	31.66	0.92	1
33	25.28	0.72	79	25.55	0.88	64	26.09	0.99	48	27.02	1.13	30	28.40	1.30	12	30.46	1.48	0
34	24.45	0.93	85	24.57	1.08	71	24.95	1.25	55	25.71	1.40	37	26.89	1.99	19	28.71	1.97	5
35	23.42	1.09	92	23.39	1.25	79	23.59	1.46	65	24.11	1.74	47	25.08	2.00	29	26.52	2.36	12
36	22.28	1.17	99	22.08	1.34	89	22.05	1.57	76	22.32	1.83	60	22.90	2.18	42	24.00	2.62	24
37	21.09	1.17	106	20.72	1.34	98	20.46	1.57	87	20.45	1.86	74	20.67	2.23	54	21.28	2.73	39
38	19.93	1.11	112	19.39	1.27	107	18.91	1.48	100	18.60	1.78	88	18.44	2.16	74	18.54	2.67	56
39	18.86	0.89	116	18.17	1.12	116	17.49	1.31	111	16.88	1.50	103	16.35	1.96	90	15.94	2.47	73
40	17.94	0.80	122	17.14	0.89	123	16.28	1.06	122	15.41	1.30	117	14.51	1.64	107	13.61	2.12	91
41	17.25	0.55	124	16.38	0.61	129	15.36	0.74	131	14.27	0.94	129	13.06	1.22	122	11.70	1.64	107
42	16.83	−0.26	126	15.92	−0.28	133	14.80	−0.35	138	13.53	−0.53	139	12.00	0.78	135	10.33	1.06	122
43	16.73	+0.07	125	15.81	+0.08	135	14.65	+0.06	143	13.26	−0.02	147	11.60	−0.17	145	9.55	−0.42	135
44	16.96	0.40	125	16.00	0.45	134	14.71	0.48	144	13.48	+0.46	151	11.71	+0.40	152	9.50	+0.25	144
45	17.52	0.72	118	16.71	0.91	131	15.60	0.89	143	14.18	0.98	152	12.39	0.95	155	10.10	0.92	149
46	18.39	1.00	112	17.69	1.13	126	16.68	1.25	139	15.33	1.85	149	13.60	1.44	154	11.34	1.52	152
47	19.52	1.22	105	18.96	1.37	119	18.09	1.53	132	16.87	1.68	144	15.27	2.84	150	13.14	2.02	150
48	20.83	1.37	98	20.43	1.53	111	19.73	1.71	124	18.69	1.90	135	17.28	2.13	143	15.38	2.38	145
49	22.26	1.43	89	22.01	1.59	101	21.50	1.78	114	20.67	2.00	125	19.52	2.28	137	17.90	2.58	137
50	23.69	1.39	80	23.61	1.54	92	23.29	1.73	103	22.69	1.97	114	21.80	2.25	122	20.54	2.01	127
51	25.04	1.25	74	25.10	1.38	82	24.97	1.58	92	24.61	1.81	101	24.03	2.10	110	23.11	2.46	115
52	26.20	1.03	67	26.38	1.15	73	26.45	1.31	81	26.31	1.52	89	26.01	1.80	97	25.46	2.16	103
53	27.10	0.74	61	27.40	0.84	66	27.59	0.96	71	27.67	1.15	78	27.64	1.40	85	27.43	1.72	92
54	27.69	0.42	56	28.07	0.49	59	28.38	0.68	63	28.62	0.73	68	28.81	0.92	75	28.89	1.18	81
55	27.95	+0.23	53	28.38	+0.12	54	28.76	+0.17	56	29.13	+0.07	61	29.48	−0.41	66	29.78	+1.60	73
56	27.88	−0.23	51	28.32	−0.23	52	28.72	−0.22	53	29.17	−0.18	56	29.63	+0.10	60	30.07	−0.00	67
57	27.50	0.51	51	28.00	0.55	50	28.32	0.57	51	28.96	0.67	53	29.28	0.87	57	29.79	0.54	64
58	26.86	0.76	52	27.22	0.81	51	27.59	0.87	51	28.02	0.92	53	28.50	0.97	57	28.98	1.04	63
59	25.99	0.94	54	26.31	1.00	53	26.59	1.09	54	26.95	1.18	55	27.34	1.29	59	27.71	1.43	66
60	24.99	−1.04	57	25.23	−1.12	57	25.42	−1.22	57	25.67	−1.34	60	25.93	−1.49	64	26.13	−1.67	71

NOTE. — When T exceeds 88, subtract 88 from it, and add 46.98 to V.

24   TABLE X.

T	0			4			8			12			16			20		
V	dv	Diff.	r	dv	Diff.	r	dv	Diff.	r	dv	Diff.	r	dv	Diff.	r	dv	Diff.	r
60	28.43	-1.62	65	29.09	-1.79	71	29.68	-2.01	79	29.91	2.19	88	29.68	-2.30	98	28.89	-2.27	105
61	26.77	1.65	74	27.22	1.88	80	27.57	2.13	87	27.60	2.34	95	27.23	2.50	101	26.45	2.50	104
62	25.12	1.60	84	25.34	1.82	89	25.43	2.07	96	25.23	2.30	101	24.69	2.48	104	23.89	2.51	104
63	23.57	1.43	92	23.58	1.53	99	23.43	1.86	104	22.99	2.08	108	22.26	2.27	106	21.42	2.32	104
64	22.25	1.16	100	22.08	1.32	106	21.70	1.52	112	21.06	1.75	114	20.14	1.87	112	19.23	1.95	105
65	21.24	0.82	105	20.94	0.92	112	19.39	1.05	118	19.58	1.18	119	18.53	1.30	115	17.52	1.39	106
66	20.61	0.42	108	20.23	-0.46	116	19.60	-0.50	121	18.70	-0.60	122	17.53	-0.63	118	16.44	-0.71	107
67	20.39	-0.02	108	20.02	+0.04	116	19.38	+0.08	122	18.47	+0.13	123	17.26	+0.12	119	16.10	+0.07	109
68	20.60	+0.41	105	20.31	0.54	113	19.75	0.67	120	18.96	0.77	122	17.77	0.90	119	16.57	0.89	110
69	21.23	0.81	100	21.09	0.99	107	20.72	1.22	114	20.10	1.45	118	19.05	1.63	117	17.85	1.66	111
70	22.21	1.12	91	22.29	1.87	98	22.19	1.68	105	21.86	2.01	111	21.02	2.27	113	19.88	2.36	111
71	23.46	1.34	81	23.83	1.65	87	24.07	2.01	94	24.11	2.42	102	23.58	2.76	107	22.55	2.91	110
72	24.89	1.46	69	25.58	1.78	74	26.21	2.19	81	26.70	2.85	91	26.53	3.05	100	25.69	3.27	108
73	26.37	1.42	56	27.39	1.75	59	28.44	2.18	67	29.40	2.66	78	29.67	3.12	92	29.08	3.40	105
74	27.74	1.27	43	29.09	1.58	44	30.57	1.99	51	32.03	2.45	64	32.78	2.96	82	32.48	3.28	100
75	28.91	1.00	31	30.56	1.26	31	32.42	1.63	37	34.36	2.08	50	35.60	2.57	71	35.65	2.93	94
76	29.74	0.61	22	31.62	0.81	18	33.83	0.91	23	36.20	1.51	37	37.92	1.96	60	38.35	2.36	87
77	30.14	+0.15	14	32.19	+0.08	8	34.64	+0.47	11	37.38	+0.79	25	39.53	1.19	49	40.37	1.59	79
78	30.05	-0.34	10	32.18	-0.32	2	34.77	-0.23	3	37.78	-0.03	15	40.30	+0.30	39	41.54	-0.70	70
79	29.46	0.83	10	31.56	0.92	1	34.18	0.95	3	37.33	0.88	7	40.33	-0.64	30	41.77	-0.28	61
80	28.39	1.29	13	30.35	1.48	0	32.87	1.54	5	36.02	1.70	3	39.02	1.58	22	40.99	1.27	52
81	26.88	1.60	19	28.60	1.97	5	30.90	2.26	5	33.93	2.44	1	36.98	2.44	17	39.24	2.19	43
82	25.01	1.99	29	26.41	2.35	13	28.36	2.75	13	31.14	3.07	3	34.14	3.18	13	36.05	3.06	35
83	22.01	2.17	42	23.90	2.61	25	25.40	3.09	13	27.80	3.53	7	30.62	3.76	12	33.22	3.67	27
84	20.67	2.33	57	21.20	2.71	40	22.18	3.26	25	24.09	3.78	15	26.63	4.13	14	29.28	4.11	22
85	18.45	2.15	74	18.48	2.65	57	18.89	3.23	39	20.24	3.81	25	22.40	4.24	17	25.00	4.33	18
86	16.36	1.96	90	15.89	2.44	74	15.71	3.03	56	16.46	3.65	37	18.16	4.14	23	20.63	4.29	16
87	14.53	1.64	107	13.59	2.09	92	12.83	2.64	72	12.94	3.27	50	14.15	3.78	30	16.41	4.03	16
88	13.08	1.23	122	11.71	1.61	108	10.42	2.11	89	9.92	2.68	64	10.60	3.22	39	12.57	3.53	19
89	12.00	0.72	135	10.36	1.03	123	8.61	1.44	104	7.57	1.96	78	7.71	2.48	49	9.34	2.84	23
90	11.64	-0.17	145	9.64	-0.30	136	7.53	-0.70	117	5.99	1.14	90	5.63	1.61	59	6.80	-1.94	29

T	48			52			56			60			64			68		
V	dv	Diff.	r	dv	Diff.	r	dv	Diff.	r	dv	Diff.	r	dv	Diff.	r	dv	Diff.	r
60	23.92	1.03	76	23.89	-0.97	70	24.00	0.95	66	24.40	-1.01	62	24.42	-0.96	59	24.72	-0.99	58
61	22.82	1.13	71	22.85	1.07	67	23.00	1.03	64	23.41	1.00	62	23.43	1.00	60	23.69	1.04	60
62	21.65	1.18	66	21.76	1.09	64	21.95	1.04	62	22.20	1.00	61	22.41	1.00	61	22.65	1.02	61
63	20.47	1.14	61	20.67	1.06	60	20.91	0.99	59	21.20	0.96	60	21.41	0.95	61	21.64	0.97	63
64	19.36	1.04	56	19.64	0.96	56	19.96	0.90	57	20.27	0.86	57	20.50	0.84	61	20.71	0.85	64
65	18.36	0.67	52	18.75	0.61	53	19.12	0.75	54	19.47	0.71	57	19.72	0.69	60	19.94	0.67	64
66	17.62	0.62	50	18.04	0.60	51	18.46	0.54	53	18.85	0.51	56	19.03	0.49	60	19.36	0.47	64
67	17.13	-0.32	50	17.57	-0.81	50	18.03	-0.29	51	18.44	-0.27	55	18.74	-0.25	58	19.00	-0.23	63
68	16.97	+0.02	51	17.41	0.00	51	17.88	-0.01	51	18.30	+0.00	54	18.62	+0.01	57	18.90	+0.03	62
69	17.16	0.38	55	17.57	+0.32	55	18.01	+0.29	52	18.43	0.28	54	18.76	0.39	56	19.07	0.32	60
70	17.72	0.74	61	18.05	0.64	57	18.45	0.59	54	18.85	0.55	54	19.19	0.56	55	19.53	0.59	58
71	18.63	1.06	68	18.85	0.94	63	19.06	0.86	58	19.53	0.81	56	19.87	0.80	55	20.24	0.81	56
72	19.85	1.84	77	19.93	1.19	70	20.16	1.08	62	20.46	1.02	58	20.78	0.99	55	21.14	0.99	55
73	21.31	1.54	87	21.23	1.37	78	21.34	1.24	68	21.56	1.15	62	21.85	1.11	56	22.22	1.11	53
74	22.92	1.63	98	22.66	1.45	86	22.63	1.31	75	22.76	1.21	66	23.00	1.18	58	23.35	1.13	53
75	24.56	1.61	109	24.13	1.44	95	23.96	1.28	82	23.98	1.19	71	24.16	1.12	61	24.48	1.08	53
76	26.15	1.50	118	25.54	1.33	104	25.22	1.19	89	25.14	1.08	77	25.24	1.00	65	25.52	0.95	55
77	27.57	1.39	127	26.80	1.15	112	26.34	1.01	96	26.15	0.90	82	26.15	0.80	69	26.38	0.74	57
78	28.73	1.00	134	27.84	0.80	119	27.25	0.77	103	26.95	0.67	89	26.87	0.57	74	27.00	0.48	60
79	29.57	0.65	139	28.58	0.58	125	27.89	0.49	109	27.49	0.39	94	27.49	0.31	79	27.43	+0.21	64
80	30.04	+0.28	141	29.00	+0.24	129	28.23	+0.18	114	27.74	+0.10	100	27.49	+0.02	85	27.43	-0.07	70
81	30.14	-0.10	141	29.07	-0.09	131	28.26	-0.12	117	27.70	-0.17	105	27.37	-0.25	90	27.22	0.35	75
82	29.85	0.47	138	28.82	0.41	131	27.99	0.40	119	27.39	0.42	109	26.87	0.00	95	26.74	0.78	81
83	29.21	0.76	132	28.26	0.68	128	27.47	0.64	120	26.86	0.64	112	26.40	0.68	100	26.06	0.76	87
84	28.29	1.04	123	27.46	0.91	124	26.79	0.83	119	26.12	0.81	114	25.72	0.92	104	25.22	0.84	93
85	27.13	1.24	115	26.45	1.07	119	25.81	0.97	117	25.24	0.92	114	24.75	0.92	108	24.28	0.96	99
86	25.82	1.33	105	25.32	1.16	112	24.79	1.04	113	24.29	0.96	114	23.80	0.94	110	23.33	0.95	104
87	24.44	1.37	94	24.13	1.18	103	23.72	1.03	103	23.32	0.95	112	22.87	0.92	112	22.37	0.90	107
88	23.07	1.32	83	22.96	1.12	95	22.72	0.98	103	22.39	0.88	109	21.99	0.82	111	21.50	0.80	110
89	21.80	1.18	73	21.88	1.00	87	21.78	0.86	97	21.56	0.75	106	21.23	0.68	110	20.78	0.62	111
90	20.71	0.97	63	20.96	-0.81	70	21.00	-0.68	91	20.88	-0.58	101	20.63	-0.49	108	20.25	-0.42	111

NOTE.—When T exceeds 88, subtract 88 from it, and add 46.98 to V.

TABLE X. 25

T	24			28			32			36			40			44		
V	δv	Diff.	r	δv	Diff.	r	δv	Diff.	r	δv	Diff.	r	δv	Diff.	r	δv	Diff.	r
60	27.74	−2.08	108	26.47	1.85	108	25.40	1.59	104	24.70	1.38	97	24.25	1.21	90	24.02	1.11	82
61	25.48	2.35	104	24.46	2.10	100	23.66	1.81	95	23.20	1.57	89	22.94	1.37	82	22.82	1.25	75
62	23.05	2.89	100	22.82	2.16	93	21.78	1.86	86	21.57	1.64	80	21.51	1.43	74	21.53	1.29	70
63	20.69	2.24	96	20.13	2.06	87	19.89	1.81	78	19.93	1.58	71	20.08	1.39	66	20.24	1.26	63
64	18.56	1.92	94	18.16	1.78	82	18.15	1.59	72	18.40	1.41	64	18.73	1.25	59	19.01	1.14	57
65	16.85	1.41	93	16.56	1.35	79	16.70	1.24	68	17.11	1.12	59	17.57	1.01	55	17.96	0.93	53
66	15.73	0.77	93	15.46	−0.79	79	15.66	0.77	66	16.16	0.73	57	16.70	0.69	52	17.14	0.66	50
67	15.31	−0.03	95	14.98	+0.13	80	15.15	0.20	67	15.65	−0.26	58	16.19	−0.28	52	16.63	−0.31	50
68	15.66	+0.75	97	15.19	0.55	84	15.25	+0.41	71	15.64	+0.26	61	16.11	+0.15	56	16.51	+0.08	53
69	16.80	1.53	101	16.14	1.30	89	15.97	1.03	78	16.17	0.80	68	16.48	0.61	62	16.78	0.48	58
70	18.71	2.23	105	17.78	1.96	96	17.31	1.63	86	17.24	1.32	78	17.33	1.07	70	17.46	0.88	65
71	21.26	2.80	109	20.05	1.52	104	19.23	2.15	97	18.80	1.78	89	18.62	1.48	81	18.54	1.25	75
72	24.31	3.21	113	22.82	2.04	112	21.61	2.54	109	20.80	2.15	102	20.28	1.80	94	19.96	1.55	85
73	27.67	3.40	115	25.92	3.17	120	24.31	2.78	120	23.09	2.37	115	22.22	2.03	107	21.64	1.76	97
74	31.11	3.35	117	29.15	3.18	127	27.16	2.83	130	25.54	2.46	128	24.33	2.12	120	23.47	1.86	109
75	34.38	3.07	116	32.28	2.98	132	29.98	2.71	140	28.00	2.38	139	26.46	2.07	132	25.35	1.83	121
76	37.26	2.58	114	35.12	2.50	135	32.59	2.41	147	30.30	2.15	149	28.47	1.89	143	27.14	1.68	132
77	39.54	1.80	110	37.48	2.00	135	34.80	1.93	150	32.30	1.77	155	30.25	1.60	151	28.72	1.43	141
78	41.04	1.05	104	39.12	1.77	132	36.46	1.33	150	33.85	1.26	158	31.67	1.21	157	30.01	1.10	147
79	41.65	+0.13	95	40.01	+0.45	126	37.47	+0.64	147	34.87	0.72	157	32.65	0.73	158	31.03	0.70	150
80	41.30	−0.83	85	40.03	−0.41	117	37.75	−0.09	140	35.29	−0.11	152	33.13	+0.12	155	31.42	+0.27	150
81	40.00	1.75	74	39.20	1.23	105	37.29	0.81	129	35.09	−0.50	144	33.09	−0.29	149	31.47	−0.17	147
82	37.81	2.57	62	37.57	2.02	100	36.13	1.46	115	34.29	1.08	132	32.55	0.78	140	31.08	0.58	141
83	34.86	3.25	50	35.17	2.69	76	34.32	2.08	99	32.94	1.56	117	31.53	1.21	129	30.30	0.86	132
84	31.31	3.75	39	32.20	3.18	59	31.98	2.54	81	31.13	1.99	100	30.13	1.56	113	29.17	1.26	121
85	27.33	4.04	28	28.62	3.49	44	29.24	2.86	63	28.97	2.27	82	28.42	1.81	97	27.78	1.48	108
86	23.23	4.09	19	25.22	3.61	29	26.27	3.01	45	26.59	2.42	63	26.51	1.95	80	26.22	1.60	94
87	19.17	3.92	12	21.60	3.52	16	23.23	2.96	29	24.14	2.42	46	24.52	1.87	64	24.58	1.63	80
88	15.39	3.53	7	18.17	3.22	6	20.34	2.76	15	21.74	2.28	31	22.56	1.88	49	22.95	1.56	67
89	12.11	2.93	4	15.16	2.76	1	17.71	2.41	4	19.56	2.02	18	20.76	1.67	36	21.46	1.39	55
90	9.52	−2.18	6	12.65	−2.16	5	15.51	−1.92	3	17.70	−1.64	8	19.22	−1.37	25	20.16	−1.15	45

T	72			76			80			84			88			92		
V	δv	Diff.	r	δv	Diff.	r	δv	Diff.	r	δv	Diff.	r	δv	Diff.	r	δv	Diff.	r
60	24.09	1.04	57	25.23	−1.12	57	25.42	1.22	57	25.07	1.34	60	25.93	1.49	64	26.13	1.67	71
61	23.91	1.08	60	24.07	1.17	61	24.15	1.28	62	24.27	1.41	66	24.37	1.58	71	24.37	1.80	77
62	22.83	1.06	63	22.90	1.14	65	22.87	1.24	68	22.85	1.38	73	22.78	1.55	79	22.54	1.79	85
63	21.78	1.00	66	21.79	1.04	69	21.67	1.13	74	21.51	1.26	80	21.26	1.42	87	20.79	1.64	94
64	20.83	0.86	68	20.81	0.86	73	20.60	0.95	79	20.33	1.03	86	19.94	1.18	95	19.36	1.36	102
65	20.05	0.67	70	20.01	0.68	70	19.77	0.70	84	19.40	0.77	92	18.89	0.86	101	18.07	0.96	110
66	19.48	0.44	70	19.44	−0.43	78	19.19	0.42	86	18.79	0.43	96	18.22	0.46	106	17.29	−0.52	115
67	19.16	−0.19	70	19.14	+0.14	78	18.92	−0.09	86	18.53	−0.06	98	17.96	−0.02	109	17.03	+0.00	118
68	19.10	+0.08	69	19.15	0.17	77	19.01	+0.26	86	18.67	+0.34	97	18.17	+0.44	109	17.32	0.57	119
69	19.32	0.37	66	19.47	0.47	74	19.43	0.59	83	19.21	0.73	94	18.84	0.80	106	18.17	1.11	116
70	19.84	0.65	63	20.09	0.75	68	20.18	0.89	78	20.12	1.08	88	19.96	1.30	100	19.53	1.58	110
71	20.61	0.87	60	20.97	0.99	65	21.23	1.16	72	20.36	1.37	81	21.43	1.62	91	21.35	2.00	101
72	21.58	1.05	56	22.06	1.16	60	22.49	1.34	65	22.76	1.57	73	23.20	1.87	80	23.53	2.29	90
73	22.70	1.15	53	23.20	1.25	54	23.90	1.43	57	24.50	1.60	61	25.16	1.97	68	25.92	2.41	78
74	23.87	1.15	49	24.56	1.24	48	25.34	1.40	48	26.18	1.63	51	27.14	1.98	55	28.34	2.37	64
75	25.01	1.08	47	25.78	1.14	43	26.70	1.27	41	27.56	1.47	40	29.03	1.75	43	30.66	2.18	50
76	26.04	0.83	46	26.85	0.85	40	27.88	1.04	34	29.13	1.31	31	30.65	1.44	30	32.69	1.81	36
77	26.88	0.70	46	27.69	0.64	37	28.79	0.74	29	30.19	0.85	23	31.92	1.03	20	34.28	1.31	23
78	27.44	0.41	48	28.23	0.36	37	29.36	+0.37	26	30.84	+0.42	17	32.71	+0.53	12	35.31	0.72	13
79	27.71	+0.12	51	28.45	−0.04	38	29.55	−0.04	26	31.04	−0.02	15	32.98	−0.00	7	35.71	+0.07	06
80	27.68	−0.15	55	28.31	+0.30	41	29.34	0.40	27	30.80	0.46	15	32.72	0.54	5	35.45	−0.58	02
81	27.35	0.46	60	27.85	0.60	46	28.75	0.76	32	30.12	0.88	18	31.92	1.03	7	34.55	1.19	02
82	26.76	0.71	67	27.11	0.87	53	27.84	1.04	38	29.04	1.28	24	30.86	1.45	12	33.08	1.71	05
83	25.94	0.90	74	26.12	1.07	65	26.68	1.26	47	27.66	1.49	33	29.03	1.77	20	31.13	2.13	13
84	24.97	1.01	82	24.98	1.18	70	25.33	1.40	57	26.06	1.65	44	27.12	1.98	31	28.82	2.41	23
85	23.92	1.06	89	23.78	1.22	79	23.89	1.43	68	24.36	1.70	56	25.08	2.05	44	26.32	2.63	36
86	22.86	1.08	96	22.54	1.18	88	22.47	1.42	79	22.66	1.65	69	23.02	2.00	59	23.77	2.50	49
87	21.85	0.90	102	21.40	1.07	95	21.14	1.24	90	21.06	1.49	82	21.08	1.83	73	21.33	2.32	64
88	20.94	0.82	107	20.40	0.90	104	19.98	1.08	100	19.67	1.25	91	19.36	1.55	87	19.14	2.01	79
89	20.20	0.68	111	19.60	0.67	110	19.00	0.77	108	18.55	0.94	105	17.97	1.18	100	17.32	1.57	92
90	19.68	0.39	113	19.06	0.40	114	18.44	−0.45	115	17.79	−0.57	114	16.99	−0.74	111	16.01	−1.04	104

NOTE.— When T exceeds 88, subtract 88 from it, and add 46.98 to V

T	0			4			8			12			16			20		
V	δv	Diff.	ṙ	δv	Diff.	ṙ	δv	Diff.	ṙ	δv	Diff.	ṙ	δv	Diff.	ṙ	δv	Diff.	ṙ
90	11.64	−0.17	145	9.64	−0.89	136	7.53	−0.70	117	5.99	−1.14	90	5.63	−1.61	59	6.89	−1.94	29
91	11.75	+0.40	151	9.58	+0.28	145	7.21	+0.09	128	5.28	−0.05	101	4.48	−0.65	69	5.35	1.06	36
92	12.43	0.05	155	10.20	0.94	150	7.70	0.87	135	5.48	+0.05	111	4.32	+0.32	79	4.78	−0.07	45
93	13.64	1.44	155	11.45	1.53	152	8.94	1.58	140	6.58	1.46	117	5.11	1.24	87	5.20	+0.84	54
94	15.31	1.84	150	13.25	2.02	150	10.85	2.18	141	8.44	2.14	122	6.79	2.07	94	6.54	1.74	64
95	17.31	2.12	143	15.49	2.98	145	13.30	2.04	139	10.06	2.76	123	9.22	2.71	100	8.67	2.45	73
96	19.54	2.32	133	18.01	2.59	137	16.12	2.91	134	13.95	3.12	123	12.21	3.16	105	11.43	2.95	83
97	21.83	2.24	121	20.64	2.59	127	19.11	2.97	127	17.19	3.25	120	15.53	3.36	108	14.57	3.22	91
98	24.03	2.08	109	23.20	2.44	115	22.07	2.84	118	20.45	3.16	116	18.93	3.35	109	17.87	3.25	98
99	26.00	1.79	96	25.52	2.13	103	24.80	2.52	108	23.51	2.85	111	22.19	3.06	109	21.07	3.03	104
100	27.62	1.40	84	27.47	1.09	92	27.12	2.04	99	26.16	2.36	101	25.06	2.58	109	23.94	2.60	109
101	28.79	0.91	74	28.91	1.05	81	28.89	1.45	90	28.24	1.73	99	27.35	1.98	107	26.27	1.98	112
102	29.45	+0.40	66	29.78	+0.56	73	30.03	0.79	83	29.63	1.01	94	28.93	1.18	105	27.91	1.25	114
103	29.60	−0.11	60	30.06	−0.01	67	30.48	+0.11	77	30.26	+0.25	90	29.71	+0.87	103	28.78	+0.45	114
104	29.24	0.58	57	29.76	0.58	64	30.25	−0.54	74	30.13	−0.49	87	29.68	−0.47	102	28.82	−0.36	114
105	28.45	0.97	57	28.94	1.05	63	29.40	1.10	73	29.29	1.15	86	28.87	1.15	100	28.07	1.10	113
106	27.30	1.28	59	27.67	1.42	66	28.03	1.57	75	27.84	1.69	87	27.38	1.76	100	26.62	1.75	111
107	25.90	1.48	64	26.10	1.67	71	26.26	1.89	79	25.92	2.07	90	25.35	2.22	100	24.58	2.24	109
108	24.35	1.57	71	24.33	1.80	77	24.26	2.05	85	23.70	2.29	94	22.95	2.48	101	22.15	2.56	107
109	22.77	1.54	79	22.51	1.77	85	22.16	2.00	92	21.34	2.82	99	20.39	2.54	103	19.50	2.67	105
110	21.27	1.41	87	20.78	1.62	94	20.14	1.89	100	19.06	2.18	105	17.86	2.40	106	16.86	2.53	104
111	19.95	1.17	95	19.26	1.25	102	18.37	1.56	108	17.02	1.81	111	15.59	2.05	109	14.44	2.20	103
112	18.92	0.84	102	18.08	0.97	110	16.98	1.14	115	15.43	1.32	116	13.75	1.52	112	12.45	1.67	102
113	18.26	0.45	106	17.32	−0.50	115	16.09	−0.59	120	14.38	−0.70	120	12.54	0.84	114	11.10	1.00	103
114	18.01	−0.02	108	17.07	+0.03	118	15.79	+0.04	124	14.03	+0.03	123	12.06	−0.05	116	10.45	−0.20	103
115	18.22	+0.43	109	17.37	0.58	119	16.15	0.65	124	14.43	0.79	124	12.43	+0.80	117	10.69	+0.75	104
116	18.87	0.89	106	18.22	1.11	116	17.17	1.83	122	15.60	1.55	123	13.66	1.06	117	11.85	1.61	106
117	20.00	1.31	100	19.58	1.59	110	18.81	1.02	117	17.42	2.25	119	15.74	2.51	116	13.91	2.48	106
118	21.48	1.63	91	20.40	2.00	101	21.00	2.41	109	20.10	2.84	113	18.58	3.15	113	16.80	3.22	107
119	23.25	1.86	81	23.57	2.28	90	23.62	2.75	99	23.19	3.26	105	22.03	3.66	108	20.35	3.81	107
120	25.19	1.06	68	25.95	+2.40	77	26.50	+2.61	86	26.61	+3.48	95	25.90	4.06	102	24.41	+4.18	106

T	48			52			56			60			64			68		
V	δv	Diff.	ṙ	δv	Diff.	ṙ	δv	Diff.	ṙ	δv	Diff.	ṙ	δv	Diff.	ṙ	δv	Diff.	ṙ
90	20.71	−0.57	63	20.96	−0.81	79	21.00	−0.68	91	20.88	−0.58	101	20.63	−0.49	108	20.25	−0.42	111
91	19.86	0.70	56	20.26	0.57	73	20.41	0.47	85	20.40	0.37	97	20.24	0.27	105	19.93	−0.20	110
92	19.31	0.38	50	19.81	−0.30	67	20.06	−0.12	80	20.14	−0.15	93	20.08	−0.04	101	19.85	+0.04	108
93	19.09	−0.06	47	19.65	−0.01	63	19.97	+0.04	75	20.13	+0.11	88	20.15	+0.19	97	20.01	0.28	104
94	19.19	+0.20	46	19.78	+0.26	60	20.14	0.29	72	20.36	0.48	84	20.45	0.41	93	20.41	0.40	100
95	18.60	0.54	47	20.17	0.50	59	20.54	0.50	70	20.79	0.52	81	20.96	0.58	89	20.99	0.66	96
96	20.26	0.76	50	20.78	0.69	60	21.13	0.60	68	21.40	0.67	78	21.61	0.70	86	21.73	0.79	91
97	21.11	0.90	55	21.55	0.81	61	21.85	0.75	68	22.12	0.74	77	22.36	0.77	82	22.56	0.82	87
98	22.06	0.94	60	22.39	0.84	67	22.63	0.77	69	22.87	0.78	76	23.14	0.75	79	23.38	0.78	83
99	23.00	0.90	67	23.23	0.79	69	23.39	−0.71	71	23.59	0.66	75	23.86	0.65	78	24.12	0.68	79
100	23.86	0.77	73	23.98	0.66	73	24.05	0.58	73	24.20	0.52	76	24.45	0.50	77	24.74	0.51	77
101	24.55	0.57	79	24.56	0.47	77	24.55	0.39	76	24.64	0.33	77	24.86	0.29	76	25.15	0.28	75
102	25.00	+0.30	84	24.92	+0.24	81	24.84	+0.19	78	24.87	+0.15	78	25.04	+0.05	77	25.31	+0.02	74
103	25.16	0.00	88	25.03	−0.03	84	24.88	−0.09	80	24.85	−0.15	80	24.97	−0.20	78	25.20	−0.25	75
104	25.01	−0.30	90	24.86	0.31	86	24.66	0.34	82	24.58	0.36	81	24.65	0.44	79	24.82	0.50	76
105	24.56	0.59	91	24.41	0.58	86	24.20	0.57	83	24.07	0.61	83	24.09	0.87	81	24.20	0.79	78
106	23.83	0.86	89	23.71	0.80	86	23.52	0.78	83	23.36	0.80	83	23.32	0.86	83	23.36	0.98	80
107	22.86	1.07	86	22.81	0.98	84	22.64	0.94	82	22.47	0.96	84	22.38	1.00	84	22.34	1.07	83
108	21.70	1.28	81	21.74	1.12	81	21.64	1.05	81	21.45	1.05	84	21.33	1.08	85	21.23	1.13	86
109	20.41	1.31	75	20.57	1.19	76	20.54	1.11	78	20.38	1.08	83	20.23	1.10	86	20.08	1.18	86
110	19.08	1.32	69	19.36	1.19	72	19.42	1.10	75	19.30	1.05	81	19.13	1.06	86	18.03	1.11	91
111	17.77	1.24	63	18.19	1.12	66	18.34	1.02	71	18.27	0.98	79	18.10	0.97	86	17.86	1.00	93
112	16.59	1.08	56	17.12	0.98	61	17.37	0.88	67	17.34	0.89	76	17.18	0.82	85	16.93	0.82	93
113	15.60	0.85	51	16.23	0.76	57	16.57	0.68	63	16.60	0.62	73	16.46	0.60	83	16.21	0.60	93
114	14.80	0.54	47	15.59	0.48	53	16.01	0.42	60	16.09	0.36	70	15.98	0.33	80	15.75	−0.30	92
115	14.52	−0.17	45	15.26	−0.14	50	15.73	−0.10	57	15.87	−0.06	66	15.80	−0.02	77	15.60	+0.01	90
116	14.56	+0.25	45	15.30	+0.23	49	15.80	+0.25	54	15.97	+0.28	63	15.94	+0.31	74	15.77	0.35	87
117	15.02	0.68	47	15.72	0.42	49	16.22	0.60	53	16.42	0.62	61	16.42	0.66	71	16.29	0.70	83
118	15.92	1.10	51	16.53	1.00	51	16.99	0.95	53	17.21	0.95	59	17.25	0.98	68	17.17	1.04	83
119	17.22	1.47	56	17.71	1.38	54	18.11	1.25	54	18.31	1.24	58	18.38	1.26	64	18.36	1.32	74
120	18.86	+1.77	64	19.19	+1.59	59	19.49	+1.47	57	19.68	+1.47	58	19.76	1.47	62	19.80	+1.52	70

Note. — When T exceeds 88, subtract 88 from it, and add 46.98 to V.

TABLE X.   27

T	24			28			32			36			40			44		
V	δv	Diff.	ř	δv	Diff.	ř	δv	Diff.	ř	δv	Diff.	ř	δv	Diff.	ř	δv	Diff.	ř
90	9.52	−2.18	6	12.65	−2.18	−5	15.51	−1.92	−3	17.70	−1.64	8	19.22	−1.37	25	20.16	−1.16	45
91	7.74	1.83	10	10.83	1.41	−5	13.86	1.83	−7	16.28	1.10	2	18.02	0.99	18	19.16	0.82	37
92	6.85	−0.42	17	9.82	−0.51	−1	12.85	0.67	−6	15.37	0.64	0	17.24	0.55	14	18.51	0.46	32
93	6.90	+0.49	26	9.60	+0.18	6	12.51	−0.01	−1	15.00	−0.09	3	16.91	−0.10	14	18.23	−0.09	30
94	7.83	1.82	36	10.17	0.92	16	12.83	+0.62	7	15.18	+0.44	9	17.03	+0.33	18	18.34	+0.27	31
95	9.53	2.01	48	11.43	1.55	29	13.75	1.17	19	15.87	0.59	18	17.56	0.71	24	18.70	0.61	35
96	11.85	2.53	61	13.27	2.05	43	15.17	1.60	32	16.96	1.25	30	18.45	1.01	33	19.55	0.87	40
97	14.59	2.86	73	15.52	2.34	58	16.04	1.87	47	18.36	1.49	43	19.58	1.21	44	20.52	1.03	48
98	17.53	2.91	85	17.95	2.46	73	18.91	1.98	63	19.93	1.58	57	20.86	1.29	56	21.60	1.09	57
99	20.42	2.76	96	20.43	2.36	86	20.90	1.90	79	21.52	1.52	72	22.15	1.24	68	22.69	1.04	66
100	23.05	2.40	105	22.68	2.05	99	22.72	1.67	92	22.98	1.34	85	23.34	1.07	79	23.68	0.89	75
101	25.23	1.87	113	24.54	1.60	109	24.24	1.30	103	24.18	1.02	96	24.34	0.81	89	24.48	0.67	83
102	26.79	1.19	118	25.89	1.04	117	25.33	0.82	112	25.02	0.63	105	24.97	0.46	97	25.02	0.37	90
103	27.62	+0.46	121	26.62	+0.39	122	25.89	+0.28	118	25.44	+0.18	111	25.26	+0.09	102	25.23	+0.03	94
104	27.71	−0.29	121	26.68	−0.27	123	25.80	−0.28	120	25.38	−0.30	113	25.15	−0.31	105	25.08	−0.32	97
105	27.04	1.01	120	26.08	0.94	122	25.34	0.88	119	24.85	0.75	113	24.65	0.69	104	24.60	0.64	97
106	25.69	1.84	117	24.85	1.48	118	24.24	1.32	115	23.88	1.16	109	23.77	1.04	101	23.80	0.94	94
107	23.77	2.12	113	23.12	1.92	113	22.71	1.70	109	22.53	1.49	103	22.58	1.32	96	22.72	1.19	90
108	21.45	2.44	108	21.01	2.23	105	20.85	1.97	101	20.90	1.72	94	21.14	1.52	88	21.42	1.36	84
109	18.89	2.57	103	18.66	2.37	98	18.77	2.12	91	19.09	1.84	85	19.54	1.63	80	20.00	1.46	77
110	16.31	2.49	98	16.27	2.32	90	16.64	2.08	82	17.22	1.83	75	17.89	1.62	71	18.51	1.46	69
111	13.91	2.21	93	14.02	2.09	83	14.61	1.90	73	15.43	1.69	66	16.30	1.51	62	17.08	1.37	61
112	11.89	1.74	90	12.08	1.69	77	12.83	1.57	65	13.84	1.42	58	14.86	1.30	54	15.77	1.18	54
113	10.42	1.11	88	10.63	1.13	73	11.47	1.10	60	12.59	1.08	52	13.70	0.96	48	14.71	0.90	48
114	9.67	−0.33	87	9.81	−0.45	71	10.63	−0.51	57	11.78	−0.53	48	12.93	0.54	44	13.97	0.54	44
115	9.75	+0.52	88	9.73	+0.33	71	10.45	+0.17	57	11.52	+0.04	47	12.61	−0.06	43	13.62	−0.12	42
116	10.71	1.42	90	10.47	1.16	74	10.97	0.89	60	11.87	0.67	50	12.81	+0.48	45	13.73	+0.35	43
117	12.58	2.38	97	12.04	1.87	79	12.23	1.62	66	12.86	1.30	56	13.57	1.03	51	14.32	0.84	47
118	15.27	3.05	97	14.40	2.70	86	14.20	2.28	74	14.46	1.89	64	14.87	1.56	57	15.40	1.30	52
119	18.67	3.67	102	17.43	3.31	94	16.80	2.85	84	16.63	2.40	75	16.68	2.01	67	16.92	1.71	60
120	22.60	4.08	106	21.01	+3.74	102	19.90	4.27	95	19.25	+2.78	87	18.89	2.36	78	18.81	+2.08	70

T	72			76			80			84			88			92		
V	δv	Diff.	ř	δv	Diff.	ř	δv	Diff.	ř	δv	Diff.	ř	δv	Diff.	ř	δv	Diff.	ř
90	19.68	−0.89	113	19.06	−0.40	114	18.44	−0.45	115	17.79	−0.57	114	16.99	−0.74	111	16.01	−1.04	104
91	19.41	−0.04	114	18.80	−0.11	116	18.15	−0.11	119	17.41	−0.17	120	16.48	−0.37	118	15.25	−0.47	114
92	19.40	+0.12	113	18.84	+0.16	117	18.21	+0.24	120	17.45	+0.24	123	16.45	+0.22	123	15.08	+0.13	120
93	19.65	0.36	110	19.18	0.47	115	18.62	0.56	119	17.88	0.62	123	16.91	0.68	124	15.50	0.70	122
94	20.15	0.61	106	19.78	0.72	111	19.33	0.84	116	18.68	0.96	120	17.80	1.06	122	16.47	1.20	121
95	20.86	0.78	101	20.62	0.91	106	20.29	1.05	111	19.79	1.21	114	19.06	1.40	117	17.90	1.61	116
96	21.71	0.89	96	21.60	1.03	99	21.43	1.19	103	21.10	1.37	107	20.60	1.61	108	19.69	1.90	108
97	22.64	0.93	92	22.67	1.06	92	22.55	1.22	95	22.51	1.41	97	22.27	1.68	98	21.69	2.02	98
98	23.57	0.88	84	23.72	0.98	86	23.87	1.15	86	23.93	1.34	86	23.96	1.61	87	23.73	1.98	86
99	24.40	0.75	79	24.66	0.64	78	24.96	0.97	77	25.22	1.16	76	25.50	1.41	75	25.69	1.74	74
100	25.07	0.55	75	25.41	0.62	72	25.82	0.71	69	26.26	0.87	66	26.79	1.09	63	27.28	1.42	61
101	25.51	0.30	72	25.90	0.34	67	26.39	0.39	62	26.97	0.50	57	27.68	0.66	52	28.48	0.94	50
102	25.68	+0.02	70	26.09	+0.01	64	26.61	+0.03	57	27.27	+0.08	50	28.12	+0.18	44	29.16	+0.39	40
103	25.55	−0.28	69	25.93	−0.32	60	26.45	−0.36	54	27.13	−0.37	46	28.04	−0.34	38	29.23	−0.24	33
104	25.13	0.56	70	25.45	0.64	63	25.90	0.72	54	26.54	0.80	44	27.44	0.84	35	28.68	0.86	29
105	24.44	0.81	73	24.66	0.92	65	25.01	1.05	56	25.54	1.18	46	26.33	1.33	36	27.51	1.45	28
106	23.52	1.02	76	23.61	1.15	69	23.81	1.31	60	24.18	1.51	50	24.79	1.72	39	25.78	1.95	31
107	22.41	1.16	80	22.46	1.31	74	22.39	1.50	74	22.53	1.75	57	22.99	2.05	46	23.61	2.34	37
108	21.20	1.24	85	21.00	1.40	80	20.81	1.61	74	20.69	1.88	66	20.74	2.21	56	21.11	2.80	46
109	19.93	1.25	89	19.58	1.40	87	19.18	1.61	83	18.77	1.90	76	18.47	2.28	68	18.42	2.71	57
110	18.70	1.19	94	18.20	1.33	92	17.58	1.53	92	16.88	1.63	88	16.19	2.19	81	15.70	2.65	70
111	17.55	1.07	98	16.92	1.18	100	16.11	1.36	101	15.12	1.63	93	14.09	2.07	94	13.12	2.45	84
112	16.56	0.88	101	15.83	0.96	100	14.86	1.10	109	13.62	1.33	110	12.24	2.66	107	10.81	2.99	99
113	15.80	0.62	103	15.00	0.68	108	13.90	0.77	116	12.45	0.95	120	10.77	1.22	119	8.95	1.59	112
114	15.32	+0.31	103	14.50	−0.32	113	13.32	−0.37	121	11.71	−0.50	128	9.80	0.69	129	7.63	0.99	124
115	15.18	−0.04	102	14.36	+0.07	107	13.15	+0.07	124	11.45	+0.01	136	9.38	−0.11	137	6.97	−0.31	133
116	15.39	0.40	100	14.63	0.48	113	13.45	0.48	125	11.72	0.54	135	9.58	+0.51	141	7.02	+0.42	140
117	15.98	0.77	96	15.31	0.87	110	14.20	0.97	123	12.84	1.54	135	10.40	1.12	142	7.81	1.14	143
118	16.20	1.11	92	16.37	1.24	105	15.39	1.39	119	13.84	1.85	125	11.81	1.68	140	9.30	1.81	143
119	18.20	1.41	86	17.78	1.55	99	16.97	1.74	112	15.61	1.95	125	13.76	2.16	135	11.42	2.36	139
120	19.73	+1.61	80	19.47	+1.78	92	18.86	+1.99	104	17.73	+2.24	116	16.13	+2.52	127	14.08	+2.82	132

NOTE.—When T exceeds 88, subtract .88 from it, and add 46.98 to V.

T	0		4		8		12		16		20		24		28		32		36		40		44	
J	δv	r	δv	r	δv	r	δv	r	δv	r	δv	r	δv	r	δv	r	δv	r	δv	r	δv	r	δv	r
0	2.20	45	1.79	36	1.69	25	2.03	15	2.79	7	3.87	2	5.09	1	6.24	3	7.15	9	7.64	17	7.75	26	7.52	35
1	2.51	52	1.83	43	1.49	33	1.58	22	2.12	12	3.03	5	4.20	2	5.41	2	6.46	6	7.14	13	7.43	21	7.44	29
2	2.88	58	2.05	50	1.47	41	1.29	30	1.57	19	2.30	10	3.36	5	4.56	3	5.72	4	6.55	9	7.08	16	7.24	23
3	3.40	54	2.41	57	1.63	48	1.22	38	1.22	27	1.70	16	2.60	9	3.73	5	4.92	4	5.88	7	6.58	12	6.94	18
4	3.99	69	2.93	64	1.98	56	1.31	46	1.05	35	1.28	24	1.97	15	2.97	9	4.14	5	5.17	7	6.02	10	6.54	15
5	4.68	72	3.59	69	2.50	63	1.62	55	1.09	44	1.04	32	1.50	22	2.32	13	3.42	9	4.47	8	5.40	9	6.07	13
6	5.42	75	4.32	74	3.15	69	2.10	62	1.32	52	1.00	41	1.17	30	1.81	21	2.76	14	3.80	10	4.77	9	5.55	11
7	6.15	76	5.13	76	3.93	74	2.74	69	1.75	61	1.17	50	1.08	38	1.44	28	2.23	20	3.17	14	4.15	11	5.00	11
8	6.90	75	5.98	78	4.79	78	3.54	75	2.38	68	1.54	58	1.16	47	1.25	36	1.82	27	2.65	19	3.59	15	4.46	12
9	7.57	73	6.82	78	5.70	80	4.41	79	3.14	74	2.10	66	1.44	56	1.27	44	1.59	34	2.23	25	3.08	19	3.96	15
10	8.18	69	7.61	76	6.62	80	5.37	81	4.02	79	2.81	73	1.91	63	1.47	53	1.52	42	1.98	32	2.67	25	3.50	19
11	8.66	65	8.31	73	7.53	79	6.37	82	5.00	82	3.67	78	2.56	70	1.87	60	1.63	50	1.88	39	2.36	31	3.11	24
12	9.04	59	8.93	68	8.35	76	7.33	81	6.04	83	4.63	82	3.37	76	2.43	67	1.94	57	1.92	47	2.26	38	2.84	29
13	9.28	53	9.41	62	9.07	71	8.25	79	7.05	83	5.66	84	4.29	80	3.16	73	2.43	64	2.15	54	2.27	44	2.68	36
14	9.35	46	9.73	56	9.66	66	9.07	74	8.05	81	6.71	84	5.20	83	4.02	78	3.05	70	2.54	61	2.42	51	2.64	42
15	9.27	39	9.89	48	10.09	59	9.76	69	8.95	77	7.74	82	6.33	83	4.96	81	3.81	75	3.07	67	2.72	58	2.74	49
16	9.03	32	9.87	41	10.34	51	10.29	62	9.73	72	8.71	79	7.37	82	5.95	82	4.67	78	3.74	71	3.16	63	2.96	55
17	8.66	26	9.67	34	10.41	43	10.65	54	10.37	65	9.56	74	8.35	79	6.96	81	5.59	79	4.51	75	3.73	68	3.34	61
18	8.14	20	9.33	27	10.29	35	10.79	46	10.82	57	10.27	67	9.25	75	7.95	79	6.56	80	5.36	77	4.40	72	3.80	65
19	7.54	15	8.81	20	9.97	28	10.75	38	11.08	49	10.81	60	10.02	69	8.87	75	7.51	78	6.24	77	5.15	74	4.37	69
20	6.84	12	8.17	15	9.48	21	10.49	29	11.12	40	11.15	52	10.63	62	9.67	70	8.40	75	7.12	76	6.05	75	5.02	72
21	6.00	09	7.44	10	8.84	15	10.05	22	10.94	32	11.28	43	11.06	54	10.33	63	9.21	70	7.97	74	6.76	75	5.72	73
22	5.34	08	6.62	8	8.07	10	9.44	15	10.56	23	11.20	34	11.28	45	10.83	56	9.90	64	8.77	70	7.55	73	6.44	73
23	4.59	00	5.77	6	7.21	6	8.66	9	9.99	16	10.89	20	11.28	37	11.14	48	10.45	58	9.45	65	8.29	69	7.16	72
24	3.90	11	4.90	6	6.29	4	7.80	5	9.26	10	10.38	18	11.09	28	11.23	40	10.82	50	10.02	59	8.97	65	7.85	69
25	3.26	15	4.11	8	5.36	4	6.82	3	8.39	5	9.72	12	10.68	21	11.12	31	11.00	42	10.41	52	9.52	59	8.47	65
26	2.75	19	3.37	11	4.44	5	5.83	2	7.43	2	8.88	6	10.09	14	10.81	24	10.99	34	10.65	45	9.96	53	9.02	60
27	2.36	25	2.71	16	3.59	8	4.84	3	6.38	1	7.94	2	9.32	8	10.31	17	10.78	27	10.72	37	10.22	46	9.44	54
28	2.10	31	2.21	22	2.83	13	3.88	5	5.35	1	6.90	0	8.42	4	9.62	11	10.38	20	10.59	30	10.34	40	9.74	48
29	2.01	38	1.85	28	2.19	18	3.04	10	4.32	3	5.85	0	7.44	1	8.81	6	9.82	14	10.28	23	10.30	33	9.90	42
30	2.06	45	1.65	36	1.71	25	2.29	15	3.37	1	4.79	2	6.39	1	7.88	3	9.09	9	9.82	17	10.09	26	9.92	33

T	48		52		56		60		64		68		72		76		80		84		88		92	
J	δv	r	δv	r	δv	r	δv	r	δv	r	δv	r	δv	r	δv	r	δv	r	δv	r	δv	r	δv	r
0	7.10	44	6.60	51	6.19	58	5.88	64	5.69	68	5.52	70	5.26	70	4.82	69	4.20	65	3.41	60	2.57	53	1.88	44
1	7.17	37	6.79	45	6.42	53	6.14	59	5.98	65	5.85	68	5.66	70	5.29	70	4.70	69	3.90	65	2.98	60	2.13	51
2	7.15	31	6.87	39	6.59	47	6.36	55	6.24	61	6.17	66	6.04	69	5.75	71	5.24	71	4.47	69	3.51	65	2.52	58
3	7.00	26	6.87	33	6.68	41	6.50	49	6.45	56	6.44	62	6.39	67	6.21	70	5.79	72	5.08	72	4.12	70	3.08	65
4	6.77	21	6.78	28	6.68	35	6.58	43	6.59	50	6.65	58	6.69	63	6.63	68	6.34	72	5.73	73	4.82	73	3.75	70
5	6.47	17	6.61	23	6.60	30	6.59	37	6.67	45	6.81	52	6.93	59	7.00	65	6.85	70	6.38	73	5.55	75	4.50	74
6	6.07	14	6.36	19	6.47	25	6.52	32	6.68	39	6.87	47	7.11	54	7.31	61	7.32	67	7.01	72	6.30	75	5.32	76
7	5.64	13	6.03	16	6.25	20	6.40	26	6.61	33	6.84	41	7.20	48	7.54	56	7.60	63	7.56	69	7.02	74	6.16	76
8	5.19	12	5.66	14	5.98	17	5.07	22	6.47	28	6.80	35	7.21	43	7.66	51	7.98	58	8.03	66	7.68	72	6.99	78
9	4.71	13	5.28	13	5.66	15	5.97	18	6.29	24	6.66	29	7.13	37	7.69	45	8.16	53	8.41	61	8.28	68	7.76	76
10	4.25	15	4.87	14	5.32	14	5.67	16	6.02	19	6.48	25	6.97	31	7.61	39	8.22	47	8.66	55	8.74	64	8.45	72
11	3.85	19	4.48	15	4.97	14	5.36	14	5.74	16	6.17	20	6.73	26	7.45	33	8.17	40	8.77	49	9.05	58	9.04	67
12	3.50	23	4.12	18	4.62	15	5.04	14	5.42	14	5.86	17	6.43	21	7.18	27	8.00	34	8.77	42	9.30	51	9.48	61
13	3.24	28	3.81	22	4.31	18	4.71	14	5.09	14	5.52	15	6.07	18	6.85	22	7.72	28	8.61	36	9.35	44	9.77	55
14	3.08	34	3.56	27	4.03	21	4.42	17	4.77	14	5.16	14	5.70	15	6.43	18	7.34	23	8.32	30	9.23	37	9.89	47
15	3.02	40	3.41	33	3.81	26	4.16	20	4.46	16	4.81	14	5.29	14	5.09	15	6.63	19	7.92	24	8.97	31	9.73	40
16	3.08	47	3.34	39	3.65	31	3.95	25	4.19	19	4.48	16	4.88	14	5.51	14	6.36	15	7.42	19	8.57	24	9.60	33
17	3.24	53	3.37	45	3.59	37	3.81	29	3.97	23	4.18	18	4.50	15	5.03	13	5.80	13	6.88	15	8.03	19	9.22	26
18	3.54	58	3.50	51	3.60	41	3.74	35	3.82	28	3.94	22	4.17	17	4.58	14	5.24	12	6.21	12	7.40	14	8.07	19
19	3.93	63	3.72	56	3.71	49	3.74	41	3.74	33	3.77	26	3.87	20	4.15	16	4.67	12	5.55	11	6.71	11	8.01	14
20	4.41	67	4.05	61	3.92	54	3.83	47	3.74	39	3.67	32	3.67	25	3.79	19	4.16	14	4.88	11	5.06	9	7.26	10
21	4.97	70	4.46	65	4.18	59	4.01	52	3.81	45	3.66	37	3.51	30	3.49	23	3.70	16	4.25	12	5.20	9	6.43	8
22	5.57	71	4.94	68	4.54	64	4.25	58	3.97	51	3.72	43	3.47	35	3.28	28	3.32	21	3.69	15	4.46	9	5.58	6
23	6.20	72	5.47	70	4.97	67	4.56	62	4.21	56	3.86	49	3.50	41	3.19	33	3.03	26	3.20	18	3.78	12	4.73	6
24	6.85	71	6.02	71	5.43	69	4.94	66	4.50	61	4.09	55	3.63	47	3.17	39	2.86	31	2.81	23	3.16	16	3.95	8
25	7.47	69	6.59	70	5.92	70	5.37	68	4.87	65	4.39	59	3.85	53	3.28	45	2.79	37	2.54	29	2.69	21	3.22	12
26	8.03	65	7.14	69	6.42	70	5.82	70	5.27	68	4.75	64	4.15	58	3.49	51	2.86	44	2.42	35	2.32	26	2.47	17
27	8.52	61	7.67	66	6.92	69	6.28	70	5.71	70	5.16	67	4.51	63	3.79	57	3.05	50	2.42	42	2.08	33	2.13	23
28	8.95	56	8.13	62	7.39	66	6.74	69	6.16	70	5.59	69	4.94	66	4.17	62	3.34	56	2.57	48	2.01	40	1.81	29
29	9.25	50	8.51	57	7.82	63	7.17	67	6.60	70	6.06	70	5.39	69	4.63	66	3.74	61	2.86	55	2.10	47	1.65	37
30	9.44	44	8.82	51	8.17	58	7.56	64	7.03	68	6.50	70	5.88	70	5.12	69	4.22	65	3.25	60	2.33	53	1.66	44

NOTE. — When T exceeds 88, subtract 88 from it, and add 1.22 to Argument J.

TABLE XI. 29

T	0		4		8		12		16		20		24		28		32		36		40		44	
J	δv	r	δv	r	δv	r	δv	r	δv	r	δv	r	δv	r	δv	r	δv	r	δv	r	δv	r	δv	r
30	2.05	45	1.65	36	1.71	25	1.20	15	3.37	7	4.79	2	6.39	1	7.88	3	9.09	9	9.82	17	10.09	26	9.92	35
31	2.27	52	1.63	43	1.41	33	1.70	22	2.54	12	3.79	5	5.34	2	6.89	2	8.26	6	9.20	13	9.72	21	9.78	29
32	2.62	58	1.77	50	1.27	41	1.29	30	1.83	19	2.88	10	4.32	5	5.86	3	7.34	4	8.47	9	9.20	16	9.50	23
33	3.10	64	2.07	57	1.33	48	1.06	98	1.32	27	2.10	16	3.36	9	4.83	5	6.36	4	7.64	7	8.58	12	9.10	18
34	3.69	69	2.55	64	1.58	56	1.03	46	0.97	35	1.48	24	2.51	15	3.87	9	5.39	5	6.75	7	7.86	10	8.58	15
35	4.36	72	3.13	69	2.00	63	1.20	55	0.85	44	1.04	32	1.82	22	3.00	13	4.44	9	5.83	8	7.06	9	7.97	13
36	5.08	75	3.82	74	2.57	69	1.56	62	0.92	52	.82	41	1.31	30	2.25	21	3.58	14	4.94	10	6.23	9	7.27	11
37	5.81	76	4.59	76	3.27	74	2.08	69	1.19	61	.79	50	.98	38	1.66	28	2.79	20	4.09	14	5.41	11	6.54	11
38	6.54	75	5.38	78	4.05	78	2.76	75	1.64	68	.9M	58	.86	47	1.25	36	2.16	27	3.33	19	4.61	15	5.80	12
39	7.21	73	6.20	78	4.90	80	3.53	79	2.26	74	1.36	66	.92	56	1.03	44	1.67	34	2.67	25	3.88	19	5.06	15
40	7.82	69	6.95	76	5.76	80	3.41	81	3.02	79	1.91	73	1.21	63	1.01	53	1.38	42	2.16	32	3.23	25	4.38	19
41	8.32	65	7.65	73	6.59	79	5.29	82	3.86	82	2.61	78	1.64	70	1.17	60	1.25	50	1.80	39	2.69	31	3.77	24
42	8.70	59	8.27	68	7.37	76	6.21	81	4.78	83	3.41	82	2.27	76	1.53	67	1.30	57	1.60	47	2.30	38	3.24	29
43	8.94	53	8.73	62	8.07	71	7.05	79	5.71	83	4.32	84	3.03	80	2.06	73	1.55	64	1.59	54	2.05	44	2.42	36
44	9.03	46	9.05	56	8.64	66	7.81	74	6.61	81	5.23	84	3.85	83	2.72	78	1.95	70	1.72	61	1.94	51	2.54	42
45	8.97	39	9.23	48	9.07	59	8.48	69	7.45	77	6.16	82	4.75	83	3.48	81	2.51	75	2.03	67	2.00	58	2.38	49
46	8.75	32	9.23	41	9.32	51	8.99	62	8.17	72	7.03	79	5.65	82	4.30	82	3.17	78	2.48	71	2.20	63	2.36	55
47	8.40	26	9.07	34	9.41	43	9.33	54	9.79	65	7.82	74	6.53	79	5.18	81	3.91	79	3.03	75	2.55	68	2.48	61
48	7.92	20	8.75	27	9.31	35	9.49	46	9.20	57	8.49	67	7.35	75	6.05	79	4.72	80	3.68	77	3.00	72	2.72	65
49	7.34	15	8.27	20	9.03	28	9.47	38	9.46	49	8.99	60	8.06	69	6.85	75	5.53	78	4.40	77	3.53	74	3.07	69
50	6.68	12	7.67	15	8.58	21	9.25	29	9.52	40	9.33	52	8.61	62	7.57	70	6.30	75	5.14	76	4.15	75	3.50	72
51	5.97	09	6.98	10	8.00	15	8.85	22	9.38	32	9.46	43	9.02	54	8.17	63	7.01	70	5.83	74	4.80	75	4.02	73
52	5.26	08	6.22	8	7.29	10	8.30	15	9.06	23	9.40	34	9.26	56	8.63	56	7.64	64	6.53	70	5.45	73	4.58	73
53	4.53	09	5.43	6	6.51	6	7.60	9	8.55	16	9.15	26	9.26	37	8.92	48	8.13	58	7.13	65	6.07	69	5.14	72
54	3.88	11	4.64	6	5.67	4	6.81	5	7.90	10	8.72	18	9.11	28	9.03	40	8.48	50	7.64	59	6.63	65	5.69	69
55	3.30	15	3.89	8	4.82	4	5.96	3	7.13	5	8.12	12	8.76	21	8.96	31	8.66	42	8.01	52	7.14	59	6.21	65
56	2.81	19	3.23	11	4.00	5	5.07	2	6.27	2	7.40	6	8.27	14	8.71	24	8.69	34	8.23	45	7.53	53	6.66	60
57	2.46	25	2.65	16	3.25	8	4.20	3	5.36	1	6.58	2	7.60	8	8.29	17	8.54	27	8.32	37	7.78	46	7.04	54
58	2.24	31	2.21	22	2.59	13	3.37	5	4.45	1	5.68	0	6.82	4	7.72	11	8.20	20	8.23	30	7.90	40	7.32	48
59	2.17	38	1.93	28	2.08	18	2.64	10	3.58	3	4.77	0	5.98	1	7.01	6	7.74	14	8.02	23	7.90	33	7.48	42
60	2.20	45	1.79	36	1.69	25	2.03	15	2.79	7	3.87	2	5.09	1	6.24	3	7.15	9	7.64	17	7.75	26	7.52	35

T	48		52		56		60		64		68		72		76		80		84		88		92	
J	δv	r	δv	r	δv	r	δv	r	δv	r	δv	r	δv	r	δv	r	δv	r	δv	r	δv	r	δv	r
30	9.44	44	8.42	51	8.17	58	7.56	64	7.03	68	6.50	70	5.88	70	5.12	69	4.22	65	3.25	60	2.33	53	1.66	44
31	9.49	37	9.01	45	8.46	53	7.90	59	7.42	65	6.93	68	6.36	70	5.65	70	4.76	69	3.74	65	2.70	60	1.84	51
32	9.43	31	9.09	39	8.65	47	8.16	55	7.76	61	7.33	66	6.82	69	6.19	71	5.31	71	4.33	69	3.21	65	2.17	58
33	9.22	26	9.07	33	8.74	41	8.34	49	8.01	56	7.66	62	7.23	67	6.69	70	5.93	72	4.94	72	3.82	70	2.68	65
34	8.91	21	8.94	28	8.72	35	8.44	43	8.19	50	7.93	58	7.59	63	7.17	68	6.52	72	5.61	73	4.48	73	3.28	70
35	8.47	17	8.67	23	8.62	30	8.45	37	8.29	45	8.11	52	7.89	59	7.58	65	7.07	70	6.28	73	5.21	75	3.99	74
36	7.95	14	8.32	19	8.41	25	8.36	32	8.30	39	8.21	47	8.11	54	7.93	61	7.56	67	6.91	72	5.94	75	4.77	76
37	7.36	13	7.89	16	8.11	20	8.18	26	8.23	33	8.22	41	8.22	48	8.18	56	7.97	63	7.48	69	6.66	74	5.56	78
38	6.73	12	7.38	14	7.74	17	7.93	22	8.05	28	8.14	35	8.25	43	8.34	51	8.28	58	7.97	66	7.32	72	6.37	78
39	6.07	13	6.84	13	7.30	15	7.59	18	7.81	24	7.98	29	8.17	37	8.39	45	8.48	53	8.35	61	7.92	68	7.10	76
40	5.41	15	6.25	14	6.82	14	7.21	16	7.50	19	7.73	25	8.01	31	8.33	39	8.58	47	8.64	55	8.34	64	7.77	78
41	4.79	19	5.68	15	6.31	14	6.78	14	7.12	16	7.41	20	7.75	26	8.15	33	8.53	40	8.77	49	8.73	58	8.37	67
42	4.22	23	5.10	18	5.80	15	6.32	14	6.72	14	7.04	17	7.45	21	7.88	27	8.36	34	8.77	42	8.96	51	8.80	61
43	3.70	28	4.59	22	5.29	18	5.85	14	6.27	14	6.62	15	7.03	18	7.53	22	8.10	28	8.63	36	9.01	44	9.09	55
44	3.30	34	4.12	27	4.81	21	5.40	17	5.83	14	6.18	14	6.60	15	7.11	18	7.72	23	8.36	29	8.93	37	9.23	47
45	3.00	40	3.73	33	4.39	26	4.96	20	5.36	16	5.73	14	6.13	14	6.63	15	7.26	19	7.98	24	8.69	31	9.20	40
46	2.82	47	3.42	39	4.03	31	4.57	25	4.97	19	5.30	16	5.62	14	6.11	14	6.74	15	7.50	19	8.31	24	9.00	33
47	2.71	53	3.23	45	3.73	37	4.23	29	4.59	25	4.88	18	5.20	15	5.59	13	6.18	13	6.93	15	7.81	19	8.64	26
48	2.80	58	3.12	51	3.54	41	3.98	35	4.28	28	4.52	22	4.77	17	5.08	14	5.60	12	6.33	12	7.22	14	8.14	19
49	2.95	63	3.12	56	3.45	49	3.80	41	4.04	33	4.21	26	4.39	20	5.61	16	5.03	12	5.67	11	6.55	11	7.52	14
50	3.21	67	3.23	61	3.42	54	3.69	47	3.86	39	3.97	32	4.07	25	4.19	19	4.48	14	5.02	11	5.84	9	6.81	10
51	3.57	70	3.42	65	3.50	59	3.67	52	3.77	45	3.82	37	3.83	30	3.83	23	3.98	16	4.39	12	5.12	9	6.05	8
52	3.99	71	3.70	68	3.66	64	3.73	58	3.75	51	3.74	43	3.67	35	3.46	28	3.58	21	3.83	15	4.42	9	5.26	6
53	4.44	72	4.05	70	3.87	67	3.86	62	3.83	56	3.76	49	3.60	41	3.38	33	3.27	26	3.36	18	3.78	12	4.48	6
54	4.93	71	4.42	71	4.17	69	4.06	66	3.96	61	3.83	55	3.63	47	3.31	39	3.06	31	2.99	23	3.22	16	3.74	8
55	5.43	69	4.85	70	4.50	70	4.31	68	4.17	65	4.01	59	3.73	53	3.34	45	2.97	37	2.72	29	2.75	21	3.11	12
56	5.89	65	5.26	69	4.82	70	4.60	70	4.43	68	4.23	64	3.93	58	3.47	51	3.00	44	2.60	35	2.42	26	2.56	17
57	6.30	61	5.67	66	5.22	69	4.92	70	4.71	70	4.50	67	4.19	63	3.71	57	3.15	50	2.60	42	2.22	33	2.15	23
58	6.67	56	6.03	62	5.57	66	5.26	69	5.04	70	4.83	68	4.52	66	4.01	62	3.40	56	2.75	48	2.19	40	1.90	29
59	6.93	50	6.37	57	5.90	63	5.57	67	5.36	70	5.17	70	4.87	69	4.39	66	3.76	61	3.02	55	2.30	47	1.83	37
60	7.10	44	6.60	51	6.19	58	5.88	64	5.69	68	5.52	70	5.26	70	4.82	69	4.20	65	3.41	60	2.57	53	1.88	44

NOTE. — When T exceeds 88, subtract 88 from it, and add 1.22 to Argument J.

TABLE XII.

T	0	4	8	12	16	20	24	28	32	36	40	44
E	δv	δv	δv	δv	δv	δv	δv	δv	δv	δv	δv	δv
0	2.33	2.21	2.09	1.95	1.83	1.74	1.65	1.62	1.61	1.61	1.65	1.69
1	2.66	2.58	2.51	2.42	2.30	2.20	2.08	2.01	1.94	1.88	1.85	1.85
2	2.88	2.85	2.81	2.77	2.67	2.58	2.43	2.32	2.20	2.10	2.02	1.97
3	2.94	2.95	2.98	2.95	2.87	2.75	2.66	2.52	2.39	2.24	2.14	2.07
4	2.88	2.93	2.06	2.95	2.87	2.76	2.67	2.53	2.40	2.28	2.17	2.10
5	2.71	2.76	2.78	2.77	2.72	2.61	2.52	2.42	2.29	2.19	2.09	2.05
6	2.47	2.52	2.49	2.48	2.42	2.31	2.24	2.16	2.08	2.00	1.95	1.91
7	2.22	2.23	2.19	2.14	2.05	1.95	1.89	1.82	1.77	1.74	1.74	1.75
8	1.98	1.99	1.01	1.81	1.71	1.59	1.53	1.46	1.48	1.48	1.50	1.56
9	1.82	1.80	1.69	1.59	1.45	1.33	1.27	1.21	1.22	1.25	1.31	1.39
10	1.75	1.72	1.63	1.50	1.35	1.23	1.15	1.08	1.09	1.13	1.20	1.28
11	1.78	1.78	1.69	1.56	1.44	1.31	1.20	1.14	1.11	1.11	1.20	1.24
12	1.91	1.90	1.91	1.82	1.72	1.57	1.45	1.35	1.30	1.26	1.29	1.33
13	2.12	2.19	2.22	2.18	2.12	2.00	1.85	1.75	1.63	1.55	1.50	1.48
14	2.33	2.45	2.58	2.61	2.60	2.53	2.38	2.24	2.08	1.92	1.82	1.74
15	2.51	2.69	2.89	3.01	3.07	3.05	2.93	2.76	2.57	2.36	2.19	2.04
16	2.60	2.83	3.11	3.33	3.46	3.49	3.40	3.25	3.04	2.78	2.56	2.37
17	2.58	2.86	3.18	3.45	3.67	3.76	3.74	3.62	3.40	3.15	2.89	2.65
18	2.43	2.71	3.07	3.41	3.66	3.83	3.86	3.80	3.61	3.38	3.12	2.86
19	2.16	2.43	2.77	3.14	3.44	3.66	3.77	3.70	3.64	3.45	3.24	2.99
20	1.80	2.03	2.34	2.66	3.00	3.26	3.45	3.51	3.47	3.37	3.21	3.01
21	1.41	1.57	1.80	2.09	2.41	2.69	2.95	3.09	3.15	3.16	3.06	2.92
22	1.03	1.11	1.24	1.46	1.75	2.05	2.33	2.55	2.70	2.81	2.80	2.75
23	0.72	0.70	0.74	0.88	1.11	1.38	1.70	1.97	2.23	2.41	2.50	2.53
24	0.52	0.43	0.37	0.42	0.56	0.83	1.13	1.43	1.75	2.02	2.19	2.28
25	0.46	0.32	0.18	0.13	0.22	0.43	0.70	1.02	1.36	1.68	1.91	2.07
26	0.58	0.38	0.19	0.10	0.11	0.25	0.48	0.79	1.11	1.44	1.72	1.89
27	0.83	0.61	0.41	0.27	0.22	0.30	0.47	0.72	1.04	1.34	1.60	1.80
28	1.18	0.97	0.78	0.60	0.51	0.55	0.65	0.85	1.10	1.37	1.61	1.81
29	1.56	1.40	1.23	1.09	0.96	0.95	0.98	1.12	1.29	1.50	1.68	1.85
30	1.97	1.83	1.71	1.59	1.47	1.42	1.41	1.46	1.55	1.69	1.83	1.95

T	48	52	56	60	64	68	72	76	80	84	88	92
E	δv	δv	δv	δv	δv	δv	δv	δv	δv	δv	δv	δv
0	1.75	1.77	1.79	1.83	1.83	1.86	1.90	1.97	2.09	2.23	2.40	2.56
1	1.86	1.86	1.85	1.89	1.87	1.91	1.94	2.01	2.15	2.33	2.55	2.75
2	1.96	1.93	1.91	1.93	1.90	1.92	1.94	2.01	2.14	2.33	2.59	2.84
3	2.01	1.97	1.94	1.92	1.90	1.89	1.89	1.94	2.05	2.24	2.51	2.79
4	2.01	1.98	1.93	1.90	1.84	1.80	1.78	1.82	1.90	2.06	2.31	2.58
5	1.98	1.94	1.88	1.81	1.77	1.69	1.64	1.63	1.68	1.80	2.00	2.25
6	1.86	1.83	1.79	1.74	1.66	1.57	1.51	1.45	1.43	1.49	1.62	1.82
7	1.71	1.72	1.69	1.62	1.55	1.45	1.36	1.27	1.18	1.19	1.23	1.36
8	1.55	1.59	1.57	1.52	1.47	1.35	1.24	1.13	1.01	0.92	0.87	0.92
9	1.42	1.48	1.47	1.46	1.40	1.30	1.20	1.05	0.89	0.74	0.61	0.55
10	1.32	1.39	1.44	1.41	1.39	1.32	1.21	1.05	0.87	0.67	0.48	0.38
11	1.32	1.37	1.44	1.44	1.43	1.37	1.29	1.15	0.95	0.74	0.51	0.35
12	1.38	1.42	1.48	1.50	1.53	1.50	1.44	1.32	1.14	0.93	0.68	0.49
13	1.50	1.52	1.59	1.62	1.65	1.67	1.63	1.53	1.39	1.20	0.98	0.78
14	1.72	1.70	1.72	1.77	1.81	1.86	1.84	1.78	1.69	1.55	1.36	1.17
15	1.97	1.90	1.91	1.94	1.97	2.03	2.04	2.02	1.97	1.89	1.76	1.60
16	2.24	2.12	2.09	2.10	2.12	2.19	2.20	2.23	2.22	2.19	2.13	2.00
17	2.47	2.34	2.26	2.23	2.25	2.30	2.33	2.37	2.40	2.41	2.41	2.32
18	2.67	2.49	2.40	2.34	2.33	2.36	2.39	2.44	2.48	2.51	2.57	2.52
19	2.79	2.61	2.48	2.39	2.36	2.38	2.38	2.43	2.47	2.53	2.59	2.56
20	2.81	2.65	2.50	2.40	2.34	2.32	2.31	2.35	2.39	2.43	2.49	2.48
21	2.75	2.62	2.46	2.37	2.29	2.25	2.23	2.28	2.25	2.28	2.31	2.29
22	2.63	2.54	2.42	2.29	2.22	2.14	2.11	2.10	2.11	2.10	2.08	2.04
23	2.49	2.42	2.32	2.21	2.13	2.06	2.02	1.99	1.95	1.90	1.86	1.79
24	2.31	2.30	2.22	2.14	2.05	1.99	1.95	1.87	1.84	1.76	1.68	1.60
25	2.15	2.17	2.14	2.07	2.03	1.94	1.92	1.87	1.81	1.70	1.59	1.51
26	2.08	2.08	2.06	2.05	2.01	1.96	1.93	1.90	1.83	1.75	1.62	1.53
27	1.97	2.03	2.04	2.06	2.03	2.02	2.00	1.97	1.92	1.87	1.75	1.58
28	1.95	2.02	2.06	2.09	2.08	2.07	2.08	2.07	2.07	2.04	1.99	1.93
29	2.00	2.05	2.11	2.15	2.15	2.16	2.18	2.21	2.23	2.25	2.26	2.23
30	2.07	2.13	2.17	2.21	2.21	2.24	2.26	2.31	2.37	2.43	2.50	2.54

NOTE. — When T exceeds 88, subtract 88 from it, and add 14.45 to E.

TABLE XII. 31

T	0	4	8	12	16	20	24	28	32	36	40	44	48
E	δv	δv	δv	δv	δv	δv	δv	δv	δv	δv	δv	δv	δv
30	1.97	1.83	1.71	1.59	1.47	1.42	1.41	1.46	1.55	1.69	1.83	1.95	2.07
31	2.28	2.20	2.13	2.04	1.94	1.86	1.80	1.81	1.84	1.00	1.97	2.07	2.16
32	2.50	2.47	2.43	2.39	2.31	2.22	2.11	2.08	2.04	2.06	2.10	2.15	2.22
33	2.58	2.57	2.60	2.57	2.49	2.39	2.30	2.24	2.19	2.14	2.16	2.19	2.23
34	2.41	2.55	2.58	2.57	2.49	2.40	2.31	2.21	2.16	2.14	2.13	2.18	2.19
35	2.39	2.40	2.40	2.39	2.34	2.22	2.16	2.08	2.01	1.99	1.99	2.07	2.10
36	2.17	2.16	2.13	2.10	2.04	1.93	1.88	1.80	1.76	1.76	1.79	1.87	1.94
37	1.94	1.89	1.83	1.76	1.67	1.57	1.51	1.46	1.43	1.46	1.54	1.65	1.73
38	1.74	1.67	1.55	1.45	1.33	1.21	1.15	1.10	1.12	1.16	1.26	1.40	1.53
39	1.62	1.52	1.37	1.23	1.09	0.95	0.89	0.83	0.86	0.91	1.03	1.19	1.34
40	1.59	1.48	1.31	1.14	0.99	0.85	0.77	0.70	0.73	0.77	0.88	1.04	1.20
41	1.68	1.58	1.41	1.24	1.08	0.93	0.82	0.76	0.73	0.75	0.88	0.96	1.12
42	1.89	1.80	1.67	1.50	1.36	1.21	1.07	0.97	0.92	0.88	0.93	1.01	1.14
43	2.14	2.09	2.02	1.90	1.78	1.64	1.49	1.37	1.25	1.17	1.14	1.16	1.24
44	2.41	2.41	2.42	2.37	2.28	2.17	2.02	1.86	1.70	1.54	1.44	1.38	1.42
45	2.63	2.71	2.79	2.81	2.79	2.71	2.57	2.40	2.19	1.98	1.81	1.68	1.65
46	2.78	2.91	3.05	3.17	3.22	3.17	3.04	2.89	2.66	2.40	2.18	1.99	1.90
47	2.80	2.98	3.18	3.35	3.47	3.48	3.40	3.26	3.04	2.77	2.51	2.27	2.11
48	2.69	2.89	3.15	3.35	3.50	3.59	3.54	3.44	3.25	3.00	2.74	2.48	2.29
49	2.46	2.65	2.89	3.14	3.32	3.46	3.49	3.42	3.28	3.09	2.86	2.61	2.41
50	2.14	2.29	2.52	2.74	2.94	3.10	3.19	3.19	3.11	3.01	2.83	2.63	2.43
51	1.75	1.87	2.02	2.21	2.41	2.59	2.73	2.79	2.81	2.80	2.68	2.54	2.37
52	1.37	1.43	1.50	1.64	1.81	1.99	2.15	2.29	2.38	2.47	2.44	2.37	2.25
53	1.08	1.04	1.04	1.10	1.21	1.38	1.58	1.75	1.93	2.07	2.14	2.15	2.11
54	0.88	0.77	0.69	0.68	0.75	0.89	1.07	1.25	1.49	1.70	1.83	1.90	1.93
55	0.82	0.68	0.52	0.43	0.44	0.53	0.70	0.88	1.14	1.38	1.57	1.69	1.77
56	0.96	0.74	0.55	0.42	0.37	0.43	0.54	0.71	0.93	1.18	1.38	1.55	1.65
57	1.21	0.99	0.77	0.61	0.50	0.52	0.57	0.72	0.90	1.12	1.30	1.46	1.59
58	1.56	1.35	1.14	0.96	0.83	0.81	0.81	0.91	1.02	1.19	1.35	1.47	1.59
59	1.94	1.78	1.61	1.45	1.32	1.23	1.18	1.22	1.29	1.36	1.46	1.55	1.66
60	2.33	2.21	2.09	1.95	1.83	1.74	1.65	1.62	1.61	1.61	1.65	1.60	1.75

T	52	56	60	64	68	72	76	80	84	88
E	δv	δv	δv	δv	δv	δv	δv	δv	δv	δv
30	2.13	2.17	2.21	2.21	2.24	2.26	2.31	2.37	2.43	2.50
31	2.20	2.23	2.27	2.25	2.29	2.30	2.37	2.47	2.57	2.71
32	2.25	2.27	2.31	2.28	2.30	2.32	2.37	2.48	2.61	2.79
33	2.27	2.28	2.30	2.28	2.27	2.27	2.30	2.41	2.56	2.75
34	2.24	2.25	2.26	2.22	2.18	2.16	2.20	2.26	2.40	2.59
35	2.18	2.18	2.17	2.13	2.07	2.02	2.01	2.04	2.16	2.32
36	2.03	2.07	2.06	2.02	1.95	1.89	1.83	1.81	1.85	1.96
37	1.86	1.93	1.94	1.91	1.81	1.74	1.65	1.58	1.55	1.59
38	1.67	1.77	1.80	1.79	1.71	1.62	1.51	1.39	1.30	1.23
39	1.50	1.63	1.70	1.72	1.66	1.56	1.43	1.27	1.12	0.97
40	1.37	1.54	1.61	1.67	1.64	1.57	1.43	1.25	1.05	0.84
41	1.29	1.46	1.60	1.67	1.69	1.65	1.51	1.33	1.12	0.87
42	1.30	1.46	1.60	1.73	1.78	1.76	1.68	1.52	1.31	1.06
43	1.34	1.51	1.66	1.81	1.91	1.95	1.89	1.75	1.58	1.36
44	1.48	1.60	1.75	1.91	2.06	2.12	2.12	2.05	1.91	1.74
45	1.64	1.73	1.86	2.03	2.19	2.28	2.34	2.33	2.25	2.14
46	1.82	1.87	1.98	2.12	2.29	2.40	2.51	2.56	2.55	2.49
47	2.00	2.00	2.05	2.17	2.36	2.49	2.61	2.70	2.77	2.77
48	2.15	2.10	2.12	2.21	2.36	2.49	2.64	2.78	2.85	2.93
49	2.25	2.14	2.13	2.18	2.30	2.44	2.59	2.73	2.85	2.95
50	2.27	2.16	2.10	2.12	2.20	2.31	2.45	2.61	2.73	2.83
51	2.24	2.12	2.03	2.03	2.07	2.17	2.29	2.43	2.54	2.63
52	2.16	2.04	1.95	1.92	1.92	1.99	2.10	2.21	2.32	2.38
53	2.04	1.94	1.87	1.81	1.80	1.84	1.93	2.01	2.08	2.12
54	1.92	1.84	1.78	1.71	1.69	1.73	1.77	1.84	1.90	1.90
55	1.79	1.76	1.71	1.67	1.62	1.66	1.69	1.75	1.78	1.77
56	1.70	1.68	1.67	1.65	1.62	1.65	1.68	1.73	1.75	1.76
57	1.65	1.66	1.68	1.67	1.66	1.68	1.71	1.78	1.81	1.83
58	1.64	1.68	1.71	1.70	1.71	1.74	1.79	1.87	1.94	1.99
59	1.70	1.73	1.77	1.77	1.80	1.82	1.89	1.99	2.09	2.20
60	1.77	1.79	1.83	1.83	1.86	1.90	1.97	2.09	2.23	2.40

TABLE XIII.

S	δv	Dif.
0	0.40	.11
4	0.51	.10
8	0.61	.09
12	0.70	.06
16	0.76	.03
20	0.79	.01
24	0.80	.03n
28	0.77	.06
32	0.71	.08
36	0.63	.10
40	0.53	.11
44	0.42	.11
48	0.31	.11
52	0.20	.09
56	0.11	.06
60	0.05	.04
64	0.01	.01n
68	0.00	.02+
72	0.02	.06
76	0.08	.07
80	0.15	.10
84	0.25	.11
88	0.36	.12
92	0.48	

Period = 89.43

Note. — When T exceeds 88, subtract 88 from it, and add 14.45 to E.

ARG.	0.0 v.	0.1 v.	0.2 v.	0.3 v.	0.4 v.
0	359° 59 30.2	0° 18 41.5	0° 37 43.8	0° 56 46.1	1° 15 48.4
1	3 10 0.4	3 29 2.0	3 48 3.6	4 7 4.9	4 26 6.2
2	6 20 9.6	6 39 9.4	6 58 9.0	7 17 8.3	7 36 7.3
3	9 29 55.1	9 48 51.9	10 7 48.4	10 26 44.4	10 45 40.1
4	12 39 5.3	12 57 58.0	13 16 50.1	13 35 41.8	13 54 32.9
5	15 47 28.8	16 6 16.2	16 25 3.0	16 43 49.2	17 2 34.7
6	18 54 54.8	19 13 35.8	19 32 16.1	19 50 55.7	20 9 34.7
7	22 1 12.7	22 19 46.3	22 38 19.2	22 56 51.3	23 15 22.6
8	25 6 12.7	25 24 38.1	25 43 2.5	26 1 26.1	26 19 48.9
9	28 9 45.6	28 28 1.8	28 46 17.0	29 4 31.2	29 22 44.4
10	31 11 42.7	31 29 48.9	31 47 54.0	32 5 58.0	32 24 1.0
11	34 11 56.2	34 29 51.6	34 47 45.8	35 5 39.0	35 23 31.0
12	37 10 18.9	37 28 2.8	37 45 45.5	38 3 27.1	38 21 7.5
13	40 6 41.3	40 24 16.2	40 41 46.8	40 59 16.2	41 16 44.4
14	43 1 6.8	43 18 26.1	43 35 44.1	43 53 0.8	44 10 16.2
15	45 53 21.5	46 10 27.8	46 27 32.7	46 44 36.3	47 1 38.6
16	48 43 21.3	49 0 17.1	49 17 8.6	49 33 58.8	49 50 47.6
17	51 31 11.5	51 47 50.6	52 4 28.4	52 21 4.8	52 37 39.7
18	54 16 40.3	54 33 5.5	54 49 29.3	55 5 51.7	55 22 12.7
19	56 59 48.9	57 16 0.0	57 32 9.6	57 48 17.8	58 4 24.6
20	59 40 35.4	59 56 32.3	60 12 27.6	60 28 21.6	60 44 14.1
21	62 18 59.1	62 34 41.6	62 50 22.6	63 6 2.3	63 21 40.5
22	64 54 59.5	65 10 27.6	65 25 54.4	65 41 19.7	65 56 43.5
23	67 28 36.6	67 43 50.4	67 59 2.9	68 14 13.8	68 29 23.4
24	69 59 50.9	70 14 50.5	70 29 48.7	70 44 45.5	70 59 40.9
25	72 28 43.3	72 43 28.8	72 58 12.9	73 12 55.6	73 27 36.9
26	74 55 15.2	75 9 46.7	75 24 16.9	75 38 45.6	75 53 13.0
27	77 19 28.1	77 33 45.9	77 48 2.2	78 2 17.2	78 16 30.8
28	79 41 24.0	79 55 28.1	80 9 30.9	80 23 32.3	80 37 32.4
29	82 1 4.8	82 14 55.6	82 28 45.0	82 42 33.1	82 56 19.9
30	84 18 32.9	84 32 10.6	84 45 46.9	84 59 21.9	85 12 55.6
31	86 33 50.9	86 47 15.7	87 0 39.1	87 14 1.3	87 27 22.3
32	88 47 1.4	89 0 13.6	89 13 24.5	89 26 34.1	89 39 42.5
33	90 58 7.2	91 11 7.0	91 24 5.6	91 37 3.0	91 49 59.2
34	93 7 11.1	93 19 58.9	93 32 45.5	93 45 31.0	93 58 15.2
35	95 14 16.3	95 26 52.3	95 39 27.2	95 52 1.0	96 4 33.6
36	97 19 25.4	97 31 50.1	97 44 13.7	97 56 36.1	98 8 57.4
37	99 22 41.9	99 34 55.4	99 47 7.9	99 59 19.3	100 11 29.6
38	101 24 8.7	101 36 11.4	101 48 13.1	102 0 13.8	102 12 13.4
39	103 23 48.9	103 35 41.2	103 47 32.4	103 59 22.7	104 11 11.9
40	105 21 45.7	105 33 27.8	105 45 8.9	105 56 49.0	106 8 28.1
41	107 18 2.1	107 29 34.3	107 41 5.6	107 52 35.9	108 4 5.3
42	109 12 41.2	109 24 3.9	109 35 25.7	109 46 46.5	109 58 6.3
43	111 5 46.1	111 16 59.6	111 28 12.1	111 39 23.7	111 50 34.4
44	112 57 19.8	113 8 24.3	113 19 27.9	113 30 30.6	113 41 32.4
45	114 47 25.2	114 58 21.0	115 9 16.0	115 20 10.1	115 31 3.3
ARG.	0.0	0.1	0.2	0.3	0.4

TABLE XIV. 33

ARG.	0.5 v.	0.6 v.	0.7 v.	0.8 v.	0.9 v.
0	1 34 50.5	1 53 52.7	2 12 54.7	2 31 56.7	2 50 58.6
1	4 45 7.2	5 4 8.1	5 23 8.8	5 42 9.3	6 1 9.6
2	7 55 6.1	8 14 4.5	8 33 2.7	8 52 0.5	9 10 58.0
3	11 4 35.4	11 23 30.2	11 42 24.7	12 1 18.7	12 20 12.2
4	14 13 23.6	14 32 13.7	14 51 3.3	15 9 52.4	15 28 40.9
5	17 21 19.6	17 40 4.0	17 58 47.7	18 17 30.7	18 36 13.1
6	20 28 12.9	20 46 50.3	21 5 27.0	21 24 3.0	21 42 38.2
7	23 33 53.0	23 52 22.6	24 10 51.4	24 29 19.4	24 47 46.5
8	26 38 10.6	26 56 31.5	27 14 51.4	27 33 10.4	27 51 28.5
9	29 40 56.7	29 59 7.9	30 17 18.2	30 35 27.4	30 53 35.6
10	32 42 2.9	33 0 3.7	33 18 3.5	33 36 2.1	33 53 59.7
11	35 41 21.8	35 59 11.5	36 17 0.1	36 34 47.5	36 52 33.8
12	38 38 46.6	38 56 24.6	39 14 1.3	39 31 36.9	39 49 11.2
13	41 34 11.3	41 51 36.9	42 9 1.3	42 26 24.4	42 43 46.2
14	44 27 30.4	44 44 43.2	45 1 54.7	45 19 5.0	45 36 13.9
15	47 18 39.6	47 35 39.2	47 52 37.5	48 9 34.4	48 26 30 0
16	50 7 35.0	50 24 21.0	50 41 5.7	50 57 49.0	51 14 30.9
17	52 51 13.3	53 10 45.5	53 27 16.3	53 43 45.7	54 0 13.7
18	55 38 32.3	55 54 50.4	56 11 7.2	56 27 22.5	56 43 36.4
19	58 20 30.0	58 36 34.0	58 52 36.5	59 8 37.6	59 24 37.3
20	61 0 5.2	61 15 54.8	61 31 43.0	61 47 29.8	62 3 15.2
21	63 37 17.2	63 52 52.5	64 8 26.4	64 23 58.9	64 39 29.9
22	66 12 5.9	66 27 26.9	66 42 46.5	66 58 4.6	67 13 21.3
23	68 44 31.6	68 59 38.3	69 14 43.6	69 29 47.4	69 44 49.9
24	71 14 34.8	71 29 27.3	71 44 18.5	71 59 8.2	72 13 56.5
25	73 42 16.8	73 56 55.2	74 11 32.3	74 26 8.0	74 40 42.3
26	76 7 38.9	76 22 3.5	76 36 26.8	76 50 48.6	77 5 9.1
27	78 30 43.1	78 44 54.0	78 59 3.5	79 13 11.7	79 27 18.5
28	80 51 31.2	81 5 28.6	81 19 24.6	81 33 19.4	81 47 12.8
29	83 10 5.3	83 23 49.5	83 37 32.3	83 51 13.8	84 4 54.0
30	85 26 28.0	85 39 59.2	85 53 29.0	86 6 57.6	86 20 24.9
31	87 40 41.9	87 54 0.3	88 7 17.5	88 20 33.4	88 33 48.0
32	89 52 49.7	90 5 55.7	90 19 0.4	90 32 3.9	90 45 6.1
33	92 2 54.2	92 15 48.0	92 28 40.6	92 41 31.9	92 54 22.1
34	94 10 58.3	94 23 40.2	94 36 21.0	94 49 0.6	95 1 39.0
35	96 17 5.1	96 29 35.5	96 42 4.6	96 54 32.7	97 6 59.6
36	98 21 17.6	98 33 36.6	98 45 54.6	98 58 11.5	99 10 27.2
37	100 23 38.8	100 35 46.9	100 47 54.0	100 59 59.9	101 12 4.8
38	102 24 11.9	102 36 9.4	102 48 5.8	103 0 1.2	103 11 55.6
39	104 23 0.0	104 34 47.2	104 46 33.3	104 58 18.5	105 10 2.6
40	106 20 6.3	106 31 43.4	106 43 19.5	106 54 54.7	107 6 28.9
41	108 15 33.6	108 27 1.1	108 38 27.5	108 49 53.0	109 1 17.6
42	110 9 25.3	110 20 43.3	110 32 0.4	110 43 16.6	110 54 31.8
43	112 1 44.2	112 12 53.1	112 24 1.1	112 35 8.2	112 46 14.5
44	113 52 33.3	114 3 33.4	114 14 32.7	114 25 31.0	114 36 28.5
45	115 41 55.8	115 52 47.3	116 3 38.1	116 14 28.0	116 25 17.1
ARG.	0.5	0.6	0.7	0.8	0.9

TABLE XIV.

ARG.	0.0	0.1	0.2	0.3	0.4
	v.	v.	v.	v.	v.
45	114 47 25.2	114 58 21.0	115 9 16.0	115 20 10.1	115 31 3.3
46	116 36 5.3	116 46 52.8	116 57 39.4	117 8 25.2	117 19 10.2
47	118 23 23.1	118 34 2.5	118 44 41.1	118 55 18.8	119 5 55.9
48	120 9 21.3	120 19 52.9	120 30 23.7	120 40 53.7	120 51 23.0
49	121 54 2.7	122 4 26.8	122 14 50.1	122 25 12.6	122 35 34.5
50	123 37 30.1	123 47 46.9	123 58 3.0	124 8 18.3	124 18 33.0
51	125 19 46.2	125 29 56.0	125 40 5.1	125 50 13.5	126 0 21.3
52	127 0 53.6	127 10 56.6	127 20 59.0	127 31 0.8	127 41 1.8
53	128 40 54.7	128 50 51.3	129 0 47.3	129 10 42.6	129 20 37.3
54	130 19 52.3	130 29 42.7	130 39 32.4	130 49 21.6	130 59 10.1
55	131 57 48.7	132 7 33.1	132 17 16.9	132 27 0.1	132 36 42.7
56	133 34 46.3	133 44 25.0	133 54 3.1	134 3 40.6	134 13 17.6
57	135 10 47.7	135 20 20.8	135 29 53.4	135 39 25.4	135 48 57.0
58	136 45 54.9	136 55 22.7	137 4 50.1	137 14 16.8	137 23 43.1
59	138 20 10.2	138 29 33.0	138 38 55.3	138 48 17.0	138 57 38.3
60	139 53 35.9	140 2 53.9	140 12 11.4	140 21 28.3	140 30 44.9
61	141 26 14.2	141 35 27.5	141 44 40.4	141 53 52.8	142 3 4.7
62	142 58 7.0	143 7 16.0	143 16 24.4	143 25 32.4	143 34 40.0
63	144 29 16.6	144 38 21.3	144 47 25.5	144 56 29.4	145 5 32.8
64	145 59 44.9	146 8 45.6	146 17 45.8	146 26 45.7	146 35 45.2
65	147 29 33.9	147 38 30.7	147 47 27.2	147 56 23.2	148 5 18.9
66	148 58 45.5	149 7 38.7	149 16 31.5	149 25 24.0	149 34 16.1
67	150 27 21.6	150 36 11.4	150 45 0.8	150 53 49.9	151 2 38.7
68	151 55 24.2	152 4 10.8	152 12 56.9	152 21 42.8	152 30 28.3
69	153 22 55.0	153 31 38.5	153 40 21.6	153 49 4.4	153 57 46.9
70	154 49 55.7	154 58 36.3	155 7 16.5	155 15 56.4	155 24 36.0
71	156 16 28.2	156 25 6.0	156 33 43.5	156 42 20.7	156 50 57.7
72	157 42 34.2	157 51 9.4	157 59 44.4	158 8 19.1	158 16 53.6
73	159 8 15.4	159 16 48.3	159 25 20.9	159 33 53.2	159 42 25.4
74	160 33 33.5	160 42 4.2	100 50 34.6	160 59 4.7	161 7 34.7
75	161 58 30.1	162 6 58.7	162 15 27.1	162 23 55.2	162 32 23.2
76	163 23 6.9	163 31 33.6	163 40 0.1	163 48 26.4	163 56 52.5
77	164 47 25.5	164 55 50.5	165 4 15.3	165 12 39.8	165 21 4.3
78	166 11 27.5	166 19 50.9	166 28 14.1	166 36 37.1	166 45 0.0
79	167 35 14.3	167 43 36.3	167 51 58.1	168 0 19.7	168 8 41.3
80	168 58 47.7	169 7 8.4	169 15 28.9	169 23 49.4	169 32 9.7
81	170 22 9.2	170 30 28.7	170 38 48.1	170 47 7.5	170 55 26.7
82	171 45 20.1	171 53 38.7	172 1 57.2	172 10 15.6	172 18 34.0
83	173 8 22.1	173 16 40.0	173 24 57.7	173 33 15.3	173 41 32.9
84	174 31 16.8	174 39 34.0	174 47 51.0	174 56 8.0	175 4 25.0
85	175 54 5.5	176 2 22.2	176 10 38.7	176 18 55.3	176 27 11.7
86	177 16 49.8	177 25 6.1	177 33 22.3	177 41 38.5	177 49 54.7
87	178 39 31.2	178 47 47.3	178 56 3.4	179 4 19.4	179 12 35.4
88	180 2 11.2	180 10 27.3	180 18 43.2	180 26 59.2	180 35 15.2
89	181 24 51.2	181 33 7.3	181 41 23.4	181 49 39.5	181 57 55.6
90	182 47 32.8	182 55 49.1	183 4 5.4	183 12 21.8	183 20 38.1
ARG.	0.0	0.1	0.2	0.3	0.4

TABLE XIV. 35

ARG.	0.5 v.	0.6 v.	0.7 v.	0.8 v.	0.9 v.
45	115 41 55.8	115 52 47.3	116 3 38.1	116 14 28.0	116 25 17.1
46	117 29 54.4	117 40 37.7	117 51 20.3	118 2 2.1	118 12 43.0
47	119 16 32.0	119 27 7.4	119 37 42.0	119 48 15.9	119 58 49.0
48	121 1 51.5	121 12 19.2	121 22 46.2	121 33 12.5	121 43 38.0
49	122 45 55.5	122 56 15.9	123 6 35.6	123 16 54.5	123 27 12.7
50	124 28 46.9	124 39 0.2	124 49 12.7	124 59 24.6	125 9 35.7
51	126 10 28.3	126 20 34.7	126 30 40.4	126 40 45.4	126 50 49.8
52	127 51 2.3	128 1 2.0	128 11 1.2	128 20 59.7	128 30 57.5
53	129 30 31.3	129 40 24.8	129 50 17.6	130 0 9.8	130 10 1.4
54	131 8 58.0	131 18 45.3	131 28 32.1	131 38 18.2	131 48 3.7
55	132 46 24.7	132 56 6.2	133 5 47.1	133 15 27.4	133 25 7.2
56	134 22 54.0	134 32 29.8	134 42 5.1	134 51 39.9	135 1 14.1
57	135 58 27.9	136 7 58.4	136 17 28.3	136 26 57.7	136 36 26.6
58	137 33 8.9	137 42 34.2	137 51 58.9	138 1 23.3	138 10 47.0
59	139 6 59.1	139 16 19.5	139 25 39.3	139 34 58.7	139 44 17.5
60	140 40 0.9	140 49 16.5	140 58 31.7	141 7 46.3	141 17 0.5
61	142 12 16.2	142 21 27.3	142 30 37.9	142 39 48.1	142 48 57.8
62	143 43 47.1	143 52 53.9	144 2 0.2	144 11 6.1	144 20 11.6
63	145 14 35.8	145 23 38.4	145 32 40.7	145 41 42.5	145 50 43.9
64	146 44 44.2	146 53 42.9	147 2 41.3	147 11 39.2	147 20 36.7
65	148 14 14.3	148 23 9.2	148 32 3.8	148 40 58.0	148 49 52.0
66	149 43 7.9	149 51 59.3	150 0 50.4	150 9 41.2	150 18 31.6
67	151 11 27.1	151 20 15.2	151 29 2.9	151 37 50.4	151 46 37.5
68	152 39 13.6	152 47 58.5	152 56 43.1	153 5 27.4	153 14 11.4
69	154 6 29.1	154 15 11.0	154 23 52.6	154 32 34.0	154 41 15.0
70	155 33 15.4	155 41 54.5	155 50 33.3	155 59 11.9	156 7 50.2
71	156 59 34.5	157 8 10.9	157 16 47.1	157 25 23.1	157 33 58.8
72	158 25 27.8	158 34 1.8	158 42 35.6	158 51 9.1	158 59 42.4
73	159 50 57.3	159 59 29.0	160 8 0.5	160 16 31.7	160 25 2.8
74	161 16 4.5	161 24 34.0	161 33 3.4	161 41 32.5	161 50 1.5
75	162 40 51.0	162 49 18.6	162 57 46.0	163 6 13.2	163 14 40.2
76	164 5 18.5	164 13 44.2	164 22 9.8	164 30 35.3	164 39 0.5
77	165 29 28.5	165 37 52.7	165 46 16.6	165 54 40.4	166 3 4.1
78	166 53 22.7	167 1 45.3	167 10 7.8	167 18 30.1	167 26 52.3
79	168 17 2.7	168 25 23.9	168 33 45.1	168 42 6.1	168 50 27.0
80	169 40 29.9	169 48 49.9	169 57 9.9	170 5 29.8	170 13 49.5
81	171 3 45.9	171 12 4.9	171 20 23.9	171 28 42.7	171 37 1.5
82	172 26 52.2	172 35 10.4	172 43 28.4	172 51 46.4	173 0 4.4
83	173 49 50.4	173 58 7.7	174 6 25.0	174 14 42.2	174 22 59.5
84	175 12 41.9	175 20 58.7	175 29 15.5	175 37 32.3	175 45 49.0
85	176 35 28.2	176 43 44.6	176 52 1.0	177 0 17.3	177 8 33.6
86	177 58 10.9	178 6 27.0	178 14 43.1	178 22 59.2	178 31 15.2
87	179 20 51.4	179 29 7.4	179 37 23.3	179 45 39.3	179 53 55.3
88	180 43 31.2	180 51 47.2	181 0 3.2	181 8 19.2	181 16 35.3
89	182 6 11.8	182 14 27.9	182 22 44.1	182 31 0.3	182 39 16.5
90	183 28 54.6	183 37 11.0	183 45 27.5	183 53 44.1	184 2 0.7
ARG.	0.5	0.6	0.7	0.8	0.9

TABLE XIV.

ARG.	0.0	0.1	0.2	0.3	0.4
	v.	v.	v.	v.	v.
90	182 47 32.8	182 55 49.1	183 4 5.4	183 12 21.8	183 20 38.1
91	184 10 17.3	184 18 34.0	184 26 50.7	184 35 7.5	184 43 24.3
92	185 33 6.3	185 41 23.6	185 49 40.9	185 57 58.2	186 6 15.6
93	186 56 1.4	187 4 19.3	187 12 37.3	187 20 55.3	187 29 13.5
94	188 19 3.9	188 27 22.7	188 35 41.5	188 44 0.4	188 52 19.5
95	189 42 15.5	189 50 35.3	189 58 55.1	190 7 15.0	190 15 35.1
96	191 5 37.6	191 13 58.5	191 22 19.5	191 30 40.6	191 39 1.8
97	192 29 11.8	192 37 34.0	192 45 56.2	192 54 18.7	193 2 41.2
98	193 52 59.5	194 1 23.1	194 9 46.9	194 18 10.8	194 26 34.8
99	195 17 2.4	195 25 27.7	195 33 53.0	195 42 18.6	195 50 44.3
100	196 41 22.1	196 49 49.1	196 58 16.2	197 6 43.6	197 15 11.1
101	198 6 0.1	198 14 29.0	198 22 58.1	198 31 27.3	198 39 56 8
102	199 30 58.0	199 39 29.0	199 48 0.1	199 56 31.5	200 5 3.1
103	200 56 17.4	201 4 50.7	201 13 24.1	201 21 57.8	201 30 31.7
104	202 22 0.1	202 30 35.8	202 39 11.7	202 47 47.8	202 56 24.1
105	203 48 7.7	203 56 45.9	204 5 24.4	204 14 3.1	204 22 42.1
106	205 14 41.8	205 23 22.8	205 32 4.0	205 40 45.5	205 49 27.3
107	206 41 44.3	206 50 28.2	206 59 12.4	207 7 56.9	207 16 41.7
108	208 9 17.1	208 18 4.1	208 26 51.4	208 35 39.0	208 44 27.0
109	209 37 21.6	209 46 12.0	209 55 2.6	210 3 53.6	210 12 44.9
110	211 5 59.9	211 14 53.7	211 23 47.8	211 32 42.3	211 41 37.1
111	212 35 13.7	212 44 11.2	212 53 9.0	213 2 7.2	213 11 5.7
112	214 5 5.1	214 14 6.4	214 23 8.0	214 32 10.1	214 41 12.6
113	215 35 35.8	215 44 41.2	215 53 46.9	216 2 53.1	216 11 59.7
114	217 6 48.0	217 15 57.6	217 25 7.6	217 34 18.1	217 43 28.9
115	218 38 43.6	218 47 57.6	218 57 12.1	219 6 27.1	219 15 42.5
116	220 11 24.7	220 20 43.5	220 30 2.6	220 39 22.3	220 48 42.4
117	221 44 53.4	221 54 17.0	222 3 41.1	222 13 5.7	222 22 30.8
118	223 19 11.9	223 28 40.6	223 38 9.8	223 47 39.5	223 57 9.7
119	224 54 22.3	225 3 56.4	225 13 30.9	225 23 6.0	225 32 41.6
120	226 30 27.0	226 40 6.6	226 49 46.7	226 59 27.4	227 9 8.6
121	228 7 28.2	228 17 13.6	228 26 59.5	228 36 46.0	228 46 33.1
122	229 45 26.3	229 55 19.7	230 5 11.6	230 15 4.2	230 24 57.4
123	231 24 29.7	231 34 27.3	231 44 25.6	231 54 24.5	232 4 24.0
124	233 4 34.9	233 14 39.0	233 24 43.8	233 34 49.3	233 44 55.4
125	234 45 46.4	234 55 57.3	235 6 8.9	235 16 21.2	235 26 34.1
126	236 28 6.7	236 38 24.7	236 48 43.3	236 59 2.7	237 9 22.7
127	238 11 38.6	238 22 3.8	238 32 29.8	238 42 56.5	238 53 24.0
128	239 56 24.6	240 6 57.5	240 17 31.0	240 28 5.4	240 38 40.5
129	241 42 27.6	241 53 8.3	242 3 49.8	242 14 32.0	242 25 15.0
130	243 29 50.4	243 40 39.2	243 51 26.8	244 2 19.2	244 13 10.4
131	245 18 35.7	245 29 32.9	245 40 30.9	245 51 29.8	246 2 29.6
132	247 8 46.4	247 19 52.3	247 30 59.1	247 42 6.7	247 53 15.3
133	249 0 25.5	249 11 40.5	249 22 56.3	249 34 13.0	249 45 30.7
134	250 53 36.1	251 5 0.4	251 16 25.5	251 27 51.6	251 39 18.7
135	252 48 21.2	252 59 55.0	253 11 29.8	253 23 5.6	253 34 42.3
ARG.	0.0	0.1	0.2	0.3	0.4

TABLE XIV. 37

ARG.	0.5 v.	0.6 v.	0.7 v.	0.8 v.	0.9 v.
90	183 28 54.6	183 37 11.0	183 45 27.5	183 53 44.1	184 2 0.7
91	184 51 41.2	184 59 58.1	185 8 15.1	185 16 32.0	185 24 49.1
92	186 14 33.1	186 22 50.6	186 31 8.2	186 39 25.9	186 47 43.6
93	187 37 31.7	187 45 50.0	187 54 8.3	188 2 26.8	188 10 45.4
94	189 0 38.6	189 8 57.8	189 17 17.1	189 25 36.5	189 33 56.0
95	190 23 55.2	190 32 15.5	190 40 35.9	190 48 56.3	190 57 16.9
96	191 47 23.2	191 55 44.6	192 4 6.2	192 12 28.0	192 20 49.8
97	193 11 3.9	193 19 26.7	193 27 49.7	193 36 12.9	193 44 36.1
98	194 34 59.0	194 43 23.6	194 51 47.9	195 0 12.6	195 8 37.5
99	195 59 10.1	196 7 36.2	196 16 2.4	196 24 28.8	196 32 55.4
100	197 23 38.8	197 32 6.6	197 40 34.7	197 49 3.0	197 57 31.5
101	198 48 26.5	198 56 56.4	199 5 26.5	199 13 56.8	199 22 27.3
102	200 13 35.0	200 22 7.0	200 30 39.3	200 39 11.8	200 47 44.5
103	201 39 5.8	201 47 40.2	201 56 14.8	202 4 49.7	202 13 24.8
104	203 5 0.8	203 13 37.6	203 22 14.8	203 30 52.2	203 39 29.8
105	204 31 21.4	204 40 0.9	204 48 40.8	204 57 20.9	205 6 1.2
106	205 58 9.4	206 6 51.8	206 15 34.5	206 24 17.5	206 33 0.8
107	207 25 26.8	207 34 12.2	207 42 58.0	207 51 44.0	208 0 30.4
108	208 53 15.3	209 2 3.9	209 10 52.8	209 19 42.1	209 28 31.7
109	210 21 36.5	210 30 28.5	210 39 20.8	210 48 13.5	210 57 6.6
110	211 50 32.3	211 59 27.9	212 8 23.8	212 17 20.1	212 26 16.8
111	213 20 4.6	213 29 4.0	213 38 3.7	213 47 3.8	213 56 4.2
112	214 50 15.4	214 59 18.7	215 8 22.4	215 17 26.5	215 26 31.0
113	216 21 6.7	216 30 14.1	216 39 21.9	216 48 30.2	216 57 38.9
114	217 52 40.3	218 1 52.0	218 11 4.2	218 16 16.9	218 29 30.0
115	219 24 58.4	219 34 14.7	219 43 31.5	219 52 48.8	220 2 6.5
116	220 58 3.0	221 7 24.1	221 16 45.7	221 26 7.8	221 35 30.4
117	222 31 56.3	222 41 22.4	222 50 49.0	223 0 16.1	223 9 43.8
118	224 6 40.5	224 16 11.8	224 25 43.6	224 35 16.0	224 44 48.9
119	225 42 17.8	225 51 54.5	226 1 31.8	226 11 9.7	226 20 48.1
120	227 18 50.5	227 28 32.9	227 38 15.8	227 47 59.4	227 57 43.5
121	228 56 20.8	229 6 9.1	229 15 58.0	229 25 47.5	229 35 37.6
122	230 34 51.2	230 44 45.6	230 54 40.7	231 4 36.4	231 14 32.7
123	232 14 24.2	232 24 25.0	232 34 26.5	232 44 28.6	232 54 31.4
124	233 55 2.2	234 5 9.7	234 15 17.8	234 25 26.6	234 35 36.2
125	235 36 47.8	235 47 2.2	235 57 17.3	236 7 33.0	236 17 49.5
126	237 19 43.6	237 30 5.1	237 40 27.4	237 50 50.4	238 1 14.1
127	239 3 52.2	239 14 21.1	239 24 50.9	239 35 21.4	239 45 52.6
128	240 49 16.4	240 59 53.1	241 10 30.5	241 21 8.8	241 31 47.8
129	242 35 58.9	242 46 43.6	242 57 29.1	243 8 15.4	243 19 2.5
130	244 24 2.5	244 34 55.5	244 45 49.3	244 56 43.9	245 7 39.4
131	246 13 30.2	246 24 31.7	246 35 34.1	246 46 37.3	246 57 41.4
132	248 4 24.8	248 15 35.1	248 26 46.3	248 37 58.5	248 49 11.6
133	249 56 49.3	250 8 8.8	250 19 29.2	250 30 50.6	250 42 12.9
134	251 50 46.7	252 2 15.7	252 13 45.6	252 25 16.5	252 36 46.3
135	253 46 20.1	253 57 58.8	254 9 38.5	254 21 19.2	254 33 1.0
ARG.	0.5	0.6	0.7	0.8	0.9

ARG.	0.0	0.1	0.2	0.3	0.4
	v.	*v.*	*v.*	*v.*	*v.*
135	252° 48 21.2	252° 59 55.0	253° 11 29.8	253° 23 5.6	253° 34 42.3
136	254 44 43.6	254 56 27.4	255 8 12.2	255 19 57.9	255 31 44.7
137	256 42 46.7	256 54 40.7	257 6 35.7	257 18 31.7	257 30 28.8
138	258 42 33.4	258 54 37.9	259 6 43.5	259 18 50.1	259 30 57.8
139	260 44 6.8	260 56 22.1	261 8 38.6	261 20 56.1	261 33 14.8
140	262 47 30.0	262 59 56.6	263 12 24.2	263 24 52.9	263 37 22.8
141	264 52 46.3	265 5 24.3	265 18 3.4	265 30 43.7	265 43 25.2
142	266 59 58.6	267 12 48.4	267 25 39.3	267 38 31.4	267 51 24.7
143	269 9 9.9	269 22 11.8	269 35 14.8	269 48 19.0	270 1 24.5
144	271 20 23.2	271 33 37.5	271 46 52.9	272 0 9.5	272 13 27.4
145	273 33 41.5	273 47 8.3	274 0 36.4	274 14 5.8	274 27 36.4
146	275 49 7.3	276 2 47.1	276 16 28.1	276 30 10.4	276 43 54.1
147	278 6 43.5	278 20 36.5	278 34 30.7	278 48 26.2	279 2 23.1
148	280 26 32.6	280 40 38.9	280 54 46.6	281 8 55.6	281 23 5.9
149	282 48 36.8	283 2 56.8	283 17 18.1	283 31 40.7	283 46 4.8
150	285 12 58.2	285 27 32.0	285 42 7.1	285 56 43.7	286 11 21.6
151	287 39 38.6	287 54 26.4	288 9 15.6	288 24 6.1	288 38 58.2
152	290 8 39.7	290 23 41.7	290 38 45.0	290 53 49.7	291 8 55.9
153	292 40 2.8	292 55 19.0	293 10 36.5	293 25 55.5	293 41 16.0
154	295 13 48.7	295 29 19.2	295 44 51.1	296 0 24.4	296 15 59.2
155	297 49 57.8	298 5 42.7	298 21 28.9	298 37 16.6	298 53 5.7
156	300 28 30.2	300 44 29.4	301 0 29.9	301 16 31.9	301 32 35.3
157	303 9 25.5	303 25 38.9	303 41 53.7	303 58 9.9	304 14 27.5
158	305 52 42.8	306 9 10.3	306 25 39.1	306 42 9.4	306 58 41.0
159	308 38 20.2	308 55 1.6	309 11 44.4	309 28 28.5	309 45 14.0
160	311 26 15.8	311 43 10.9	312 0 7.3	312 17 5.0	312 34 4.2
161	314 16 26.7	314 33 35.2	314 50 44.9	315 7 55.9	315 25 8.3
162	317 8 49.5	317 26 10.8	317 43 33.4	318 0 57.3	318 18 22.5
163	320 3 19.6	320 20 53.5	320 38 28.5	320 56 4.8	321 13 42.3
164	322 59 52.4	323 17 38.2	323 35 25.2	323 53 13.3	324 11 2.6
165	325 58 22.0	326 16 19.2	326 34 17.5	326 52 16.8	327 10 17.2
166	328 58 42.1	329 16 49.9	329 34 58.7	329 53 8.6	330 11 19.4
167	332 0 45.3	332 19 3.1	332 37 21.7	332 55 41.3	333 14 1.8
168	335 4 23.8	335 22 50.6	335 41 18.2	335 59 46.7	336 18 16.0
169	338 9 28.9	338 28 3.8	338 46 39.5	339 5 15.9	339 23 53.1
170	341 15 51.2	341 34 33.4	341 53 16.2	342 11 59.6	342 30 43.7
171	344 23 21.1	344 42 9.4	345 0 58.2	345 19 47.6	345 38 37.6
172	347 31 47.7	347 50 41.1	348 9 35.0	348 28 29.2	348 47 23.9
173	350 41 0.4	350 59 57.8	351 18 55.5	351 37 53.5	351 56 51.8
174	353 50 47.7	354 9 47.9	354 28 48.3	354 47 49.0	355 6 49.8
175	357 0 58.0	357 19 59.9	357 39 1.9	357 58 3.9	358 17 6.0
176	0 11 19.6	0 30 21.9	0 49 24.2	1 8 26.5	1 27 28.6
ARG.	0.0	0.1	0.2	0.3	0.4

TABLE XIV. 39

ARG.	0.5	0.6	0.7	0.8	0.9
	v.	v.	v.	v.	v.
135	253° 46 20.1	253° 57 58.8	254° 9 38.5	254° 21 19.2	254° 33 1.0
136	255 43 32.5	255 55 21.3	256 7 11.1	256 19 1.9	256 30 53.8
137	257 42 26.9	257 54 26.1	258 6 26.3	258 18 27.6	258 30 30.0
138	259 43 6.7	259 55 16.4	260 7 27.4	260 19 39.4	260 31 52.6
139	261 45 34.5	261 57 55.4	262 10 17.4	262 22 40.5	262 35 4.7
140	263 49 53.9	264 2 26.1	264 14 59.4	264 27 33.9	264 40 9.5
141	265 56 7.8	266 8 51.6	266 21 36.6	266 34 22.7	266 47 10.1
142	268 4 19.2	268 17 15.0	268 30 11.9	268 43 10.0	268 56 9.4
143	270 14 31.2	270 27 39.1	270 40 48.3	270 53 58.7	271 7 10.4
144	272 26 46.6	272 40 7.1	272 53 28.8	273 6 51.8	273 20 16.0
145	274 41 8.3	274 54 41.6	275 8 16.1	275 21 51.9	275 35 29.0
146	276 57 39.0	277 11 25.3	277 25 12.9	277 39 1.8	277 52 52.0
147	279 16 21.3	279 30 20.9	279 44 21.8	279 58 24.0	280 12 27.6
148	281 37 17.7	281 51 30.8	282 5 45.2	282 20 1.0	282 34 18.2
149	284 0 30.2	284 14 57.1	284 29 25.3	284 43 54.9	284 58 25.8
150	286 26 0.9	286 40 41.7	286 55 23.8	287 10 7.3	287 24 52.3
151	288 53 51.6	289 8 46.4	289 23 42.6	289 38 40.3	289 53 39.3
152	291 24 3.5	291 39 12.5	291 54 22.9	292 9 34.6	292 24 48.1
153	293 56 37.8	294 12 1.2	294 27 25.9	294 42 52.1	294 58 19.7
154	296 31 35.4	296 47 13.0	297 2 52.1	297 18 32.6	297 34 14.6
155	299 8 56.2	299 24 48.1	299 40 41.5	299 56 36.4	300 12 32.6
156	301 48 40.1	302 4 46.4	302 20 54.1	302 37 3.1	302 53 13.7
157	304 30 46.5	304 47 7.0	305 3 28.8	305 19 52.1	305 36 16.7
158	307 15 14.1	307 31 48.5	307 48 24.4	308 5 1.6	308 21 40.2
159	310 2 0.9	310 18 49.2	310 35 38.8	310 52 29.8	311 9 22.1
160	312 51 4.6	313 8 6.4	313 25 9.5	313 42 14.0	313 59 19.7
161	315 42 21.9	315 59 36.8	316 16 53.1	316 34 10.6	316 51 29.4
162	318 35 48.9	318 53 16.5	319 10 45.4	319 28 15.6	319 45 47.0
163	321 31 21.0	321 49 0.9	322 6 42.0	322 24 24.3	322 42 7.8
164	324 28 53.0	324 46 44.6	325 4 37.3	325 22 31.1	325 40 26.0
165	327 28 18.7	327 46 21.3	328 4 24.9	328 22 29.6	328 40 35.3
166	330 29 31.3	330 47 44.2	331 5 58.0	331 24 12.8	331 42 28.6
167	333 32 23.2	333 50 45.5	334 9 8.8	334 27 32.9	334 45 57.9
168	336 36 46.1	336 55 17.1	337 13 48.8	337 32 21.4	337 50 54.8
169	339 42 31.0	340 1 9.7	340 19 49.0	340 38 29.1	340 57 9.8
170	342 49 28.4	343 8 13.8	343 26 59.7	343 45 46.2	344 4 33.4
171	345 57 28.0	346 16 19.0	346 35 10.4	346 54 2.4	347 12 54.8
172	349 6 19.0	349 25 14.6	349 44 10.5	350 3 6.7	350 22 3.4
173	352 15 50.5	352 34 49.4	352 53 48.6	353 12 48.1	353 31 47.8
174	355 25 50.7	355 44 51.9	356 3 53.2	356 22 54.6	356 41 56.3
175	358 36 8.1	358 55 10.4	359 14 12.7	359 33 14.9	359 52 17.3
176	1 46 30.9	2 5 32.9	2 24 34.9	2 43 36.8	3 2 38.7
ARG.	0.5	0.6	0.7	0.8	0.9

ARG.	0.0	0.1	0.2	0.3	0.4	ARG.
	Log r.	Log r.	Log r.	Log r.	Log r.	
0	9.4878495	9.4878506	9.4878540	9.4878597	9.4878677	0
1	.4879630	.4879868	.4880129	.4880413	.4880719	1
2	.4883030	.4883494	.4883980	.4884489	.4885020	2
3	.4888674	.4889361	.4890070	.4890801	.4891553	3
4	9.4896531	9.4897437	9.4898364	9.4899314	9.4900284	4
5	.4906558	.4907678	.4908819	.4909981	.4911164	5
6	.4918699	.4920027	.4921376	.4922744	.4924133	6
7	.4932890	.4934419	.4935968	.4937536	.4939124	7
8	9.4949055	9.4950777	9.4952518	9.4954277	9.4956055	8
9	.4967111	.4969017	.4970941	.4972883	.4974843	9
10	.4986967	.4989048	.4991146	.4993261	.4995392	10
11	.5008526	.5010772	.5013033	.5015311	.5017604	11
12	9.5031688	9.5034088	9.5036503	9.5038933	9.5041378	12
13	.5056345	.5058889	.5061447	.5064018	.5066603	13
14	.5082391	.5085068	.5087757	.5090459	.5093173	14
15	.5109715	.5112513	.5115323	.5118145	.5120977	15
16	9.5138206	9.5141115	9.5144035	9.5146965	9.5149905	16
17	.5167756	.5170765	.5173783	.5176811	.5179848	17
18	.5198255	.5201353	.5204459	.5207574	.5210697	18
19	.5229598	.5232775	.5235959	.5239150	.5242348	19
20	9.5261681	9.5264925	9.5268176	9.5271434	9.5274697	20
21	.5294400	.5297703	.5301012	.5304325	.5307644	21
22	.5327660	.5331012	.5334369	.5337730	.5341095	22
23	.5361371	.5364763	.5368159	.5371558	.5374961	23
24	9.5395439	9.5398862	9.5402288	9.5405716	9.5409147	24
25	.5429781	.5433227	.5436675	.5440125	.5443577	25
26	.5464318	.5467779	.5471242	.5474705	.5478170	26
27	.5498973	.5502442	.5505912	.5509382	.5512852	27
28	9.5533676	9.5537146	9.5540617	9.5544086	9.5547556	28
29	.5568361	.5571826	.5575290	.5578753	.5582215	29
30	.5602963	.5606417	.5609869	.5613320	.5616769	30
31	.5637431	.5640868	.5644303	.5647736	.5651167	31
32	9.5671706	9.5675121	9.5678534	9.5681944	9.5685351	32
33	.5705740	.5709128	.5712514	.5715896	.5719276	33
34	.5739488	.5742845	.5746199	.5749550	.5752897	34
35	.5772908	.5776231	.5779549	.5782865	.5786176	35
36	9.5805963	9.5809247	9.5812527	9.5815802	9.5819074	36
37	.5836615	.5841857	.5845094	.5848328	.5851556	37
38	.5870835	.5874032	.5877225	.5880412	.5883596	38
39	.5902594	.5905743	.5908888	.5912027	.5915162	39
40	9.5933864	9.5936963	9.5940057	9.5943146	9.5946230	40
41	.5964622	.5967669	.5970710	.5973746	.5976777	41
42	.5994846	.5997839	.6000826	.6003807	.6006783	42
43	.6024521	.6027457	.6030388	.6033313	.6036232	43
44	9.6053625	9.6056503	9.6059376	9.6062243	9.6065104	44
45	.6082144	.6084963	.6087777	.6090584	.6093385	45
ARG.	0.0	0.1	0.2	0.3	0.4	ARG.

ARG.	0.5	0.6	0.7	0.8	0.9	ARG.
	Log r.	Log r.	Log r.	Log r.	Log r.	
0	9.4878779	9.4878904	9.4879051	9.4879221	9.4879414	0
1	.4881048	.4881399	.4881773	.4882170	.4882589	1
2	.4885573	.4886140	.4886747	.4887367	.4888009	2
3	.4892328	.4893125	.4893914	.4894784	.4895647	3
4	9.4901276	9.4902290	9.4903325	9.4904381	9.4905458	4
5	.4912368	.4913593	.4914838	.4916105	.4917392	5
6	.4925543	.4926972	.4928422	.4929891	.4931381	6
7	.4940731	.4942357	.4944003	.4945668	.4947352	7
8	9.4957852	9.4959667	9.4961501	9.4963353	9.4965223	8
9	.4976820	.4978815	.4980827	.4982856	.4984902	9
10	.4997540	.4999705	.5001886	.5004083	.5006296	10
11	.5019913	.5022237	.5024577	.5026932	.5029303	11
12	9.5043837	9.5046310	9.5048798	9.5051299	9.5053815	12
13	.5069201	.5071813	.5074438	.5077076	.5079727	13
14	.5095900	.5098639	.5101390	.5104153	.5106928	14
15	.5123821	.5126677	.5129543	.5132420	.5135307	15
16	9.5152856	9.5155816	9.5158786	9.5161766	9.5164756	16
17	.5182894	.5185948	.5189012	.5192084	.5195165	17
18	.5213828	.5216966	.5220113	.5223267	.5226429	18
19	.5245553	.5248765	.5251984	.5255209	.5258441	19
20	9.5277967	9.5281242	9.5284523	9.5287810	9.5291102	20
21	.5310968	.5314297	.5317631	.5320969	.5324312	21
22	.5344465	.5347838	.5351216	.5354597	.5357982	22
23	.5378366	.5381775	.5385186	.5388601	.5392019	23
24	9.5412581	9.5416016	9.5419454	9.5422894	9.5426337	24
25	.5447030	.5450485	.5453941	.5457399	.5460858	25
26	.5481635	.5485101	.5488568	.5492036	.5495504	26
27	.5516323	.5519793	.5523264	.5526735	.5530205	27
28	9.5551025	9.5554493	9.5557961	9.5561429	9.5564895	28
29	.5585676	.5589136	.5592595	.5596052	.5599508	29
30	.5620217	.5623663	.5627108	.5630551	.5633992	30
31	.5654596	.5658023	.5661447	.5664869	.5668289	31
32	9.5688756	9.5692158	9.5695558	9.5698955	9.5702349	32
33	.5722652	.5726026	.5729396	.5732763	.5736127	33
34	.5756241	.5759582	.5762919	.5766252	.5769582	34
35	.5789484	.5792787	.5796087	.5799383	.5802675	35
36	9.5822342	9.5825605	9.5828864	9.5832119	9.5835369	36
37	.5854781	.5858001	.5861216	.5864427	.5867633	37
38	.5886774	.5889948	.5893116	.5896280	.5899440	38
39	.5918292	.5921416	.5924536	.5927650	.5930760	39
40	9.5949308	9.5952382	9.5955450	9.5958512	9.5961570	40
41	.5979802	.5982822	.5985836	.5988845	.5991848	41
42	.6009753	.6012718	.6015677	.6018631	.6021579	42
43	.6039146	.6042053	.6044955	.6047851	.6050741	43
44	9.6067958	9.6070807	9.6073651	9.6076488	9.6079319	44
45	.6096180	.6098970	.6101753	.6104530	.6107301	45
ARG.	0.5	0.6	0.7	0.8	0.9	ARG.

ARG.	**0.0** Log r.	**0.1** Log r.	**0.2** Log r.	**0.3** Log r.	**0.4** Log r.	ARG.
45	9.6082144	9.6084963	9.6087777	9.6090564	9.6093385	45
46	.6110066	.6112925	.6115577	.6118324	.6121064	46
47	.6137377	.6140074	.6142765	.6145450	.6148128	47
48	.6164068	.6166703	.6169331	.6171953	.6174568	48
49	9.6190128	9.6192699	9.6195264	9.6197822	9.6200374	49
50	.6215551	.6218058	.6220558	.6223052	.6225540	50
51	.6240330	.6242772	.6245208	.6247637	.6250060	51
52	.6264459	.6266836	.6269206	.6271570	.6273927	52
53	9.6287932	9.6290243	9.6292548	9.6294845	9.6297137	53
54	.6310746	.6312991	.6315229	.6317461	.6319685	54
55	.6332895	.6335073	.6337245	.6339410	.6341568	55
56	.6354379	.6356491	.6358596	.6360694	.6362786·	56
57	·9.6375196	9.6377241	9.6379279	9.6381310	9.6383335	57
58	.6395343	.6397321	.6399292	.6401256	.6403214	58
59	.6414819	.6416730	.6418634	.6420531	.6422421	59
60	.6433623	.6435466	.6437303	.6439133	.6440957	60
61	9.6451756	9.6453532	9.6455302	9.6457065	9.6458821	61
62	.6469216	.6470925	.6472627	.6474323	.6476012	62
63	.6486005	.6487647	.6489282	.6490911	.6492532	63
64	.6502122	.6503697	.6505265	.6506827	.6508381	64
65	9.6517568	·9.6519076	9.6520577	9.6522071	9.6523559	65
66	.6532344	.6533785	.6535219	.6536646	.6538067	66
67	.6546450	.6547824	.6549191	.6550552	.6551906	67
68	.6559891	.6561198	.6562499	.6563793	.6565080	68
69	9.6572663	9.6573904	·9.6575137	9.6576365	9.6577585	69
70	.6584769	.6585943	.6587110,	.6588271	.6589425	70
71	.6596210	.6597318	.6598419	.6599513	.6600601	71
72	.6606988	.6608029	.6609064	.6610092	.6611114	72
73	9.6617104	9.6618079	9.6619048	9.6620010	9.6620966	73
74	.6626560	.6627469	.6628372	.6629268	.6630157	74
75	.6635355	.6636198	.6637035	.6637865	.6638689	75
76	.6643493	.6644271	.6645042	.6645806	.6646564	76
77	9.6650973	9.6651665	9.6652390,	9.6653089	9.6653782	77
78	.6657798	.6658444	.6659084	.6659718	.6660344	78
79	.6663967	.6664548	.6665122	.6665690	.6666251	79
80	.6669482	.6669997	.6670506	.6671008	.6671504	80
81	9.6674343	9.6674793	9.6675237	9.6675674	9.6676105	81
82	.6678553	.6678938	.6679317	.6679689	.6680054	82
83	.6682110	.6682430	.6682743	.6683050	.6683351	83
84	.6685017	.6685272	.6685520	.6685762	.6685997	84
85	9.6687273	9.6687463	9.6687646	9.6687823	9.6687993	85
86	.6688877	.6689002	.6689120	.6689232	.6689337	86
87	.6689832	.6689892	.6689945	.6689992	.6690032	87
88	.6690138	.6690133	.6690121	.6690103	.6690078	88
89	9.6689793	9.6689723	9.6689646	9.6689563	9.6689473	89
90	.6688798	.6688663	.6688521	.6688373	.6688218	90
ARG.	**0.0**	**0.1**	**0.2**	**0.3**	**0.4**	ARG.

TABLE XV.   43

ARG.	0.5	0.6	0.7	0.8	0.9	ARG.
	Log r.	Log r.	Log r.	Log r.	Log r.	
45	9.6096180	9.6098970	9.6101753	9.6104530	9.6107301	45
46	.6123798	.6126527	.6129248	.6131964	.6134674	46
47	.6150801	.6153467	.6156127	.6158780	.6161427	47
48	.6177177	.6179780	.6182377	.6184967	.6187551	48
49	9.6202920	9.6205459	9.6207991	9.6210518	9.6213038	49
50	.6228021	.6230496	.6232964	.6235426	.6237881	50
51	.6252476	.6254886	.6257289	.6259685	.6262076	51
52	.6276278	.6278622	.6280959	.6283289	.6285614	52
53	9.6299422	9.6301700	9.6303971	9.6306236	9.6308494	53
54	.6321904	.6324115	.6326320	.6328518	.6330710	54
55	.6343720	.6345865	.6348004	.6350135	.6352261	55
56	.6364871	.6366949	.6369021	.6371086	.6373144	56
57	9.6385353	9.6387365	9.6389369	9.6391367	9.6393358	57
58	.6405165	.6407109	.6409047	.6410978	.6412902	58
59	.6424305	.6426182	.6428052	.6429916	.6431773	59
60	.6442773	.6444583	.6446387	.6448183	.6449973	60
61	9.6460570	9.6462313	9.6464049	9.6465778	9.6467500	61
62	.6477694	.6479370	.6481039	.6482701	.6484356	62
63	.6494147	.6495756	.6497357	.6498952	.6500541	63
64	.6509929	.6511471	.6513004	.6514532	.6516054	64
65	9.6525040	9.6526514	9.6527982	9.6529442	9.6530897	65
66	.6539481	.6540888	.6542289	.6543682	.6545070	66
67	.6553254	.6554594	.6555929	.6557256	.6558577	67
68	.6566361	.6567635	.6568902	.6570162	.6571416	68
69	9.6578799	9.6580007	9.6581207	9.6582401	9.6583588	69
70	.6590573	.6591713	.6592848	.6593975	.6595096	70
71	.6601682	.6602756	.6603824	.6604885	.6605940	71
72	.6612129	.6613137	.6614139	.6615134	.6616122	72
73	9.6621915	9.6622857	9.6623793	9.6624722	9.6625644	73
74	.6631040	.6631916	.6632786	.6633649	.6634505	74
75	.6639506	.6640317	.6641121	.6641918	.6642709	75
76	.6647315	.6648060	.6648798	.6649530	.6650255	76
77	9.6654467	9.6655147	9.6655819	9.6656485	9.6657145	77
78	.6660964	.6661578	.6662185	.6662786	.6663380	78
79	.6666806	.6667354	.6667896	.6668431	.6668959	79
80	.6671993	.6672476	.6672953	.6673423	.6673886	80
81	9.6676529	9.6676917	9.6677358	9.6677763	9.6678161	81
82	.6680413	.6680766	.6681111	.6681451	.6681784	82
83	.6683645	.6683932	.6684213	.6684488	.6684756	83
84	.6686226	.6686449	.6686665	.6686874	.6687077	84
85	9.6688156	9.6688314	9.6688464	9.6688608	9.6688746	85
86	.6689436	.6689528	.6689614	.6689693	.6689766	86
87	.6690066	.6690094	.6690114	.6690129	.6690137	87
88	.6690047	.6690009	.6689965	.6689914	.6689857	88
89	9.6689377	9.6689274	9.6689165	9.6689019	9.6688927	89
90	.6688057	.6687890	.6687715	.6687535	.6687348	90
ARG.	0.5	0.6	0.7	0.8	0.9	ARG.

ARG.	0.0	0.1	0.2	0.3	0.4	ARG.
	Log r.	Log r,	Log r.	Log r.	Log r.	
90	9.6688798	9.6688663	9.6688521	9.6688373	9.6688218	90
91	.6687154	.6686954	.6686747	.6686534	.6686314	91
92	.6684858	.6684593	.6684321	.6684042	.6683757	92
93	.6681911	.6681581	.6681244	.6680900	.6680550	93
94	9.6678314	9.6677918	9.6677516	9.6677108	9.6676692	94
95	.6674064	.6673603	.6673136	.6672662	.6672181	95
96	.6669162	.6668636	.6668103	.6667564	.6667019	96
97	.6663608	.6663017	.6662419	.6661814	.6661203	97
98	9.6657399	9.6656742	9.6656078	9.6655408	9.6654732	98
99	.6650534	.6649811	.6649082	.6648347	.6647604	99
100	.6643013	.6642225	.6641430	.6640629	.6639821	100
101	.6631835	.6633981	.6633120	.6632253	.6631380	101
102	9.6625998	9.6625079	9.6624153	9.6623219	9.6622280	102
103	.6616503	.6615517	.6614524	.6613525	.6612520	103
104	.6606347	.6605295	.6604236	.6603171	.6602099	104
105	.6595528	.6594410	.6593285	.6592153	.6591015	105
106	9.6584046	9.6582861	9.6581670	9.6580472	9.6579267	106
107	.6571899	.6570618	.6569390	.6568125	.6566854	107
108	.6559086	.6557768	.6556443	.6555112	.6553774	108
109	.6545605	.6544220	.6542829	.6541430	.6510026	109
110	9.6531457	9.6530005	9.6528547	9.6527082	9.6525611	110
111	.6516640	.6515121	.6513596	.6512064	.6510526	111
112	.6501153	.6499567	.6497975	.6496376	.6494770	112
113	.6484995	.6483342	.6481683	.6480017	.6478344	113
114	9.6468165	9.6466445	9.6464718	9.6462985	9.6461245	114
115	.6450664	.6448877	.6447083	.6445282	.6443475	115
116	.6432490	.6430636	.6428775	.6426907	.6425032	116
117	.6413645	.6411724	.6409795	.6107860	.6405919	117
118	9.6394128	9.6392139	9.6390144	9.6388142	9.6386133	118
119	.6373940	.6371884	.6369822	.6367753	.6365677	119
120	.6353082	.6350960	.6348830	.6346695	.6344552	120
121	.6331557	.6329368	.6327172	.6324970	.6322761	121
122	9.6309367	9.6307111	9.6304849	9.6302581	9.6300305	122
123	.6286512	.6284190	.6281862	.6279527	.6277186	123
124	.6262999	.6260612	.6258218	.6255817	.6253410	124
125	.6238829	.6236376	.6233917	.6231452	.6228980	125
126	9.6214011	9.6211494	9.6208970	9.6206440	9.6203903	126
127	.6188549	.6185968	.6183380	.6180786	.6178185	127
128	.6162450	.6159805	.6157154	.6154497	.6151833	128
129	.6135720	.6133013	.6130299	.6127580	.6124855	129
130	9.6108372	9.6105603	9.6102829	9.6100048	9.6097261	130
131	.6080413	.6077584	.6074749	.6071908	.6069062	131
132	.6051858	.6048970	.6046076	.6043177	.6040272	132
133	.6022718	.6019772	.6016821	.6013864	.6010902	133
134	9.5993008	9.5990007	9.5987000	9.5983988	9.5980970	134
135	.5962751	.5959696	.5956635	.5953569	.5950498	135
ARG.	0.0	01.	0.2	0.3	0.4	ARG.

TABLE XV.   45

ARG.	0.5	0.6	0.7	0.8	0.9	ARG.
	Log *r*.	Log *r*.	Log *r*.	Log *r*.	Log *r*.	
90	9.6688057	9.6687890	9.6687715	9.6687535	9.6687348	90
91	.6686088	.6685855	.6685615	.6685370	.6685117	91
92	.6683466	.6683168	.6682864	.6682553	.6682235	92
93	.6680194	.6679831	.6679461	.6679086	.6678703	93
94	9.6676271	9.6675842	9.6675408	9.6674966	9.6674518	94
95	.6671694	.6671201	.6670701	.6670194	.6669681	95
96	.6666466	.6665908	.6665343	.6664771	.6664193	96
97	.6660585	.6659961	.6659330	.6658693	.6658049	97
98	9.6654048	9.6653358	9.6652662	9.6651959	9.6651250	98
99	.6646856	.6646100	.6645338	.6644570	.6643795	99
100	.6639006	.6638185	.6637357	.6636523	.6635682	100
101	.6630499	.6629612	.6628719	.6627819	.6626912	101
102	9.6621334	9.6620381	9.6619421	9.6618455	9.6617482	102
103	.6611507	.6610469	.6609463	.6608431	.6607392	103
104	.6601020	.6599935	.6598843	.6597745	.6596640	104
105	.6589870	.6588719	.6587560	.6586396	.6585224	105
106	9.6578056	9.6576838	9.6575613	9.6574382	9.6573144	106
107	.6565576	.6564291	.6563000	.6561702	.6560397	107
108	.6552430	.6551078	.6549720	.6548355	.6546983	108
109	.6538614	.6537196	.6535771	.6534340	.6532902	109
110	9.6524132	9.6522647	9.6521155	9.6519657	9.6518152	110
111	.6508980	.6507428	.6505869	.6504304	.6502732	111
112	.6493158	.6491539	.6489913	.6488280	.6486641	112
113	.6476664	.6474978	.6473284	.6471585	.6469878	113
114	9.6459498	9.6457745	9.6455985	9.6454218	9.6452444	114
115	.6441661	.6439840	.6438013	.6436179	.6434338	115
116	.6423151	.6421263	.6419369	.6417468	.6415560	116
117	.6403970	.6402015	.6400054	.6398085	.6396110	117
118	9.6384118	9.6382096	9.6380067	9.6378031	9.6375989	118
119	.6363595	.6361506	.6359410	.6357307	.6355198	119
120	.6342403	.6340247	.6338085	.6335915	.6333740	120
121	.6320545	.6318323	.6316094	.6313858	.6311616	121
122	9.6298023	9.6295733	9.6293437	9.6291135	9.6288827	122
123	.6274838	.6272483	.6270122	.6267754	.6265380	123
124	.6250996	.6248576	.6246149	.6243715	.6241275	124
125	.6226501	.6224016	.6221525	.6219027	.6216522	125
126	9.6201360	9.6198811	9.6196255	9.6193693	9.6191124	126
127	.6175579	.6172965	.6170346	.6167721	.6165088	127
128	.6149163	.6146487	.6143805	.6141116	.6138421	128
129	.6122123	.6119385	.6116641	.6113891	.6111135	129
130	9.6094468	9.6091669	9.6088864	9.6086053	9.6083236	130
131	.6066209	.6063351	.6060486	.6057616	.6054740	131
132	.6037360	.6034444	.6031521	.6028592	.6025658	132
133	.6007933	.6004960	.6001980	.5998995	.5995004	133
134	9.5977947	9.5974918	9.5971884	9.5968845	9.5965801	134
135	.5947422	.5944340	.5941253	.5938162	.5935064	135
ARG.	0.5	06.	0.7	0.8	0.9	ARG.

ARG.	0,0 Log r.	0.1 Log r.	0,2 Log r.	0.3 Log r.	0.4 Log r.	ARG.
135	9.5962751	9.5959696	9.5956635	9.5953569	9.5950498	135
136	.5931962	.5928855	.5925742	.5922624	.5919502	136
137	.5900661	.5897504	.5894342	.5891175	.5888003	137
138	.5868873	.5865668	.5862459	.5859246	.5656027	138
139	9.5836625	9.5833376	9.5830123	9.5826866	9.5823604	139
140	.5803947	.5800657	.5797362	.5794064	.5790762	140
141	.5770869	.5767541	.5764208	.5760873	.5757531	141
142	.5737427	.5734065	.5730699	.5727329	.5723958	142
143	9.5703662	9.5700269	9.5696873	9.5693475	9.5690073	143
144	.5669612	.5666193	.5662772	.5659348	.5655923	144
145	.5635323	.5631883	.5628441	.5624997	.5621551	145
146	.5600845	.5597389	.5593932	.5590474	.5587015	146
147	9.5566237	9.5562771	9.5559303	9.5555836	9.5552367	147
148	.5531548	.5528078	.5524607	.5521137	.5517666	148
149	.5496847	.5493378	.5489911	.5486143	.5482977	149
150	.5462196	.5458736	.5455278	.5451821	.5448366	150
151	9.5427669	9.5424226	9.5420785	9.5417346	9.5413909	151
152	.5393341	.5389922	.5386506	.5383094	.5379684	152
153	.5359293	.5355906	.5352524	.5349145	.5345770	153
154	.5325607	.5322262	.5318921	.5315586	.5312255	154
155	9.5292377	9.5289082	9.5285793	9.5282510	9.5279233	155
156	.5259694	.5256459	.5253231	.5250010	.5246795	156
157	.5227654	.5224489	.5221332	.5218183	.5215042	157
158	.5196359	.5193275	.5190199	.5187132	.5184074	158
159	9.5165916	9.5162922	9.5159939	9.5156964	9.5154000	159
160	.5136428	.5133536	.5130654	.5127764	.5124925	160
161	.5108005	.5105225	.5102458	.5099702	.5096958	161
162	.5080756	.5078100	.5075457	.5072827	.5070211	162
163	9.5054792	9.5052270	9.5049763	9.5047270	9.5044791	163
164	.5030224	.5027848	.5025487	.5023141	.5020811	164
165	.5007157	.5004937	.5002733	.5000546	.4998375	165
166	.4985699	.4983646	.4981609	.4979590	.4977589	166
167	9.4965951	9.4964074	9.4962215	9.4960374	9.4958552	167
168	.4948008	.4946317	.4944644	.4942991	.4941357	168
169	.4931962	.4930465	.4928987	.4927531	.4926093	169
170	.4917895	.4916600	.4915326	.4914072	.4912839	170
171	9.4905882	9.4904796	9.4903731	9.4902688	9.4901666	171
172	.4895986	.4895115	.4894266	.4893439	.4892633	172
173	.4888264	.4887613	.4886984	.4886377	.4885793	173
174	.4882757	.4882329	.4881924	.4881541	.4881181	174
175	9.4879495	9.4879293	9.4879114	9.4878958	9.4878824	175
176	.4878499	.4878524	.4878572	.4878643	.4878736	176
ARG.	0.0	01.	0.2	0.3	0.4	ARG.

TABLE XV. 47

ARG.	0.5 Log r.	0.6 Log r.	0.7 Log r.	0.8 Log r.	0.9 Log r.	ARG.
135	9.5947422	9.5944340	9.5941253	9.5938162	9.5935064	135
136	.5916374	.5913241	.5910104	.5906961	.5903814	136
137	.5884826	.5881645	.5878459	.5875268	.5872073	137
138	.5852805	.5849578	.5846346	.5843110	.5839870	138
139	9.5820338	9.5817068	9.5813794	9.5810516	9.5807234	139
140	.5787456	.5784146	.5780832	.5777515	.5774194	140
141	.5751191	.5750845	.5747496	.5744143	.5740787	141
142	.5720583	.5717205	.5713823	.5710439	.5707052	142
143	9.5686669	9.5683263	9.5679854	9.5676442	9.5673028	143
144	.5652495	.5649064	.5645632	.5642198	.5638762	144
145	.5618104	.5614655	.5611205	.5607753	.5604300	145
146	.5583554	.5580092	.5576630	.5573166	.5569702	146
147	9.5518898	9.5545429	9.5541959	9.5538489	9.5535019	147
148	.5514195	.5510725	.5507255	.5503785	.5500316	148
149	.5479511	.5176046	.5472582	.5469119	.5465657	149
150	.5444912	.5441460	.5438010	.5434561	.5431114	150
151	9.5410475	9.5407043	9.5403614	9.5400187	9.5396762	151
152	.5376277	.5372873	.5369473	.5366076	.5362683	152
153	.5342399	.5339032	.5335669	.5332311	.5328957	153
154	.5308929	.5305609	.5302293	.5298982	.5295677	154
155	9.5275961	9.5272695	9.5269436	9.5266182	9.5262935	155
156	.5243587	.5210386	.5237192	.5234005	.5230826	156
157	.5211907	.5208781	.5205663	.5202554	.5199452	157
158	.5181025	.5177985	.5174954	.5171932	.5168919	158
159	9.5151016	9.5148102	9.5145168	9.5142245	9.5139332	159
160	.5122076	.5119239	.5116413	.5113599	.5110796	160
161	.5094227	.5091508	.5088801	.5086106	.5083425	161
162	.5067607	.5065017	.5062440	.5059877	.5057328	162
163	9.5012327	9.5039877	9.5037441	9.5035021	9.5032615	163
164	.5018496	.5016196	.5013912	.5011645	.5009393	164
165	.4996220	.4994083	.4991961	.4989857	.4987770	165
166	.4975605	.4973638	.4971689	.4969758	.4967845	166
167	9.4956748	9.4954963	9.4953196	9.4951448	9.4949718	167
168	.4939743	.4938148	.4936572	.4935016	.4933479	168
169	.4924676	.4923279	.4921903	.4920546	.4919211	169
170	.4911627	.4910436	.4909266	.4908117	.4906989	170
171	9.4900665	9.4899686	9.4898729	9.4897793	9.4896879	171
172	.4891850	.4891089	.4890349	.4889632	.4888937	172
173	.4885231	.4884692	.4884174	.4883679	.4883207	173
174	.4880841	.4880529	.4880236	.4879966	.4879719	174
175	9.4878713	9.4878625	9.4878559	9.4878517	9.4878497	175
176	.4878853	.4878991	.4879153	.4879338	.4879544	176
ARG.	0.5	0.6	0.7	0.8	0.9	ARG.

Argument of Latitude.				Reduction to the Ecliptic.	Log Diff. for 1″.	Var. in 100 Years.	Argument of Latitude.				Reduction to the Ecliptic.	Log Diff. for 1″.	Var. in 100 Years.
−	+	−	+				−	+	−	+			
0	180	180	360	0 0.0	7.8725	0.00	45	135	225	315	12 51.9	+5.4437	0.43
1	179	181	359	0 26.8	7.8722	0.01	46	134	226	314	12 51.5	−6.3680	0.43
2	178	182	358	0 53.6	7.8714	0.02	47	133	227	313	12 50.2	6.6917	0.43
3	177	183	357	1 20.4	7.8702	0.04	48	132	228	312	12 48.0	6.8783	0.43
4	176	184	356	1 47.0	7.8684	0.05	49	131	229	311	12 44.8	7.0060	0.42
5	175	185	355	2 13.6	7.8660	0.07	50	130	230	310	12 40.6	7.1055	0.42
6	174	186	354	2 39.9	7.8630	0.09	51	129	231	309	12 35.6	7.1849	0.42
7	173	187	353	3 6.1	7.8595	0.10	52	128	232	308	12 29.6	7.2519	0.41
8	172	188	352	3 32.0	7.8555	0.12	53	127	233	307	12 22.7	7.3088	0.41
9	171	189	351	3 57.7	7.8509	0.13	54	126	234	306	12 15.0	7.3596	0.41
10	170	190	350	4 23.1	7.8456	0.14	55	125	235	305	12 6.3	7.4047	0.40
11	169	191	349	4 48.2	7.8401	0.15	56	124	236	304	11 56.7	7.4146	0.40
12	168	192	348	5 12.9	7.8338	0.17	57	123	237	303	11 46.2	7.4811	0.39
13	167	193	347	5 37.2	7.8266	0.18	58	122	238	302	11 34.9	7.5137	0.39
14	166	194	346	6 1.2	7.8190	0.19	59	121	239	301	11 22.7	7.5437	0.38
15	165	195	345	6 24.7	7.8107	0.21	60	120	240	300	11 9.7	7.5715	0.37
16	164	196	344	6 47.7	7.8018	0.22	61	119	241	299	10 55.9	7.5972	0.36
17	163	197	343	7 10.3	7.7920	0.24	62	118	242	298	10 41.3	7.6207	0.35
18	162	198	342	7 32.3	7.7814	0.25	63	117	243	297	10 25.8	7.6424	0.35
19	161	199	341	7 53.8	7.7700	0.26	64	116	244	296	10 9.7	7.6628	0.34
20	160	200	340	8 14.7	7.7582	0.28	65	115	245	295	9 52.7	7.6818	0.33
21	159	201	339	8 35.1	7.7450	0.29	66	114	246	294	9 35.1	7.6995	0.32
22	158	202	338	8 54.8	7.7308	0.30	67	113	247	293	9 16.7	7.7158	0.31
23	157	203	337	9 13.8	7.7160	0.31	68	112	248	292	8 57.6	7.7311	0.30
24	156	204	336	9 32.2	7.6999	0.32	69	111	249	291	8 37.9	7.7454	0.29
25	155	205	335	9 49.9	7.6825	0.33	70	110	250	290	8 17.6	7.7588	0.28
26	154	206	334	10 6.9	7.6641	0.34	71	109	251	289	7 56.6	7.7711	0.27
27	153	207	333	10 23.1	7.6443	0.35	72	108	252	288	7 35.1	7.7828	0.25
28	152	208	332	10 38.6	7.6230	0.36	73	107	253	287	7 13.0	7.7936	0.24
29	151	209	331	10 53.3	7.5996	0.37	74	106	254	286	6 50.3	7.8034	0.22
30	150	210	330	11 7.2	7.5747	0.37	75	105	255	285	6 27.2	7.8125	0.21
31	149	211	329	11 20.3	7.5479	0.38	76	104	256	284	6 3.6	7.8212	0.20
32	148	212	328	11 32.6	7.5182	0.38	77	103	257	283	5 39.5	7.8288	0.18
33	147	213	327	11 44.1	7.4863	0.39	78	102	258	282	5 15.0	7.8359	0.17
34	146	214	326	11 54.7	7.4506	0.39	79	101	259	281	4 50.2	7.8425	0.16
35	145	215	325	12 4.4	7.4117	0.40	80	100	260	280	4 24.9	7.8484	0.14
36	144	216	324	12 13.3	7.3680	0.41	81	99	261	279	3 59.4	7.8538	0.13
37	143	217	323	12 21.2	7.3188	0.41	82	98	262	278	3 33.5	7.8583	0.11
38	142	218	322	12 28.3	7.2639	0.42	83	97	263	277	3 7.4	7.8625	0.10
39	141	219	321	12 34.4	7.2003	0.42	84	96	264	276	2 41.1	7.8661	0.09
40	140	220	320	12 39.7	7.1231	0.43	85	95	265	275	2 14.5	7.8689	0.08
41	139	221	319	12 44.0	7.0292	0.43	86	94	266	274	1 47.8	7.8715	0.06
42	138	222	318	12 47.4	6.9091	0.43	87	93	267	273	1 21.0	7.8735	0.04
43	137	223	317	12 49.8	6.7404	0.43	88	92	268	272	0 54.0	7.8746	0.03
44	136	224	316	12 51.3	6.4607	0.43	89	91	269	271	0 27.0	7.8754	0.01
45	135	225	315	12 51.9	5.4437	0.43	90	90	270	270	0 0.0	7.8757	0.00

TABLE XVII.   49

Argument of Latitude.		Latitude.	Log Diff. for 1″.	Var. in 100 Years.	Argument of Latitude.		Latitude.	Log Diff. for 1″.	Var. in 100 Years.
180	0	0 0 0.0	9.0860	0.00	135	45	4 56 40.1	8.9371	5.01
179	1	0 7 18.8	9.0859	0.12	134	46	5 1 48.8	8.9294	5.09
178	2	0 14 37.4	9.0857	0.25	133	47	5 6 52.1	8.9215	5.18
177	3	0 21 55.8	9.0854	0.37	132	48	5 11 49.7	8.9133	5.27
176	4	0 29 13.8	9.0849	0.49	131	49	5 16 41.7	8.9048	5.35
175	5	0 36 31.3	9.0843	0.61	130	50	5 21 27.9	8.8959	5.43
174	6	0 43 48.1	9.0836	0.74	129	51	5 26 8.2	8.8868	5.51
173	7	0 51 4.1	9.0828	0.86	128	52	5 30 42.7	8.8773	5.58
172	8	0 58 19.2	9.0818	0.98	127	53	5 35 11.1	8.8675	5.66
171	9	1 5 33.3	9.0807	1.10	126	54	5 39 33.3	8.8573	5.74
170	10	1 12 46.2	9.0794	1.22	125	55	5 43 49.4	8.8467	5.81
169	11	1 19 57.7	9.0780	1.34	124	56	5 47 59.2	8.8357	5.88
168	12	1 27 7.9	9.0765	1.47	123	57	5 52 2.7	8.8243	5.95
167	13	1 34 16.4	9.0748	1.59	122	58	5 55 59.7	8.8125	6.02
166	14	1 41 23.3	9.0731	1.71	121	59	5 59 50.2	8.8002	6.09
165	15	1 48 28.3	9.0711	1.83	120	60	6 3 34.2	8.7874	6.15
164	16	1 55 31.4	9.0690	1.95	119	61	6 7 11.5	8.7740	6.21
163	17	2 2 32.4	9.0668	2.07	118	62	6 10 42.1	8.7601	6.27
162	18	2 9 31.1	9.0645	2.18	117	63	6 14 5.9	8.7456	6.33
161	19	2 16 27.6	9.0620	2.30	116	64	6 17 22.9	8.7304	6.38
160	20	2 23 21.5	9.0593	2.41	115	65	6 20 32.9	8.7146	6.44
159	21	2 30 12.9	9.0565	2.52	114	66	6 23 36.0	8.6980	6.49
158	22	2 37 1.6	9.0536	2.64	113	67	6 26 32.1	8.6806	6.54
157	23	2 43 47.4	9.0505	2.76	112	68	6 29 21.1	8.6623	6.59
156	24	2 50 30.3	9.0472	2.87	111	69	6 32 3.0	8.6431	6.64
155	25	2 57 10.1	9.0438	2.99	110	70	6 34 37.6	8.6229	6.68
154	26	3 3 46.7	9.0402	3.10	109	71	6 37 5.1	8.6015	6.72
153	27	3 10 20.0	9.0365	3.21	108	72	6 39 25.3	8.5789	6.76
152	28	3 16 49.9	9.0326	3.32	107	73	6 41 38.1	8.5549	6.80
151	29	3 23 16.1	9.0285	3.43	106	74	6 43 43.6	8.5293	6.83
150	30	3 29 38.7	9.0243	3.54	105	75	6 45 41.7	8.5020	6.87
149	31	3 35 57.6	9.0199	3.64	104	76	6 47 32.3	8.4727	6.90
148	32	3 42 12.5	9.0153	3.75	103	77	6 49 15.5	8.4411	6.93
147	33	3 48 23.3	9.0105	3.85	102	78	6 50 51.1	8.4070	6.95
146	34	3 54 30.1	9.0055	3.95	101	79	6 52 19.3	8.3697	6.98
145	35	4 0 32.6	9.0004	4.05	100	80	6 53 39.8	8.3286	7.00
144	36	4 6 30.7	8.9950	4.16	99	81	6 54 52.8	8.2835	7.02
143	37	4 12 24.4	8.9895	4.26	98	82	6 55 58.1	8.2327	7.04
142	38	4 18 13.5	8.9837	4.36	97	83	6 56 55.8	8.1751	7.06
141	39	4 23 57.9	8.9777	4.45	96	84	6 57 45.8	8.1085	7.07
140	40	4 29 37.5	8.9716	4.55	95	85	6 58 28.2	8.0295	7.08
139	41	4 35 12.2	8.9651	4.65	94	86	6 59 2.9	7.9328	7.09
138	42	4 40 41.9	8.9585	4.74	93	87	6 59 29.9	7.8081	7.10
137	43	4 46 6.6	8.9516	4.85	92	88	6 59 49.2	7.6321	7.11
136	44	4 51 26.0	8.9445	4.92	91	89	7 0 0.7	7.3313	7.11
135	45	4 56 40.1	8.9371	5.01	90	90	7 0 4.6	∞	7.11

Arg.	.0 Log Diff. v.	.1 Log Diff. v.	.2 Log Diff. v.	.3 Log Diff. v.	.4 Log Diff. v.	.5 Log Diff. v.	.6 Log Diff. v.	.7 Log Diff. v.	.8 Log Diff. v.	.9 Log Diff. v.
0	9.05779	9.05779	9.05778	9.05777	9.05775	9.05773	9.05771	9.05768	9.05764	9.05760
1	9.05756	9.05751	9.05746	9.05740	9.05734	9.05728	9.05721	9.05713	9.05705	9.05697
2	9.05688	9.05679	9.05669	9.05659	9.05648	9.05637	9.05626	9.05614	9.05601	9.05588
3	9.05575	9.05561	9.05547	9.05533	9.05517	9.05502	9.05486	9.05470	9.05453	9.05436
4	9.05418	9.05400	9.05381	9.05362	9.05343	9.05323	9.05303	9.05282	9.05261	9.05239
5	9.05217	9.05195	9.05172	9.05149	9.05125	9.05101	9.05077	9.05052	9.05027	9.05001
6	9.04975	9.04948	9.04922	9.04894	9.04866	9.04838	9.04810	9.04781	9.04751	9.04721
7	9.04691	9.04660	9.04629	9.04598	9.04566	9.04534	9.04501	9.04468	9.04435	9.04401
8	9.04367	9.04333	9.04298	9.04263	9.04227	9.04191	9.04155	9.04118	9.04081	9.04044
9	9.04006	9.03968	9.03929	9.03891	9.03852	9.03812	9.03772	9.03732	9.03691	9.03650
10	9.03609	9.03567	9.03526	9.03483	9.03441	9.03398	9.03354	9.03311	9.03267	9.03223
11	9.03178	9.03133	9.03088	9.03042	9.02997	9.02951	9.02904	9.02857	9.02810	9.02763
12	9.02715	9.02667	9.02619	9.02570	9.02521	9.02472	9.02422	9.02372	9.02322	9.02272
13	9.02221	9.02170	9.02119	9.02068	9.02016	9.01964	9.01912	9.01859	9.01806	9.01753
14	9.01700	9.01647	9.01593	9.01539	9.01485	9.01430	9.01375	9.01320	9.01265	9.01210
15	9.01154	9.01098	9.01042	9.00986	9.00929	9.00872	9.00815	9.00758	9.00700	9.00642
16	9.00581	9.00526	9.00467	9.00409	9.00350	9.00291	9.00232	9.00173	9.00113	9.00053
17	8.99993	8.99933	8.99873	8.99812	8.99751	8.99690	8.99629	8.99568	8.99507	8.99445
18	8.99383	8.99321	8.99259	8.99197	8.99135	8.99072	8.99009	8.98946	8.98883	8.98820
19	8.98757	8.98694	8.98630	8.98566	8.98502	8.98438	8.98374	8.98309	8.98245	8.98180
20	8.98115	8.98050	8.97985	8.97920	8.97855	8.97790	8.97724	8.97658	8.97593	8.97527
21	8.97461	8.97395	8.97329	8.97263	8.97196	8.97130	8.97063	8.96997	8.96930	8.96863
22	8.96796	8.96729	8.96662	8.96595	8.96527	8.96460	8.96392	8.96325	8.96257	8.96189
23	8.96121	8.96053	8.95985	8.95917	8.95849	8.95781	8.95713	8.95645	8.95577	8.95508
24	8.95440	8.95372	8.95303	8.95235	8.95166	8.95097	8.95029	8.94960	8.94891	8.94822
25	8.94753	8.94684	8.94615	8.94546	8.94477	8.94408	8.94339	8.94270	8.94201	8.94131
26	8.94062	8.93993	8.93924	8.93854	8.93785	8.93716	8.93646	8.93577	8.93508	8.93438
27	8.93369	8.93300	8.93230	8.93161	8.93092	8.93022	8.92953	8.92883	8.92814	8.92744
28	8.92675	8.92606	8.92536	8.92467	8.92397	8.92328	8.92259	8.92189	8.92120	8.92050
29	8.91981	8.91912	8.91842	8.91773	8.91704	8.91635	8.91566	8.91496	8.91427	8.91358
147	8.92024	8.92093	8.92163	8.92232	8.92301	8.92370	8.92440	8.92509	8.92578	8.92648
148	8.92717	8.92786	8.92856	8.92925	8.92994	8.93064	8.93133	8.93203	8.93272	8.93342
149	8.93411	8.93480	8.93550	8.93619	8.93688	8.93758	8.93827	8.93896	8.93965	8.94035
150	8.94104	8.94173	8.94242	8.94312	8.94381	8.94450	8.94519	8.94588	8.94657	8.94726
151	8.94795	8.94864	8.94933	8.95002	8.95070	8.95139	8.95208	8.95276	8.95345	8.95413
152	8.95482	8.95550	8.95619	8.95687	8.95755	8.95823	8.95891	8.95959	8.96027	8.96095
153	8.96163	8.96231	8.96298	8.96366	8.96433	8.96501	8.96568	8.96636	8.96703	8.96770
154	8.96837	8.96904	8.96971	8.97037	8.97104	8.97170	8.97237	8.97303	8.97369	8.97435
155	8.97501	8.97567	8.97633	8.97698	8.97764	8.97829	8.97895	8.97960	8.98025	8.98090
156	8.98155	8.98220	8.98284	8.98349	8.98413	8.98477	8.98541	8.98605	8.98669	8.98732
157	8.98796	8.98859	8.98922	8.98985	8.99048	8.99111	8.99173	8.99236	8.99298	8.99360
158	8.99422	8.99484	8.99545	8.99606	8.99667	8.99728	8.99789	8.99849	8.99910	8.99970
159	9.00030	9.00090	9.00149	9.00209	9.00268	9.00327	9.00386	9.00445	9.00503	9.00562
160	9.00620	9.00678	9.00735	9.00793	9.00850	9.00907	9.00964	9.01021	9.01077	9.01133
161	9.01189	9.01245	9.01300	9.01355	9.01410	9.01464	9.01518	9.01572	9.01626	9.01680
162	9.01733	9.01786	9.01839	9.01891	9.01944	9.01996	9.02047	9.02099	9.02150	9.02201
163	9.02252	9.02302	9.02353	9.02402	9.02452	9.02501	9.02550	9.02599	9.02648	9.02696
164	9.02744	9.02791	9.02839	9.02886	9.02932	9.02978	9.03024	9.03070	9.03115	9.03160
165	9.03205	9.03249	9.03293	9.03337	9.03381	9.03424	9.03467	9.03509	9.03551	9.03593
166	9.03635	9.03676	9.03717	9.03757	9.03797	9.03837	9.03876	9.03915	9.03954	9.03992
167	9.04030	9.04067	9.04105	9.04141	9.04178	9.04214	9.04249	9.04284	9.04319	9.04354
168	9.04388	9.04422	9.04445	9.04488	9.04521	9.04553	9.04585	9.04617	9.04648	9.04679
169	9.04709	9.04739	9.04769	9.04798	9.04826	9.04855	9.04883	9.04910	9.04938	9.04965
170	9.04991	9.05017	9.05042	9.05067	9.05092	9.05116	9.05140	9.05163	9.05186	9.05209
171	9.05231	9.05253	9.05274	9.05295	9.05315	9.05335	9.05355	9.05374	9.05393	9.05411
172	9.05429	9.05446	9.05463	9.05480	9.05496	9.05512	9.05527	9.05541	9.05556	9.05570
173	9.05583	9.05596	9.05609	9.05621	9.05632	9.05644	9.05654	9.05665	9.05675	9.05684
174	9.05693	9.05702	9.05710	9.05717	9.05725	9.05732	9.05739	9.05744	9.05749	9.05754
175	9.05759	9.05763	9.05767	9.05770	9.05773	9.05775	9.05777	9.05778	9.05779	9.05779
176	9.05779	9.05778	9.05777	9.05776	9.05774	9.05771	9.05768	9.05765	9.05761	9.05757